THE MISSING DIPLOMAT

PRAXTON

#6

N.S. HOWARD

THE MISSING DIPLOMAT
Copyright © 2022 by N.S. Howard

ISBN: 978-1-955784-69-6

Melange Books, LLC
White Bear Lake, MN 55110
www.melange-books.com

Published in the United States of America.

Cover Design by Lynsee Lauritsen

GLOSSARY OF TERMS

The Star Hawk series begins after the fourth Praxton novel, A Vote For Change. For those unfamiliar with the Praxton universe, I have listed on the next page a few of the terms used in this book.

Alliance Worlds: The Alliance worlds comprised approximately half of the human worlds. The government is located on Mars, although Earth with its large population has the most voting power. Most of the Alliance worlds reside within fifty light years from Earth.

Rebel Worlds: Any world not part of the Alliance worlds. Some Rebel worlds formed a loose association with other Rebel worlds but most live independently. The Rebel worlds are located outside of the Alliance worlds boundary, although a few are in close proximity. There is only minor trade between the Rebel and Alliance worlds.

Praxton: Formerly a Rebel world, Praxton is known for requiring women to wear collars and obeying their male guardians. Alliance forces invaded Praxton to free the women from perceived slavery. The battle did not go as the Alliance forces expected, resulting in Praxton becoming part of the Alliance Worlds, but keeping many of their unique culture and social customs.

Charter of Conduct Office: A bureaucratic Alliance world government department. The Charter of Conduct Office was created with the premise that human conflicts occurred because of differences in the social and culture of various people. If everyone spoke the same language and acted the same, conflicts would end. The authority of the Charter of Conduct Office increased to the point of ruling even on the alcohol content of wine and the caffeine in tea. The Charter of Conduct ordered Alliance forces to invade Praxton, a political disaster for the Alliance government. Afterward, the Charter of Conduct Office powers were sharply curtailed.

Pirates: Spaceships use hyperspace to jump to their destinations. It takes enormous energy to make a jump, such that most ships require a series of jumps to reach their final destination. Using advanced algorithms, pirate ships try to estimate where passenger and cargo ships will jump to between their destinations. Until the ship can recharge their jump engines, they can be attacked by pirates. Goods are the most sought-after commodity, although pirates will take women as slaves on occasion. It is generally accepted that if the spaceship does not resist the theft, it will be allowed to continue on its journey. If the spaceship is small and transporting wealthy passengers, it may be taken to a rebel world where a ransom has to be paid for the release of the passengers. Pirating is not considered illegal among the Rebel worlds.

The Wave: Earth and the rest of the solar system sent out many colony ships to habitable planets. All the planets agreed to have Earth as the governing body, sending representatives to vote on regulations and laws. Then an unknown phenomenon spread from the galactic core. The Wave destroyed electrical and electronic devices. Order was restored many years after. However, many of the planets that were the most distant decided not to rejoin the Earth dominated government, even though Earth agreed to move the governing body to Mars. Individual Rebel worlds, such as Praxton, deciding on their own laws they chose to adhere to.

Gene therapy: Advances in biology gave everyone access to gene therapy. Besides medical treatment, many people used gene therapy to improve their looks. The result was it became difficult to determine a person's age and many people appeared far younger than their years. For most people, gene therapy was very expensive due to the high tax.

Viewscreen: This device replaces mirrors and windows. For mirrors, cameras are placed so that the viewer can see their normal mirror image, plus sides and rear view. For windows, the viewscreen can give the same image as a window. The advantage is the thin membrane is mounted on a hard surface, making the danger of broken glass windows on spacecraft obsolete. The viewscreen gives the illusion of a three-dimensional image and can expand or shrink the image.

Guardian: On Praxton, a guardian was head of the household, responsible for all women who resided with him. He was in charge of their well-being as well as discipline. On the Star Hawk the tradition is continued, although ranks are still observed. If a woman on the ship accepts a man as a guardian, she is expected to obey him and accept discipline from him. As on Praxton, a woman can have only one guardian, but a male may be guardian to more than one female.

Star Hawk, Book One: The Star Hawk has adopted the Praxton cultural standards, which includes male superiority, the appreciation for female beauty and the need for discipline to maintain order. The ship's unforms follows Praxton customs. Men wear loose fitting clothing with military style boots. Women wear short skirts, a vest- style top, collar, wrist and ankle cuffs. Thin chains connect to the cuffs, usually loose. The Star Hawk continues its mission to visit Rebel worlds to stop pirating, the kidnapping of Alliance citizens, and to promote trade. Despite being a warship, the Star Hawk is mandated to use diplomacy to achieve its goals.

Personnel in Star Hawk:

Admiral: Noreen Howling (not based on ship)
Rear Admiral: Rosetta Harley (not based on ship)

Military Personnel on Ship:

Captain: Julius Elmwood
First Officer (Commander, 1st class): Morgan Regan
Steermaster (Commander, 2nd class): Nicole Redding
Communication Officer (Commander, 3rd class): Janice Madison
Commander, Senior weapons officer: Kelly Walling
Second Commander, weapons officer: Rickey Spelling
Senior Female: Khloe Levit
Communication Technician: first class, Teela Mezcal
Calibration Technician: Mitch Gallow
Senior Female, second class: Narcel Cannith

Other Ranks:

Lieutenant (1st, 2nd, 3rd class- includes Senior Female)
Warrant Officer (1st, 2nd, 3rd class)
Sergeant (1st Sergeant, Master Sergeant)
Cadet (1st, 2nd, 3rd class)

Non-military personnel:

Senior Technician: Derik Holton
Food and beverage manager: Diana Adoria
Technician (1st, 2nd)
Maintenance, Hospitality

[1]

CAPTAIN JULIUS ELMWOOD sat at the head of the table in the meeting room that included the Star Hawk's executive officers, plus Senior Diplomat Tiffany Harris and Charter of Conduct Officer Paul Thyssen.

He decided against any preliminary announcements or congratulations on the successful competition of their first mission, knowing they were eager to learn about their next one. "General Noreen Howler has instructed the Star Hawk is to proceed to the planet Divinus in the star system Coelum. Once we arrive there, we are to negotiate an agreement with the authorities governing Divinus to reduce or eliminate their trade with pirates. This can be accomplished by offering increased trade with the Alliance worlds. What we will not be doing is making any overt military threats for non-compliance regarding trade to the pirates. The belief is the Hawk Star will be sufficient to show the Alliance worlds are not standing pat to the pirate raids."

Steermaster Nicole Redding ventured information on Divinus' location. "The planet is at the edge of the Scutum-Centaurus arm of our galaxy. It will require three hyperspace jumps to reach there. Divinus is about one-quarter of the distance within the Rebel space boundary from the Alliance worlds."

"What type of government do they have? I believe it's a monarchy but I'm not sure," Communication Officer Janice Madison asked.

"That's a good question," Morgan Regan responded. "And yes, you're partially right regarding the government. The High Reeve is the king's representative, and he appoints military advisors for most government decisions. King Louis the Fourth, although still in good health, has passed over his authority to his oldest son, Prince Francis. I suspect our negotiations will be with the military advisors, but Prince Francis will have to sign off on important agreements."

Kelly Walling, in charge of the weapons of the Star Hawk, interjected, "If the military has a role in government decision making, can we assume they have a large military presence as well? I hope we're not expected to assume they will have only peaceful aspirations."

"Your concerns are noted, and we need to be wary of an attack," Elmwood answered. "The plan is for the Star Hawk to jump to the perimeter of the Coelum system and proceed to Divinus under normal propulsion. When they detect us, we will inform them we have arrived to discuss trade. We should be far enough away from their system that we can neutralize any attack if any occurs."

Diplomat Harris looked at her tablet. "Divinus already does some minor trade with a few Alliance worlds. These trades are not sanctioned or forbidden by the Alliance government. It is noted that in the past Divinus has facilitated the ransom payment of Alliance citizens captured by pirates. Divinus allows pirates to use its facilities to sell goods and slaves. Since they are close to the border with Alliance space, it makes sense to use Divinus as one of the Rebel worlds to initiate trade contracts with."

"That is correct." Elmwood nodded. "I will point out that the Rebel worlds don't act as one entity, but support each other through special agreements and arrangements. While we can establish a trade agreement with one world, it does not mean we'll have access to the other worlds. There is another matter concerning pirates. If possible, we would like Divinus to agree to stop taking Alliance citizens from pirates. It would be a stretch to believe they would agree not to take goods taken by pirates, but protecting our citizens is our priority."

"Just how big is the slave trade on the Rebel worlds?" Madison asked.

"Unfortunately, it is rather large." Elmwood frowned and continued. "The pirates will capture slaves from any world, Alliance or Rebel. They seek alliance citizens as there is less likelihood of anyone searching for them once they reach Rebel space. Slaves in the Rebel worlds are part of the economic reality. They perform free labour and are sold and purchased as needed. Most are women, as men are more resistant to training. On Divinus, few are used as sex slaves, with the majority used for housekeeping, hospitality industry, and certain types of administrative work. The slaves are not mistreated but they lack any freedom."

"Who will go on the trade mission?" Morgan asked.

Elmwood replied, "Morgan, I would like you to lead the trade mission and choose the personnel."

The meeting ended, and Morgan headed toward the exit.

Charter of Conduct Officer Thyssen caught up with her. "I believe the Charter of Conduct Office should be represented at this meeting. The Charter of Conduct is an important document that helps unify all the Alliance worlds and would be a good basis to use in negotiations with the Divinus government."

Morgan stopped walking to face him. *How do I tell him the Charter of Conduct is one reason why the Rebel worlds don't want to join the Alliance? His presence won't help the negotiations.* "I will consider your request, but I have to limit how much personnel I bring on our first meeting. I'll discuss it later with you."

"Very well. I believe I can help bring a positive influence on the meeting by stressing how the Office of Conduct strives to ensure fairness in all aspects of society."

Yeah, by a million regulations. No, thank you. She returned to the command centre and went up to Elmwood. "Thank you for giving me the mission to Divinus."

"You're welcome. This mission is important and has the potential to test your leadership abilities. I see you as being a captain of your own ship someday, and these situations will help you prepare for that role. Having said that, I must admit I'm a tad jealous you are leading the team to negotiate a trade agreement with an important Rebel world."

"No pressure at all. But thank you for your confidence in me."

Janice Madison, the Communication Officer, announced, "Captain, you have a secure call from General Howling's office. She wishes to speak to you immediately."

"I'll take it in the meeting room." Captain Julius Elmwood left from his position at the back of the command centre. It was a short walk to the meeting room, and he stared at the holographic image of General Noreen Howler.

"Captain, I wanted to contact you before you left Alliance space. Communication will be more difficult without the repeater stations we have in our own territory."

"Understood."

"We have been monitoring activity and communications within the Rebel worlds' area of influence. What we have determined is that there is an increasing amount of cooperation among the Rebel worlds, such as trade agreements and a commitment to support each other in case of military conflict."

"I see. That could have implications with our own intrusion into Rebel world space and to reach agreements with them."

"That is our view as well. The Rebel world economy overall is getting stronger. There are many factors for this. One aspect is the activity of the pirates taking cargo and citizens from Alliance ships. The goods provide immediate economic benefit while the citizens are turned into slaves to provide free labour. The pirate attacks have increased over the past year. It is obviously a profitable enterprise for them."

"That is not good news." Elmwood commented.

"No, but you need to be aware of the situation as you move deeper into Rebel world space."

"Thank you for the information, general." Elmwood returned to the command centre, going to Steermaster Nicole Redding. "I assume you have plotted the jump sequence to the New Kairon star system, the first jump to the Coelum system."

"Yes, sir. I can execute the sequence at any time."

"Very good. Let's allow time for all personnel to have lunch first. Initiate the first jump at fourteen hundred."

"Yes, sir." She understood his comment concerning lunch. The hyperspace jump would bother some crew members. Although scientists could not determine the reason for it, some people had stomach issues immediately after a jump. Older crew members were less bothered by it, and some never had issues with the effects of the jump. "I will make an announcement of a jump thirty minutes in advance."

Elmwood next went over to his First Officer, Morgan Regan. "Morgan, shall we go for lunch? There are a few matters we need to discuss."

"Of course, Master Julius." Morgan was careful to follow the Praxton custom of always addressing a male with a salutation. Failure to do so would be considered a sign of disrespect and subject her to discipline. They adopted the Praxton customs on the Star Hawk, and Alliance crew members had to adjust to the unusual social aspects. One other was the ship's uniform. The women's uniform had shoes with a higher heel than normal for Alliance worlds. The skirt was shorter, and the top was more of a vest, held by two buttons on the back at each end of an open oval. The lower arms were covered by 'phantom sleeves', a sleeve from the wrist to the elbow and held by an elastic material. The other parts of the women's uniform comprised of a collar and four matching cuffs. While not mandatory, most women added decorative chains to the cuffs. The chains often went from the wrist cuffs to the ring in the collar or to a chain belt. The women from Praxton often added additional chains, such as between the ankle cuffs. Other women would add a leash to the collar, holding the loose end on their wrist.

Elmwood informed Janice Madison she had the command centre and exited with Morgan. He led her to his private dining room and not the executive officer dining lounge.

Morgan sensed the conversation might not be entirely on the ship's next mission. She hesitated at the entrance and removed her shoes. On Praxton, women removed footwear when entering a home. Although the private dining room could be used for executive dining at the captain's discretion, she decided to view the room as if it was his personal residence.

Elmwood sat and gestured for Morgan to join him. Praxton customs dictated males walked ahead of females, sat first and were attended to first. "Lunch will be served shortly."

She noted that he had ordered lunch and decided what they would be eating. Another Praxton custom was for the male to order food at a restaurant, and she saw this was an occasion where he was prepared to act as a Praxton male. She had hoped he would want to establish a closer relationship with her and become her guardian. "May I ask why you want to see me?"

"One is to tell you that you have done a tremendous job as my first officer. You showed command capabilities on our first mission. As we enter Rebel territory, I want you to know you have my full confidence to act when I'm not available."

"Thank you, Master Julius."

Two servers entered the room, one pushing a cart. Both were women and Morgan saw their uniforms were the same as her own except in colour, blue grey as opposed to her own dark blue. The collar, used to show rank, was not as wide as her own. Servers were part of a contract with military to provide service to non-critical operations. The military found there were insufficient personnel interested in a military career and contracted out some duties. The woman in charge of hospitality service on the Star Hawk was from Praxton and insisted on full compliance of the Praxton culture, adding additional chains to their cuffs.

The servers poured wine, served plates of food, and departed.

Elmwood continued. "Returning to a discussion on our first mission, we had an incident that needs to be addressed."

Morgan took a sip of her pinot grigio. "Yes, sir. Do you mean the time I saw you naked?" On the mission, they rescued Elmwood after being accused of being a demon. He was whipped while nude, and Morgan was part of a shuttle crew that saved him. Under Praxton law, it was illegal for a female to look at a naked male who is not her guardian.

"Yes. There were mitigating factors. One, is that it was not possible for you to rescue me without seeing me undressed. You ordered the other females on the shuttle to turn their heads away from me. However, you continued to stare at me as I dressed."

"Yes, Master Julius, I couldn't help myself. If the same situation arose again, I must confess I would have difficulty resisting looking at you again." Her memory returned to his body with red whip marks. Her eyes were drawn to his trimmed pubic area, to his chest, and to his sky-blue eyes. Those eyes had seen where she was looking at.

"I understand. I didn't mind you seeing me naked. However, the fact is under Praxton rules you need to be disciplined. As captain of the Star Hawk, I should not let my personal feelings interfere with your punishment. I have some leeway in the discipline, and I have given it some thought."

Morgan ate, drank, and listened. "I hear you, Master Julius. Whatever you decide I'm sure will be fair."

"Since you saw me naked after they had whipped me, I have decided the same for you would be appropriate. The whip I will use will be a grade two."

Morgan knew the grade two of the four grades would barely sting. Grade one was akin to felt strips and not considered punishment. "Understood, sir. When and where will this occur?" *Is he going to publicly whip me?*

"In my suite after dinner. On Praxton, females are often punished in front of others, but this time I will do so privately. Unless you prefer a whipping where others can observe you." He grinned.

"Maybe another time." Morgan laughed. The thought of being naked in front of others made her pulse race faster.

"Very good. On Praxton, when a male finds a female attractive and wants to pursue with the objective of being her guardian, he will notify her of his intention. Morgan, I want to be your guardian. You may inform me now if you're not interested and I won't follow through on this path."

Morgan found her words sticking in her throat. "Master Julius, I would very much like you to be my guardian."

"I understand. We should follow the proper custom of myself giving you small orders. I need to exert my control over you through discipline, such as a spanking. If, over a period, you still wish for me to be your guardian, we can take the next step."

"I look forward to it, Master Julius."

"Then after tonight's punishment, I will start giving you small instructions."

[2]

TEELA MEZCAL SAT in front of her monitoring station, studying the three-dimensional graphs representing the various sensor inputs. She knew during the afternoon the hyperspace jump would take them to a supposedly empty star system, or at least one devoid of human life. If there were anything unexpected, she and the other crew members monitoring the sensors would notify the command centre. She relaxed as she checked the layout. Her mind drifted to Mitch Gallow, who was in charge of calibration of the sensors. She had become close to him over the weeks and now deferred to him in their relationship. He acted in the traditional Praxton way of courting her by giving her small orders. That included bringing a leash with her to work and at lunchtime he would use the leash to escort her to the dining room.

A second order was for her not to wear panties for the rest of the week. She complied, feeling pleased at his interest in her. Last week, he filled in a double shift for an absent employee preventing them from spending evenings together. She longed for the time they could be alone. In the case of the Star Hawk, it would have to be in his quarters, as males could not spend more than a few minutes in the women's quarters. Male visits were limited to escort or meet with a female crew member. Part of the restriction was due to the females often being undressed in the common room.

Teela considered the Praxton custom of dating rather odd. Males exerted their authority by giving females orders to follow. If the female didn't wish to follow the orders, it told him she wasn't interested in him. After a period of following orders, the male would begin mild discipline. That included spankings or a light whipping. The female would often show a submissive attitude toward him, such as kneeling by where he sat, allowing him to lead her by a leash, have him handcuff her wrists and ask what he would like to see her wear. Before he would ask to become her guardian, she would show she could please him, typically by performing oral sex.

So far, he has been rather nice with his orders. I wish we could have some alone time together. The girls in the common area are teasing me when he'll make the big move on me. I hope it's soon.

"Time for lunch."

Teela looked up at Gallow, tall with dark hair and a shadow on his face. She slipped the end of the leash off her wrist and handed it to him. "Are you growing a beard, Master Mitch?"

"I thought I'd try it for a few days and see how it looks." He led her out of the room and down the hallway to the lunchroom, taking her to a table where he hooked the end of the leash behind her chair.

Teela waited, knowing the Praxton custom of hooking a leash hooked behind the chair meant she wasn't allowed to leave. Gallow went to the self-serve counter and loaded a tray with their lunch. He didn't ask what she wanted and chose for them. It was another of the quirky Praxton customs that the male had the right to decide what the female could have to eat. Teela didn't mind, deciding it made her feel taken care of.

Gallow brought back soup and sandwiches. She thanked him for the meal and waited until he had started on his own meal before eating.

"Master Mitch, we've been going out together for a few weeks. I was wondering when we might spend some time alone."

"I was thinking of that as well. Those double shifts took away a lot of time we could spend together. We have also had a few yellow standby alerts that cut into free time."

Teela nodded. Yellow standby meant be prepared for immediate action. That included the avoidance of alcohol and personal interaction behind closed doors. "I know. I just hope we can make up for lost time soon. I would like to please you." *There, I said it. I want to give you a blow job so we can get on the path to sharing a room.*

He stopped eating. "I would like that very much too. I would also like to give you a spanking."

"I want one that makes my ass red so I can show it off to the females in the common room." Teela blushed.

"A status symbol?"

"Sort of. The girls appreciate what a red bottom means."

She was glad Gallow gave her the end of the leash back to her when he escorted her to her station. Putting it behind the workstation chair would have restricted her to sitting there. By handing her the leash end, she could leave by herself for a coffee break or to go to the restroom.

She heard the announcement for a jump in thirty seconds and focused on the monitor in front of her. Hyperspace jumps didn't bother her at all. Most of those in the room had done many jumps as well and were accustomed to its effects. Gallow was one of those in the room who suffered from the jump, describing it as if he had too much greasy food to eat. It didn't stop him from his tasks, although she teased him about having a sensitive stomach. She hoped the teasing would result in mild discipline for her, but he took it good naturedly.

The screen changed, a fresh set of graphs appeared, and she analyzed them. "Ms. Karlson, could you please come here? I believe I see an abnormality."

Lieutenant Karlson stood behind her, peering at what seemed to be dancing coloured mountains. "What am I supposed to be seeing?"

"Those four blue points. They're too close together to be natural."

"Oh, I see what you mean. They might be spaceships near the fifth planet of the system. I'll notify the command centre."

Teela continued to study the abnormality, deciding they were artificial. An announcement from the ship's communication officer grabbed her attention.

"Yellow standby is now in effect. The next hyperspace jump will not proceed as planned. Instead, the Star Hawk will investigate the possibility of hostile spacecraft in the vicinity."

Gallow went over to her. "Nice job in catching the abnormality. It has put us in another yellow standby condition."

"Sorry. Let's hope this isn't too serious."

"MORGAN, what do you make of this?" Elmwood peered at his monitor.

"Four ships of various sizes. I would guess they're pirate ships. They haven't changed position yet, so they're unlikely aware of us."

"I concur. I suspect they choose to be near a gas giant planet to help hide their location from any passing ships. Our new sensor technology is proving to be useful already. Let's make our way to them. Deflector shields up in case they fire first."

"Make our velocity point five of the speed of light." Elmwood spoke to Steermaster Nicole Redding. "That will bring us to them in about an hour."

"I wonder when they will detect us and what their reaction will be?" Morgan asked.

"Those are good questions. I'm curious how good our stealth capabilities are for that class of spaceships. Second, I wonder if they'll fight or flee."

At nine hundred kilometres away, the four spaceships noticed the Star Hawk.

Elmwood went to his workstation and called out to the communication officer. "Janice, send those ships a signal we wish to communicate." The ships were visible on his monitor and were all a different size, age and style. None of them were large enough to pose any threat to the Star Hawk.

Elmwood listened to new information in his earpiece from Lieutenant

Karlson. "Captain, three of the ships are preparing to jump. The fourth has not charged up for a jump. None of them have weapons ready."

A few minutes later, the worried look of a woman appeared on his screen. Her clothes didn't appear to be a uniform, but instead a stylized jacket suitable for formal discussions. The brunette had long, unkept hair. Her face was sharp boned, giving her a haunted look.

"I'm Captain Dee Solson. What do you want?"

"I'm Captain Julius Elmwood of the Alliance spaceship, the Star Hawk. We are investigating pirate activities that have occurred in Alliance space."

"We are not in Alliance space right now."

"But if we inspect the contents of your ships, I suspect we will discover you have been."

"Captain Elmwood, we are just poor traders of various goods. Some of them may have originated from Alliance worlds, but isn't that expected from trading?" She bit her lower lip.

Elmwood frowned. "Let me give you my thoughts on this. You and your group of ships are pirates. I suspect you just did a raid in Alliance space and jumped here, preparing to jump again to reach trading worlds. But one of your ships has mechanical problems and cannot jump until repairs are made. You, being the good captain, are not prepared to leave one of your ships and crew behind."

"We have heard pirates are severely punished by Alliance world authorities. Is there a way to convince you to leave us alone?"

"Those rumours may be true. I will give you an option. First, how many captured Alliance citizens do you have?"

He saw her turn her head to side, conversing with someone. She shrugged her shoulders, still talking to the unseen crew member.

"Captain, we have eight women on board. So, if you use weapons on us, they could die as a result."

"My intention is not to blow you or any of your ships apart. However, here is what you will do. You will pilot the ship carrying the women to the Star Hawk. Then you and I will have a meeting. Understood?"

Solson looked apprehensive. "Will you release me afterward?"

"We will see you aboard the Star Hawk in thirty minutes. Elmwood out."

Morgan looked at Elmwood. "You aren't planning to keep her as a prisoner, are you?"

"No. But I thought it would help her have empathy for those women they captured. They don't know what's happening. She should have the same worry."

Elmwood observed two pirate ships join. He assumed it was to transfer either the captured women or Solson from one ship to the other. The older looking ship arriving at the Star Hawk was constructed like a long tube with a balloon-like front end. It was also the one that didn't have jump capabilities working.

Elmwood, Khloe, medical staff and several armed military personnel waited as the airlocks opened and revealed the anxious face of a blonde woman. Behind her stood several women. All had their wrists handcuffed and secured to a waist belt. They wore an orange coverall that appeared made of paper. A wire rope went from each waist belt of the women to the next.

"Welcome aboard the Alliance spaceship, the Star Hawk. You are safe and will be returned to the Alliance space." Elmwood greeted the women.

"Thank God. I thought I would be made into a slave." The blonde cried as she stepped forward along with the others. After the cuffs and wire rope were removed, they went to the medical room to be examined.

Elmwood saw not all the women were adults. Two appeared to be the age he would consider teenagers. It surprised him they looked less concerned than the older females. He noted the orange coverall was the only clothes they had to wear. He ordered a female soldier to escort them to the women's quarters afterward so they could rest while new clothes were prepared for them.

The only other person to exit from the pirate ship was Captain Dee Solson. She stood at the adjoining airlock, waiting for what was to happen next.

Elmwood stood and glared at her. "You were going to sell these women as slaves? Some are too young to be called adults." He turned and walked, beckoning her to follow. He reached a meeting room near the command centre where Solson, Morgan and the military personnel followed.

He spoke to the military officer in charge. "Wait outside." Next, he pointed at Solson. "Sit."

Solson sat.

Elmwood stared at her. "Do you have anything to say before I consider what to do with you?" He studied Solson sitting across from him, looking like she didn't believe she would return to her ship.

"I'm sorry that you see us just as pirates trying to steal from Alliance ships and to take your citizens as slaves. I can't speak for other pirates, but our group tries to be careful. We avoid damaging any Alliance ship we encounter. We don't take every piece of cargo. Just commercial products from large corporations. We take women as slaves but spare others. If you check with the women you just rescued, you will find out we didn't take any women with small children. Captain Elmwood, our group of pirates came from poor worlds. Pirating is the only way we can make a living."

"They're not just women. Some of those you took are girls by Alliance standards."

"Young women, or girls if you prefer, are the easiest to train as slaves. They survive the emotional experience much better, and we receive higher pay for them. I'm sorry, it's the economics of trade."

"So what is your value as a slave?" Elmwood snapped at her. "What would you be worth if we sold you?"

She shrugged and gave a thin smile. "Not much. I'm too old and too stubborn to be of any use as a slave."

"I appreciate your honesty." He found her self-depreciating humour disarming. "Still, I have a decision to make about you and your group. I will inform you we can detect when any ship is preparing for a hyperspace jump. The Star Hawk can send out a strong enough electromagnet high frequency pulse that will disable any jump capabilities."

"Then I ask for mercy. Keep me, and let my crew go, and I will tell you everything I know about the Rebel worlds and how pirates operate."

"Morgan, record what information she has. I will be back."

━━

Morgan Regan took down the information Solson revealed. A server brought in water, coffee and snacks. Morgan noted that Solson was quick to eat.

"Hungry?"

"We pack little provisions for our trips to Alliance territory. Space is a premium and we need it for any goods we capture."

"So where do you take the women afterward?"

"There are various places. If we have only a couple of slaves to sell, we just take them to one of the slave purchasing traders. If we have six or more, then it's more worthwhile to deal with one of the slave training corporations. The biggest ones are on the planet Kijira."

"It seems the slave market is profitable."

"Those women are worth more than the rest of the cargo we took. I don't like to do it, but it's how we make a living. You're wearing a collar and cuffs. Were you a slave once?"

"No. This is an Alliance ship, but we follow Praxton customs."

"Praxton. A former Rebel world. So, do you like wearing a collar? Do you have to obey men?"

"I like the collar. I obey only those of higher rank than myself."

"Hmm. It's unusual to see an officer wearing a collar. Still, I think it looks kind of sexy and pretty. I suppose that's one reason it is decorative. It looks nice. You're a very beautiful woman with the cuffs and collar."

"Thanks."

"Can you help me with your captain? I don't want to go to prison. Please. Anything I can do for you in return?"

Okay, so that was the reason for the compliments. "Sorry, Dee. The captain will decide by himself. If he asks, I'll tell him you were cooperative and gave me information willingly."

Elmwood returned. He sat and looked at Solson. "I have some good news for you. The women you took as slaves are all in good health and told me you did not abuse them. The ship you arrived in has now been repaired and is ready for hyperspace."

"Thank you. Does that mean you're going to let me go?"

"It does. I hope you understand that I can, and should, take you and each of your companions as prisoners and have you tried as pirates. I'm going to give your group one chance, and one chance only, to make a living as traders and not as pirates."

"Yes, Captain Elmwood. I assure you we'll stop being pirates. Thank you, thank you, thank you." Her voice strained with emotion.

"My first officer will escort you back to your ship."

Morgan led her back to her ship.

"Your captain is a fair man."

"He is."

"You said you only obey those of a higher rank than yourself. Did you mean that only in a military sense, or do you obey him on a personal level as well?"

Morgan hesitated before answering. "It is what you think it is. We have a personal connection. I see him as one in control of me."

"Then good luck. I'm sorry I was coming on to you to get sympathy from you. But you are beautiful. I meant that." She stepped inside her ship. "I better leave before he changes his mind."

"Stay out of trouble. No more pirating."

Morgan returned to the command centre. She confronted Elmwood. "Okay, you let her and her ships go. Why do I think it wasn't just to be nice?"

"I felt sorry for her in a way. She didn't look rich. She offered herself in exchange for her crew's safety. I think in the right circumstances, she could be a decent person. Anyway, we downloaded all kinds of information from their ship's control system. We know where it has been and the routes it travelled. We repaired the hyperjump equipment for them, but also inserted a tracking device. That may come handy later, especially if they enter Alliance space to do any pirating."

"That's good."

"True," said Elmwood. "They'll also inform others of the encounter they had with the Star Hawk and how we tracked them down. It may put fear into other pirates."

"We can only hope," said Morgan. "Do we now take the women back to the Alliance territory?"

"Yes, I've informed our steermaster which world was their original destination. We'll take them there and return to our mission."

[4]

DIANA ADORIA, the food and beverage manager on the Star Hawk, was having a difficult time concentrating on the latest formula for soft flour used in pastries. The complex chemistry of the flour could be adjusted by the refinement of certain proteins. She pushed a hand through her dark hair, annoyed how her relationship with Senior Technician Derik Holton had become so difficult. She was one of the few Alliance citizens on a civilian contract on the Star Hawk. Her expertise on developing formulas for food and beverages had already improved many of the offerings on the spaceship. When she came on board, she tried to follow what she knew of the Praxton customs and wore the appropriate clothing, including a collar and cuffs. But Holton, who saw her as an invasion of his responsibility for food preparation, found fault with her behaviour. Within a few days, he had spanked her and ordered her to act more like a Praxton female.

She enlisted the help of Lieutenant Khloe Levit, who was in charge of all female accommodation and behaviour, to stop what she considered bullying by Holton. Khloe informed her Holton's behaviour was possibly a sign he wanted to be her guardian, and that he liked her. Diana accepted the Praxton custom that the male showed dominance and gradually enjoyed a relationship with him, one that included allowing him to enter her suite early one morning to watch her shower and later prepare breakfast for him.

Everything was fine until she dropped by his office to find a female technician kneeling by his desk. His excuse that Praxton males could have more than one female only infuriated her more. Her final words on the matter were that their relationship was to be a monogamous one, and he had to romance her like an Alliance woman.

She studied the formula of the three-dimensional image on the screen, moving up the proportions of the starch.

"Diana."

She looked up at Holton. "Yes, Master Derik." She kept her voice neutral.

"We seem to be at an impasse in our relationship. At least I don't know what's going on."

"Master Derik, I have done my best to act like a proper Praxton female. I will add I went through a difficult learning process of being punished for reasons I didn't understand. No one explained to me all the nuances of how to act like a proper female. Overall, I believe I have done very well in accommodating your desires. I am drawing the line where you feel that only I have to adapt to your wants. This is what's going on. If you want me, then you can have only me. Not another woman on the side. Second, I want to be treated like an Alliance woman occasionally. I believe I'm being very reasonable in this."

Holton let out a long breath. "What is wrong if a female wants to keep me company in my office?"

"None at all, if she's sitting in a chair drinking a tea. But if you want a kneeling female in a submissive pose next to you, it better be me."

"She wasn't naked, or even topless. She was just in a normal position for a female near a male."

"If she was naked, we wouldn't be having this conversation."

"I'm still confused. The Hawk Star is governed by Praxton culture. I'm merely following those rules."

"And I'm only following my own rules I use to survive. I will act, as you put it, like a proper Praxton female. But that doesn't mean I must accept whatever rules you have in a relationship."

"What do you suggest so we can carry on? I will do my best to change."

"I honestly don't know." She frowned. "I will contact Khloe Levit and ask her to meet us. Perhaps she can come with a solution."

"Please do that. Diana, I really want to make this work between us."

Diana watched him leave and contacted Khloe, who agreed to meet them in a lounge after work.

———

Diana saw Khloe wave at her in one of the executive lounges. The lounge was reserved for senior officers, which also included Diana and senior technicians, such as Holton.

"Hi, I hope you weren't waiting long." Diana sat.

"Not at all. Big problem with Master Derik?"

"Yes, I think so anyway. He doesn't see any problem with having more than one relationship with women at the same time."

Khloe took a drink of her merlot. "On Praxton, males can have several females in their household. He likely is looking at it from that point of view."

"I'm sure he is. But where I'm from, that is not considered normal."

"Fair enough. Is that the only problem?"

"No. I also want him to romance me a little like I was an Alliance woman. He said he doesn't know what that means."

"Okay, here's Master Derik. Let's have a drink and see if we can talk some sense into this."

A few minutes later, Derik sipped at his scotch whiskey. "I am serious about Diana. I just don't know what I'm supposed to do next."

"If you're serious about Diana, does that mean you wish to be her guardian?" asked Khloe.

"Yes, I want to be her guardian."

"Diana, do you wish to have Master Derik pursue you with the intention of being your guardian? Providing he meets certain conditions?"

"Yes." She looked at Derik. "But as Khloe stated, there are conditions."

"Great, we can go over those conditions." Khloe smiled. "But the main thing is that both of you will try. Now, Master Derik, Diana, are you willing to make a compromise to help things work out?"

Derik nodded.

"Yes," Diana answered. "Depending what those are."

Two rounds of drinks later, Khloe announced, "Okay, here's the deal we have so far. Master Derik is officially pursuing Diana with intentions to be her guardian. Master Derik will endeavour to use Alliance world social customs with Diana. He may have other females kneel and act submissive in his presence, as long as they are not undressed or be in his private suite. If he becomes Diana's guardian, he may not have another female in his household without her permission. Agreed?"

Diana and Holton nodded.

"Okay, Master Derik, because he intends to be her guardian, can give her reasonable orders to follow and to give her appropriate discipline." She looked at Diana. "Under Praxton rules, those reasonable orders and discipline can cover a wide range of activities. You cannot refuse to follow them, other than declaring you are not interested in him being your guardian. You can refuse to have sex with him, not allow him into your suite or follow orders that compromise with your duties on the Star Hawk. Other than that, you should obey him."

"I understand. How long does this go on for?"

"That's up to both of you. Traditionally, a few weeks to a few months. When, and if, you decide to accept him as your guardian, be prepared for the next part of the Praxton custom. You will be punished publicly while nude during a special party. At the end you're collared, and he is your guardian."

"Wonderful. I prefer a white dress and vows."

Khloe grinned. "You can always have both."

Holton stood. "Diana, I shall be at your suite at oh-seven hundred tomorrow to escort you for breakfast. I will give you a few rules to follow at that time."

He left and Khloe looked at Diana. "I don't know about you, but I'm curious what rules he's going to give you to follow."

Diana frowned. "Likely restrictions on what I can wear. He likes me with fewer clothes on."

"That's okay. I'm guessing you'll enjoy what he wants to do to you."

Diana checked the time. It was five minutes to seven in the morning, which meant she had exactly five minutes before Derik Holton showed up at her suite. She looked at the full length viewscreen one more time. Her blouse was long sleeved with lace cuffs. The lace also went down the front in the centre of the blouse. Other than the lace, the material was see-through, enough so that her nipple jewellery was visible, including the chain that went between them. Her dark skirt was short but loose fitting with pleats. She attached chains from her wrist cuffs to the front of a black belt with an oversized buckle. *All good, if a little revealing. But this is a Praxton culture, so just about anything goes.*

The door chime announced it was seven o'clock, and she opened the door to see Holton. "Good morning, Master Derik. Would you like to come in and have a cup of coffee before we leave?"

"That would be nice." He sat at the kitchen table, watching her as she poured coffee. "That top looks very nice on you."

"Thank you." She carried the cups to the table. She remembered the Praxton custom of lifting the back of her skirt before she sat. "You know, I don't need a clock with you. You do everything precisely by the minute."

"I like exactness. I suppose that results from being a technician that requires high precision in the job."

"It's a good quality to have. Does that mean your rules for me are going to be exact as well?"

"Yes. I've made a list of rules for you to follow. I believe they are reasonable. They allow you freedom but also show I'm in control of you."

"May I ask what the rules are?" She smiled and took a drink of her coffee.

"I might as well tell you now. One is that whenever we are together, I will have you on a leash. You must have one in your possession at all times."

"Yes, Master Derik. I will get one before we leave."

"I would like to see wider collars on you, just my preference. I notice you wear simple collars, but I would prefer to see you in ones that are more pronounced."

"Yes, sir. I will look at ordering wider collars."

"You have a lovely body and shouldn't be shy in showing it off. Therefore, at twenty-one hundred hours, you must remove your top. Wherever you are."

Diana held back her first retort. "Yes, Master Derik. At nine p.m. I must be topless."

22

"I like it when females wear a proper amount of chains. I will leave it up to your discretion along with the collar and cuffs. However, I shall warn you I believe female discipline needs to carried out regularly. Your manner of dress and behaviour will be factors on how hard the discipline will be."

"Yes, Master Derik, I understand." She stood. "I will obtain a leash." She went upstairs and clipped a leash onto her wrist cuff, preferring that to her collar. *This is a little strange being ordered to wear a leash and to go topless at an appointed hour. Although there are odd customs throughout human history. It would be exciting to be topless in one of the ship's lounges. At least I'd have an excuse to do so. 'No, it isn't the wine, I'm under orders to be half naked.'*

They left her suite, with Holton holding the end of her leash. The leash wasn't long, and she walked alongside of him. Holton led the way to a dining lounge where she sat, listening to him as he ordered her breakfast for her.

"I don't get to order my breakfast?"

"No, you're under my control. I will take care of you."

She nodded, glad he at least ordered food she liked.

After breakfast, he led her to her office, stopping in front of her desk.

"Are you wearing panties?"

"Yes. Do you want me to remove them?"

"No, I will do that." He dropped to his knees and lifted his hands under her skirt, pulling the thin fabric down.

She stepped out of them. "Am I allowed to wear panties in the future?"

"Yes, although occasionally I'll remove them if you wear them. I'll warn you it may happen in public places." He stuffed the panties into his pant pocket.

"I'll remember that, Master Derik." She waited for him to leave and went and sat in front of her monitor. She turned on her computer and made a call to Khloe.

"Hey, what's up?"

"I've some questions about the orders Master Derik gave me."

"Okay. What's the problem?"

"He's ordered me to remove my top by nine o'clock each night, no matter where I am. What are the rules for partial nudity on the ship?"

Khloe giggled. "So, you're worried about the rules of being partially naked and not actually being naked in public?"

"It sounds that way, doesn't it?" Diana laughed. "But I don't want to get into trouble for exposure."

"Okay, the rules for males are simple. No nudity outside of their bedrooms. For females, a few more rules. Military officers must have their uniforms close by at all times. After their shifts, females may remove part, or all of their uniforms, in public if they should wish to do so. But the uniform must remain close by in case of an emergency. Contract females may also remove part of their uniform but are not required to have it close by. Technically, they can walk around ship naked after their shift. You're a civilian, so the same applies to you."

"What you're saying after my workday ends, I can go topless."

"Yes. But not while on duty, unless you're being disciplined. During a shift a female can be stripped to be punished, but she must get dressed afterward."

"Lovely. So, I'm in the clear if I was in a lounge after nine o'clock and removed my top."

"If you're going to take off your top, I want to be there when it happens." Khloe laughed.

"Thanks. It may take a few drinks for me to have that courage." Diana ended her call with Khloe. *It's going to be hard to concentrate on work this morning.*

[5]

CAPTAIN ELMWOOD LOOKED across the table in the executive dining room, smiling at the eight women looking back at him. The women were rescued from the pirates, and before they returned to their original destination, they were invited to dinner with the captain and his first officer.

The pirates had taken the women's clothes and personal possessions, giving them only an orange coverall to wear. Lieutenant Khloe Levit, in charge of the women's quarters, arranged for temporary accommodation and new clothes. The women wanted to express their gratitude for their rescue to the captain and to the crew of the Star Hawk. Khloe arranged for a dinner with the captain.

The dinner was a formal affair, with wine and various dishes served by the hospitality staff. The conversation was light, and Elmwood asked each woman where she was originally from. Often, he indicated he was familiar with that world and added his perspective of it. He felt his guests were studying him, and he hoped the dinner wouldn't last too long. It didn't help when Morgan, sitting next to him, whispered, "I think some of these women would like to give you a private thank you for being rescued."

He whispered back, "You should feel fortunate I have delayed your discipline because of this rescue. But it has not been forgotten."

A woman asked, "Captain, I understand this is an Alliance world military ship. However, the uniforms I see seem to be of a style found on Praxton. Why is that?"

He looked back at the red-haired woman, recalling she was from a world known for their prestigious universities. She acted and spoke of a higher education. He noted that she was one of three women wearing a collar, a black one with a modest metal ring in the centre. "That is very observant of you. Yes, this is an Alliance ship, and yes, we follow Praxton social customs on this ship. The reason for that is that a large segment of the crew comes from Praxton, and we decided they would feel more comfortable with Praxton style of clothes."

"I like the female uniforms." She smiled. "They are feminine compared to most military uniforms. And I think your uniform adds to your stature."

Another woman, who had been rather quiet and hadn't disclosed her home world, asked him where the Star Hawk would journey to after it dropped the previously kidnapped women.

He looked at the dark-skinned woman with an abundance of long, dark hair. "Ms. Ellis, the Star Hawk will visit several Rebel worlds. Our mission is one of peace and to negotiate trade agreements. So, for the foreseeable future, we will be in Rebel world territory."

"Forgive me for asking, but isn't that dangerous? One ship to travel among hostile planets?"

"Thank you for your concern. However, the Star Hawk is well armed, and we don't expect the Rebel worlds to be hostile unless we provoke them. I assure you we don't have any intention of starting a battle."

She nodded, appearing to be deep in thought.

Elmwood was feeling the conversation had the potential of becoming uncomfortable. He saw several other women were looking at him with a hint of amusement on their faces. He was glad when desserts arrived, breaking the conversation.

He whispered to Morgan, "Can we pretend there's a ship emergency so I can leave?"

She laughed. "Come on, don't you like being the centre of attention?"

"Not in this case."

As is on cue, an announcement came on. "Yellow Standby. Thirty minutes to a hyperspace jump."

"Ladies, please excuse me." Elmwood stood. "I must prepare the ship for the hyperspace jump." He walked to the exit and turned to wave goodbye, seeing Morgan roll her eyes at him.

He entered the command centre, and the steermaster looked at him. "You didn't need to return here from your dinner. We can handle the jump without you."

"Believe me, I would rather be here than there."

"Really? Dinner with all those lovely ladies?"

"More like swimming in a pool with sharks."

[6]

DIANA ENTERED one of the theatres on the Star Hawk with Derik. She felt the slight tug on her wrist from the attached leash as he guided her to a pair of empty seats near the middle on the elevated seating. The seating was comfortable with red fabric and the rows followed in a curve pattern, allowing an excellent vantage point anywhere to see the stage. The theatre was almost full for the dance and music performance. The performers were a mix of crew members and musicians. At other times, performances in the theatres consisted of combinations of crew members and holographic artists.

She sat, remembering not to tug down the tight skirt she was wearing, as per Praxton customs. The hemline rose, showing off her long legs. Her sleeveless top was green fabric with a single button at the neckline to hold it together. As she walked, the top opened like a cape, baring her midriff and part of her breasts.

The other part of her Praxton fashion included a collar and cuffs. She followed Derik's request, wearing a wide collar that inhibited her head movement. A short, thick chain that was matched by a similar, but longer chain between her ankle cuffs, joined her wrist cuffs. The chain looked heavy but was of a lightweight material. When he commented on how she looked, she replied, her decision to wear the restrictive items was done to appease him, not mentioning her own desire to experiment with wearing them.

Derik rested a hand on her thigh as the lights above the audience dimmed. The stage lights came on, and the curtains parted, revealing a six-person orchestra sitting at the back, and two female dancers in front. The music ensemble consisted of four stringed instruments, a flute and a small set of drums. The two men wore red shirts and black pants, while the women wore a red gown with a single strap on the left shoulder that bared their right breast.

The dancers wore strips of wide colourful ribbons attached to a band that went around their shoulders, revealing and covering the naked bodies underneath. Holographic lights made the stage appear as if it was a meadow with blue skies.

Diana watched the two dancers perform a ballet style of dancing to the music she recognized as one of the lighter classical pieces. She felt Derik's hand as his fingers moved in circles, slowly moving up her leg. She looked around the dark interior and concluded no one could see them. She focused her attention back on the dancers as they touched hands, pivoting away just as they moved closer. The flute player stood and increased the volume of the instrument. Diana noticed the red gown reached the floor on the right side but was bare from high on the left hip down. She thought it created an interesting effect of a red cloth that contrasted with the pale skin of the flute player.

The first song ended, and Diana applauded along with the others in the audience, although she felt restricted with her hand movements by the chain between her wrists. The second song was slower paced than the first piece, and the dancers made longer and exaggerated movements. The barefooted flute player walked in small steps to the front of the stage and the dancers circled around her. Occasionally, the dancers joined hands and pressed their bodies against each other. There was also a moment where the dancers exchanged a kiss and hands reached past the ribbons to touch each other.

It was an erotic dance, and Diana guessed Derik was likely enjoying it more than she was. Still, she found the music and dancing intoxicating to her senses. She felt warm as his hand slid higher up her leg, reaching the hem of her skirt. She considered pushing his hand away and whispering, 'not here'. But with her wrists handcuffed with a chain, she felt he was in control, and it was not her place to refuse him.

The slow second song ended, moving to the fast pace of the final piece. The musician stepped in a small circle as she played. The dress was revealing on the back, exposing half of her back on the right. The dancers trailed after her, now in constant contact. They rolled on the floor as they rubbed their bodies together.

Diana watched a dancer arch her back as she lifted her back off the floor. It was at that moment she felt Derik's hand push between her thighs. She gasped.

The dancers rolled on the floor and lay still as the music ended. Slowly they stood to the applause from the audience. The rest of the orchestra stood and came forward as well to join in.

"That was a very interesting dance," Diana remarked.

"Yes, I thought so." He stood and helped her up. "Let's go for a nightcap."

She noted that he didn't ask if she wanted a drink, only informed her they were to do so. They went to an executive lounge near her suite, where he guided her to a table near a wall sized viewscreen showing ocean waves sliding onto a beach. Before they sat, he undid one of her wrist chains.

"Take off your top."

Diana nodded and undid the single button to her top. It slid down her arms and she draped it over the back of her chair. She held up her wrists, and he joined the chain back to the cuff. She stood, waiting for him to sit first.

He sat and looked at her. "I'm pleased you didn't object to my request of taking off your top."

"I decided you were in control right now and didn't want to risk a spanking by disobeying." She felt her nipples tighten as she gazed into his eyes. *He wants to spank me. Right here and now.* She looked around the lounge and saw three other women were bare breasted. As time passed on the ship, it had become a more common occurrence to see topless women in the evening. She didn't feel exposed, but more aware of the chains between her wrist and ankle cuffs.

He ordered the drinks, and she had to use both hands to lift her glass.

"That was an interesting performance in the theatre. Were you aware there would be nude women dancing?"

"I wasn't surprised by the description given earlier. I heard that the flute player was excellent and had won numerous awards for her past performances. On Praxton, many live performances have partially nude women in them. It is accepted as part of the art of live theatre."

She smiled. "But no nude men?"

He shrugged, "There isn't much demand to see naked men."

"Maybe they're asking the wrong gender." Diana laughed. "I would love to see you naked."

"Maybe someday." He chuckled. "But for now, let's keep to what Praxton does best. Lovely ladies in cuffs, collars and not much else."

She grinned. "Since you put it that way." She lifted her hands to the top of her head and spread apart her elbows. "Is this what you had in mind?"

He stared at her, finally choking out, "I don't believe you fully appreciate how beautiful you are."

She lowered her arms. "So just what are you going to do to have me?"

He finished his drink. "I'm working on it."

After a small bite to eat and another drink, he stood. "I guess I should escort you back to your room now. The morning will arrive soon enough."

"Do I put my top back on now?"

"No, I'll carry it." He undid one wrist cuff chain. "Turn around."

Diana obeyed, and he secured her wrists behind her back.

"Now we can go."

Diana saw a few glances at her as he led her topless, with her wrists behind her back. Her engorged nipples were in full view of everyone, and she blushed, knowing it exposed her desires.

They arrived at her door, and she waited for him to undo her wrist chains.

"That was a lovely evening. I like these chains on you. They look much more secure that the thin ones." He kissed her on the lips, lingering as he teased her with his tongue. "I will pick you up tomorrow morning. I want to share some thoughts with you at breakfast." He undid the wrist cuff chain.

She exchanged several more kisses with him, and she went inside her suite. *Damn. I need him in my bed right now. Or right here in the living room.*

I know he's teasing me. She took off her shoes and skirt and lay on the couch. Her hand reached between her legs, and she eased her fingers at the edges of her clitoris. She imagined being back in the lounge. Derik using his strength to pull off her skirt, leaving her naked as he placed her over his lap. With everyone watching, he gave her a long, hard spanking. *Oh, that would be so nice.*

[7]

MORGAN APPROACHED Elmwood in his executive room as he studied reports on a tablet. She paused at the entrance until he acknowledged her by looking up from where he sat.

"Excuse me, captain, but a woman we rescued from the pirates is requesting an urgent meeting with you."

"Really? Did she specify what it is about?"

"No, only that she only wanted to meet with you and not any of the other ship personnel."

"I see. Who is this woman?"

"She only gave her name as Ellis. She's the dark-skinned, tall woman with the long straight hair."

"Very well." Elmwood sighed. "Arrange for a meeting with her here. Make it in two hours time." He paused. "This better be urgent and not some frivolous method to get attention."

⸻

Morgan escorted Ellis down the hallway to Elmwood's executive office. At the entrance, Ellis paused only briefly, before stepping around the table and extending her hand to him, waiting for him to respond.

Elmwood stood, unsure of what she expected him to do. He took her hand and shook it. "Ms. Ellis, how can I be of assistance to you?"

"Captain Elmwood, I believe you may be the only person in this universe who can help me."

"Really? How so?" He gestured to a chair. "Perhaps we should sit down." He looked at Morgan. "You better join us."

Ellis sat. "I'm not from here. Not from anywhere in this universe. The fact is, I come from another universe all together. For the past six Earth years, I have been searching for a way home."

Elmwood sat for a moment, questioning what she had said. "You're not from this universe? How is that possible?"

"Captain, I cannot give you any better explanation than relate what happened. My full name is Nallix Sorlity Tality Ellis, Emira of Tellany. Tellany is my home world and is located beyond what would be Alliance world space, several light years past the planet Haven."

Elmwood knew Haven was the furthest planet from Sol, the last planet colonized before the Wave. That there were habitable planets past Haven wouldn't surprise him, as humans were still making a slow expansion outward. "Ms. Ellis, if that is how you wish me to address you, are you saying you are from a world we have yet to discover?"

"You're unlikely ever to discover it. In my universe, Tellany was one of a group of worlds we were in control over. The Wave your universe suffered from had a much less effect on us and our technology. The technology in this universe is below from the one we lived in. I was in a position of power and high status and thus had many comforts afforded me. I boarded a private spacecraft for a brief trip to a neighbouring world. Only the pilot, my personnel attendants and myself were aboard for the short journey. To make a long story short, my ship slipped out of the universe I was living in and into yours. You may address me as Ms. Ellis, or if you prefer, Emira Nallix." She paused. "Or just Nallix."

"You said you lived in our universe for six years. Have you told anyone else what happened?"

"No. I wasn't sure what would become of me if I did. I sold some of my jewellery to maintain a comfortable lifestyle. I know enough about astrophysics to understand a return to my universe would require an extremely rare set of circumstances. I decided I needed to find a way to live, and not just survive, in this universe. My pilot and attendants were less comfortable in this universe and were reluctant to adapt to living here. I gave my pilot and attendants permission to continue to find a way home, leaving them enough resources to live comfortably. I doubt they will succeed, as the conditions to jump between universes are extremely rare.

"I travelled between planets on passenger ships. At each planet I investigated if there were any reports of travel between alternate universes. So far, I have only uncovered speculation of cross universe travel. Then, as you know, the passenger ship I was on was attacked by pirates.

"Now I realize I'm in a position where your spaceship may provide me with a means to discover a method to return home. If not, it will be better than roaming your universe in passenger ships."

"Ms. Ellis, this is not a passenger ship. As much as I would like to help you, I believe you would be better telling the proper authorities what happened to you. They may be able to help you."

"Captain Elmwood. Do not take me for a fool. The authorities would either not believe me or subject me to various tests. You have an opportunity to help me. Only you, and this ship, have a chance to give my life a purpose. You may even find a way for me to return home. I must reiterate I'm appealing to you to help me. You, and the Star Hawk, are my best, and perhaps only chance." She reached into her hair, removing a gem woven inside. "Here. Take this to one of your scientists. Ask them what it is, and where it might be found. They will tell you they don't know where it came from."

Elmwood studied the blue gem that almost seemed to glow by itself. "Very well, I will have it examined. If you were to stay on the Star Hawk, what would you do?"

She smiled gently, appearing amused, as if he was a child asking a silly question. "Whatever you wished me to do, Captain Elmwood. I am not used to washing floors, but I assure you I can learn whatever tasks you may need done. I'm highly educated, and you should take advantage of that."

Elmwood stood. "Morgan, take this gem to our lab, and find out exactly what it is. Tell them it's a priority. In the meantime, escort Ms. Ellis to her quarters and confine her there."

Morgan returned with the gem and analysis, handing it to Elmwood. "Okay, this little blue stone is very interesting. Very interesting might be an understatement. It's extremely rare and found on only four planets in the Alliance worlds and in small quantities. It has unique electrical and magnetic properties, making it valuable for specialized quantum computers. A couple of these gems could buy a small spaceship."

"Really? She must have a dozen of these gems in her hair."

Morgan raised her eyebrows. "Is she single and does she like women?"

"Shame on you." Elmwood laughed. "Come, let's converse with her and you can help me decide if she's telling the truth. Instead of my office, let us meet in a less formal setting. Escort her to the executive lounge."

———

Elmwood entered the lounge, seeing Morgan and Ellis waiting for him. He sat and ordered a rye whisky. He passed over the gem to her. "That is a very unusual gem."

"I had more gems, but the pirates took those." She looked at Morgan and back Elmwood. "Captain, are you wanting to ask me questions as well?"

"A few. You claim to be from another universe. How is that you look like us and speak the same language?"

"I don't know why I appear to have the same physical characteristics, except it seems our universes are just an alternate reality of each other. Maybe the people are even clones. I never came across anyone the same in this universe as my own, but I obviously haven't met everyone. As far as speaking the same language, I learned your language during the time I spent in your universe."

"You stated you want to stay on the Star Hawk. How will that help you? Of what benefit will you be to the ship?"

"This ship is moving to different worlds far beyond than just the Alliance worlds. I believe it'll give me a better chance to discover a way to return home, perhaps just by accident. As for helping the Star Hawk... I'm smart and I know things, things that only could be learned in another universe. I can assist your ship's councillor."

"We don't have a councillor."

"Maybe you do now." She gave a short toss of her hair and smiled. "If you don't mind me being forward."

"Other than your gems, do you have any other proof you're from a different universe?" Morgan studied the woman's reaction to her question.

"Captain, I can tell you about planets you have yet to discover. I can inform you of alien species you will eventually contact. But it may come down to you trusting that I'm telling you the truth."

"Trust is something that has to be built up."

"I disagree. Trust can also be a feeling a person is being sincere."

"There is that. I will have a conversation with General Howler and discuss this situation." He turned his head to speak to Morgan. "Would you see if Ms. Ellis is aware and comfortable with the ship's regulations?"

"Of course, sir."

After Elmwood left, Morgan focused her attention on Ellis. "If you're permitted join the Star Hawk, are you prepared to adhere to our regulations, procedures and dress code?"

"It seems I have little choice but to say yes. However, in my universe I have the title of Emira, which is used in royalty. I assure you I'm familiar with following protocol and regulations, even ones that don't seem to make any sense. As for the uniform, I'm not averse to displaying my body. My husband, the Emir, often had me stay in my quarter's nude, even on occasions when there were visitors to the palace. The uniform is not a concern to me, although I will admit I have never worn a collar before." She smiled. "Where I come from, that was reserved for slaves. Yours look much more comfortable and elaborate."

"Good. We follow Praxton world traditions here on the ship. That means males are given an elevated status. For example, all men must be given a salutation. If you wish to use their first name, then you must use master first."

Ellia had an amused smile on her lips. "Men like signs of respect, warranted or not. Yes, I can show proper respect when needed."

"Good, because failure to do so can lead to discipline, such as a spanking." She watched her reaction.

"Really? I have never been spanked in my life. If you don't mind my saying so, it seems women on this ship have to be rather careful how they act."

"It's true. There's more to explain to you, but let's wait until the captain returns." She paused. "What did you wear in your universe?"

"I was of royalty, so I had my choice of some rather unique clothes. Everything from elaborate gowns with jewels woven into the fabric, to fine cloths that that barely covered my body. Some of my outfits were only of precious metal chains. I have noticed some people have tattoos. They are also seen in my universe. However, since I'm of elevated status, I have coloured metal designs mated with my skin."

"That sounds rather exotic. Was it painful?"

"It was done while I was barely conscious." She lifted her top, revealing a gold image of a head of tiger-like beast with the rest of the creature's image disappearing around her side.

"Wow. That is beautiful."

"Thank you. I have other markings as well." She dropped the hem of her top. "The captain has returned."

Elmwood sat at the table. "I have good news for you, Ms. Ellis. My conversation with General Howler concluded with you being accepted to work on the Star Hawk. We believe, if in fact you are from another universe, the knowledge we can obtain from you will be best kept from Alliance Security Forces." He frowned. "Information with them is a one-way street. That being said you have a responsibility to the Star Hawk. One, be honest. Do not hold back information that will put us in danger or help us. Two, accept the culture of this ship as your own."

"I agree to those terms."

"Excellent. You will be given the status of Special Envoy. You will study up on the various planets we will visit and advising the best approach to meeting them."

"I look forward to that task."

"Welcome aboard." He stood. "Morgan will show you to your suite."

"That was a quick decision." Morgan smiled. "Let's have a drink while your room is being prepared and you can tell me more about those metal designs on your body."

Captain Julius Elmwood stood with First Office Morgan Regan at the doorway to the Eagle One shuttle, saying goodbye to women hostages. The trip to rendezvous with the passenger ship Oasis was taking them out of Rebel territory and costing them three days of travel.

"Now we can get back to our mission," Elmwood commented after the shuttle door closed.

"I agree. It does feel good to have rescued those women from slavery. It also put the fear into the pirates we can chase them down if they do attack Alliance ships."

"True. And we ended up with a new member of the crew."

The Eagle One slid out of the hanger and into space, turning sharply against the backdrop of stars.

"I hope Nallix is who she says she is and not pretending." Regan heard the humming noise as the shuttle bay doors closed. A force field ensured the air stayed within the ship to allow shuttles to enter and leave the ship, but the bay doors added extra protection against a possible attack.

"You don't trust her? Those crystals she had are very rare. It seems to correlate with her tale of coming from another universe."

"Yes, but maybe it's also an elaborate hoax."

"If it's a hoax, how did she know we would be rescuing her from the pirates?"

"I don't know. It's just something about her mannerism that irks me."

"That may be true, but we can use her expertise. As far as her mannerism is concerned, she's from a different world than us. It may be a case we need to help her adjust to our world."

"Hmm. Speak of the devil." She pointed up ahead to where Nallix was walking in their direction.

Elmwood called out to her. She stopped, turned and smiled at them.

"Captain, First Office, did you see the rest of hostages off? I said my goodbyes to them at breakfast earlier. They were so relieved to be going back home."

"Yes, they have left. We're waiting for the shuttle to return and then resume our journey." Elmwood stopped walking as he conversed with her. "Would you like to join us for a coffee?"

"That would be wonderful."

Elmwood escorted Nallix with Regan following behind, frowning.

The executive dining room was busy, with the drone of the many voices discussing issues.

Nalliz sat first at the table, followed by Elmwood and lastly Regan.

"Are our dining facilities similar to those in your universe?" Elmwood asked.

"I can only compare them to my experiences as a member of the royal family. I don't mean to sound negative about your ship, but these dining rooms are quite primitive. Too many people for each dining room, which increases the noise to unacceptable levels. The furniture here is more functional than comfortable. The saving grace is food is of good quality. However, I must say the environment is less than ideal. I will say again, I am used to higher standards than this universe has to offer." She smiled.

"Perhaps you may have to adjust your standards to that of non-royalty. This is a military ship, and our resources are designed for the practical and not for luxury." Regan retorted.

Elmwood gave a quick look at Regan. "I believe what First Office Regan is meaning to say is we have different priorities being a military ship, but it is enlightening to learn of different cultures."

"Thank you, captain. I'm sorry if I upset your first officer. I have a tendency to be direct when answering questions. I must learn to temper my responses."

Elmwood stood. "I need to return to the Command Centre. The shuttle should be returning soon."

Regan stood as well. "I best be going as well."

After they left the dining room, Elmwood spook quietly to her. "Morgan, that was not an appropriate response you gave to Nallix. She is not familiar with our customs and may not always speak as expected."

"Yes, sir. I understand what you are saying."

"Good. It's alright to be proud of the ship and the crew, but let's make sure we deliver our viewpoints politely."

"Yes, sir. I'm looking forward to our next mission."

[8]

ELMWOOD PEERED at a monitor in the Command centre as the Star Hawk completed its hyperspace jump just outside the orbit of the seventh planet, approximately eight A.U. from the Coelum star system.

"Inform me of any signal we receive." Captain Elmwood spoke to the Communication Officer, Janice Madison.

"Yes, sir." Madison touched various controls on her console. A few moments later, she announced, "Ship sensors have picked up satellite detection posts. Since we are not in stealth mode, they should have seen us, and will report our presence."

"Very good. Steermaster, maintain a speed of point five light speed toward the planet Divinus."

Minutes passed and Madison informed Elmwood there was an incoming message. "It's from General Edward McQuaid, head of Divinus Inner Space Security."

Elmwood sat at his console. "Very good. Route the call here."

The monitor showed a clean-shaven man of average height, dressed in a dark blue uniform with gold-colour trim. He stood with a rigid posture.

"General McQuaid, I am Captain Julius Elmwood of the Alliance ship the Star Hawk. We are not here for any military reasons but to engage in trade discussions."

"Trade discussions using a military ship? We do not have any record of the Alliance worlds requesting trade negotiations."

"The Alliance worlds currently do not have any formal method of contacting any of the Rebel worlds. Therefore, we are using the Star Hawk to approach the Rebel worlds. I'm sure you can appreciate our concern for any Alliance ship entering the Rebel world's jurisdiction. The Star Hawk is here only to defend our diplomatic team."

"A very large defence. What type of trade is on your agenda?"

"The Alliance worlds produce a wide range of products I'm sure would interest Divinus. Part of our interest in establishing trade is to reduce the amount of pirating of Alliance ships. It is a practice that requires a resolution."

McQuaid gave a small nod of his head, acknowledging the veiled threat of a required resolution. "Very well, Captain Elmwood. I will contract the authorities regarding your request for trade discussions. You may proceed toward Divinus but must stop at ten million kilometres away. Is that understood?"

"Yes, General McQuaid."

Elmwood broke the connection. "Steermaster, proceed to a point ten million kilometres away from Divinus."

Madison reported, "Sir, a dozen military craft are moving toward the Star Hawk."

"That's to be expected. Put the ship on Yellow Standby."

Just over an hour later, another message came in for Elmwood from Divinus. Elmwood took the message at his console again. This time, the monitor showed a woman wearing a conservative business suit who sat behind a desk.

"I am Elizabeth Harold of the Divinus Trade Authority Office. I understand you represent an Alliance worlds delegation interested in pursuing formal trade negotiations."

"Yes, Ms. Harold. While I am the captain of the Star Hawk, Senior Diplomat Tiffany Harris will lead the trade delegation. She has the authority to conclude trade contracts for all Alliance worlds."

"I see. This is most unusual to be conducting high-level trade negotiations on such short notice. It makes one wonder if there's an additional motive for these trade talks." Harold didn't show any emotion as she spoke.

"To be clear, the trade negotiations can be just a start of our dialogue. The Star Hawk has a mandate to initiate trade and goodwill toward the Rebel worlds. It is the Alliance worlds' view that the Rebel and Alliance worlds are coming to a period where hostilities are becoming a possibility. Pirate attacks on Alliance ships are increasing and that is a practice that is unacceptable."

"That sounds very close to a threat."

"You asked if there is an additional motive for these talks. I provided you with one. Simply said, the present status of pirate ships raiding Alliance vessels needs to end. Our request for trade negotiations with Divinus is one step toward that goal. I want to be clear on this. We will leave peacefully if you decide against meeting with us."

Harold spread her fingers, holding her hands close together as she tapped the fingers against one another. She took a deep breath. "Well, captain, your words are carefully contrived to sound like they are just a point of view of good intentions. I doubt if we asked the Star Hawk to leave, it would be the last we saw of an Alliance warship. I have scheduled a meeting tomorrow afternoon and I will send you details later of the meeting. However, you will be required to send a shuttle with your delegation. We do not want the Star Hawk to be any closer, for obvious reasons."

"Understood. Thank you for your agreement to a meeting." Elmwood closed the connection and sighed. "She would make a good poker player. Cancel the Yellow Standby. We're going to be here a while."

———

First Officer Morgan Regan entered the Eagle Two shuttle. She had a discussion with Elmwood and Harris on the number of personnel to take and which shuttle type to take. The Falcon shuttles held five crew members and were comfortable to sit in. The larger Eagle shuttles could hold ten and were lightly armoured. The interior was not as comfortable, but could obtain a higher speed than the smaller shuttles. She decided the ability to arrive sooner at Divinus negated the less comfortable seating. The larger shuttle would also allow for additional personnel besides the negotiating team. Elmwood and Harris agreed the Eagle shuttle with its military capabilities would show Divinus the Alliance resolution in stopping pirating.

Besides Morgan and Senior Diplomat Harris, the Eagle Two contained a pilot, two middle level diplomats, a military officer and Sensor Readings Tactician Teela Mezcal.

Morgan instructed the pilot. "Okay, Lieutenant Fremont, take us to Divinus." She settled back in her seat. She watched as the shuttle slide out of the hanger where the other shuttles waited on angled ramps, facing the exit doors. She looked over at Harris as she studied her tablet, preparing for the meeting in a few hours. Her assistants, a man and a woman, were doing the same thing, but were also quietly conversing as they sat next to each other. The military officer at the rear of the shuttle appeared to be nervous, sitting stiffly. Morgan considered his addition to the shuttle unnecessary, other than to show their hosts the Alliance was taking the negotiations seriously and protecting their interests.

Harris, sitting across the aisle from Morgan, put down her tablet. "How did Paul take being excluded from the talks?"

She considered the Charter of Conduct Officer's face when she rejected his request to accompany them to the trade talks. "He was disappointed, of course. He was reluctant to accept that the Charter of Conduct viewpoint wouldn't be beneficial at our initial meeting."

"I feel sorry for him. He doesn't have many friends on the ship. The Charter is very important to him, and he wasn't allowed to bring its merits to this meeting."

"Do you think having Paul along would help at these meetings?"

"Heavens, no. The Charter is one reason the Rebel worlds refused to join the Alliance. I just feel for him. He looks so sad sometimes."

Morgan agreed. "Yes, I know what you mean. We've tried to include him when we see him, but he doesn't fit in easily." She pointed at the tablet. "Are you ready for the meeting?"

"As much as I can be. There are too many variables to plan for every eventuality. I'm trying to make sure I know their customs and how to respond properly."

"Anything in particular?"

"The ones we are meeting are part of the military and are very formal with titles and actions. The royal family, which oversees the military, enjoys rituals and a lot of pomp. The civilians dress and act very casual. There doesn't seem to be much contact between the military and the civilians."

"Since we're meeting the military for the meetings, I guess we're to act on the formal side."

"Yes. I suspect they will be taken aback by your ship's uniform. The diplomat uniforms are more conservative, but yours will open their eyes." She smiled. "That may be a good thing." She considered her own uniform. She wished it was more fashionable and fitted in better with the ship's uniform. She remembered the excitement she felt in being offered the position of Senior Diplomat on the Star Hawk. She knew she was likely chosen because she was single and willing to travel on a military vessel into the Rebel worlds territory. That, and not having a serious relationship she would have to leave behind. More established diplomats were reluctant to leave the safety of employment on Alliance world planets. She had hoped to fit in better with the Star Hawk crew, but her uniform and position seemed to place her outside the social circles on the ship. She wished for better relationships on the Star Hawk, but suspected that may take more time.

The Eagle Two landed on the roof of a spaceport the size of a small town. The building wasn't high, less than a hundred stories, but its large surface area allowed for various cargo ships to land. A part of the roof met their exit doors, and Harris and the others entered the government building without stepping outside.

A delegation led by Elizabeth Harold, which included several military officers among the official representatives, met them.

Harold shook hands with Harris. "Welcome to Divinus. Allow me to escort your party to your private quarters. You may wish to freshen up before our meeting at fourteen hundred. If you require any additional services, we will be glad to accommodate you the best we can."

They arrived at several suites that allowed access to each other through privacy doors. Morgan contacted the Star Hawk, showing their present location and that the meeting was scheduled soon. The pilot and the military officer protected the Eagle shuttle against intrusion.

Ten minutes before the meeting was to begin, two military officers escorted them to the meeting room, several floors below their suite. The meeting room differed from what Harris expected to see. Instead of a large table with functional chairs surrounding it, there was a small round table in the centre of the room. Around the table were eight armchairs, each with an attached side table that could be shifted to the front to function as a desk. Each arm also had a provision to hold a beverage.

Harris noted each chair was made of a different hue of pastel colours. She and the others stood by the chairs, waiting for the chime for the meeting to come to order. Elizabeth Harold touched a control on her wrist, and a chime sounded. Everyone sat and waited for her to begin the meeting.

"May the powers that be allow for a positive outcome for all those present at this meeting." Elizabeth Harold looked around at those seated. "This meeting is to look for a mutual satisfying agreement for trade between the Alliance worlds and the Divinus. Ms. Tiffany Harris, do you have an opening statement?"

"Yes, I do." Harris knew Divinus culture for meetings required hope for a positive outcome. "We trust these meetings will lead to a better understanding of the wants and desires of Divinus and the Alliance worlds, leading to an exchange of goods and ideas." She saw Harold give a nod of approval. The meeting could now begin on the agenda.

Almost an hour later into the meeting, Elizabeth Harold objected. "I am sorry, but your request to stop any Alliance citizen from being traded as a slave on Divinus is not practical. Who would pay for the loss of the slave? How would we determine the slave was originally from an Alliance world? Slaves often come part of a trade shipment. How do we accept part of the cargo, and not the slaves? The administration of such a request would be expensive and difficult."

Harris didn't want to get into a discussion on how slavery was wrong and why it was banned on the Alliance worlds. That would set up barriers to other negotiation items. "Perhaps we can work out a compromise. I agree trying to find individual Alliance citizens among a group of slaves would be difficult. However, when a pirate ship comes to Divinus with a cargo comprising only Alliance goods and with slaves, can we not agree there is a likelihood those slaves are from the Alliance worlds?"

Harold conferred with her three other representatives. "For the sake of this discussion, I will support that assertion."

"Then, if you were to confiscate the slaves from the pirates, the Alliance worlds would reimburse you for obtaining their release. We would not ask for the cargo to be returned, only the Alliance citizens."

"That is something we can consider. However, once we take slaves from the pirates, they would soon stop bringing slaves to Divinus and go to the next Rebel world."

"That is true. But it means a longer journey for them and makes it less worthwhile to kidnap Alliance citizens for slavery. We intend going to every nearby Rebel world and offering the same option of returning Alliance citizens. We believe we can eventually stop the pirates from capturing our citizens."

"But you're not concerned about the cargo?"

"We are. But our priority is the safety of our people. Eventually, we hope to stop the pirates from attacking any Alliance ships. We aren't there yet."

"We have recently received information that the Star Hawk hunted down some pirate ships that had stopped to undergo repairs. It appears you freed slaves but didn't destroy the pirate ships, which seems to be unusual. My question is, how did you track the pirate ships? Is this technology reliable enough to track all pirate ships?"

Harris would not reveal it was by luck they came across the pirate ships. "I'm sorry, but that technology is still classified, even from me. However, I will say that although we could've easily destroyed the pirate ships, the Alliance worlds are not interested in revenge. We cannot have peace by using destruction to achieve it."

"A very good point. It is now time for lunch. We can resume our meeting afterward." She pressed a control on her wrist and a double chime sounded. "Allow me to lead you to the dining room."

Tiffany Harris was glad the dining room was more conventional than the meeting room. She picked a chair at an oval black table and waited as servants brought in various dishes for the guests to choose from. Harris returned a smile to a woman who offered a plate of vegetables.

Wine was poured, although most of the participates only sipped at the beverage.

Elizabeth Harold casually asked if the meal was satisfactory. "Some food you may find unique in flavour, as we have spices that only grow on Divinus." She looked at Morgan. "Have you enjoyed the meal, First Officer Regan?"

"Yes, it is very good."

"And was the service good as well?"

"Yes, they did a fine job of presenting the various plates."

"They are slaves. We use them for various tasks. You may have noticed they are happy."

"That may be true," Morgan responded. "Perhaps they would be even happier if they had a choice in what they do."

"A clever retort." Elizabeth smiled. "Forgive me for saying so, but doesn't your collar represent slavery?"

"Not the way you think it does. I'm a slave to the Star Hawk. The ship is my first master, and the collar represents my allegiance to her."

"Interesting. Your collar and uniform remind me of Praxton. That seems unusual on an Alliance ship."

"The Star Hawk is an Alliance ship but was built at Praxton. A large part of the crew came from Praxton and we adopted their customs, such as clothing."

"A former Rebel world supplying an Alliance battleship. That's something I never expected to see."

"Our human universe is changing. I believe both Praxton and the Alliance worlds were better joining together."

The lunch ended, and they made their way back to the meeting room. Tiffany walked next to Morgan and spoke in a low voice.

"That was a good promotion of our goal of extending Alliance world agreements."

"Thank you."

"But I was curious when you said the Star Hawk was your first master. Is there a second one? Such as Captain Elmwood?"

"No comment."

Elizabeth Harold looked at her tablet and raised her head to look at Tiffany Harris. "Ms. Harris, I did not expect our meetings would reach this point in our discussions so soon. I would like to state the main points we have arrived at. First, Divinus agrees to, when practical to do so, to confiscate Alliance goods from pirates, Divinus will also protect and return Alliance citizens captured for slavery. Divinus will also permit up to six Alliance customs officers to assist Divinus in determining illegal pirating. In return for these considerations, Alliance worlds will allow unrestricted trading of textiles, food, beverages and entertainment with Divinus. In addition, Divinus may purchase, or trade for, up to one billion metric tons of purified titanium and one billion metric tons of purified tungsten."

"Yes, those are the key items in my notes as well. I have the authority to sign this trade agreement, but I understand your side needs royal assent."

"That is correct. Normally, this is just a formality, but because this agreement is with the Alliance worlds, it may take longer to study all the details. Would the Star Hawk be willing to wait until the agreement can receive royal assent? This may take two days."

"Yes, we will wait until Divinus is satisfied with the terms. In the meantime, would you and negotiating team like to come to the Star Hawk tomorrow for dinner? It will give us a chance to further our understanding of each other."

"We would be honoured to visit your ship."

[9]

CAPTAIN ELMWOOD SAT with Senior Diplomat Harris and First Officer Regan in the executive meeting room.

"Thank you for bringing me up to date regarding the negotiations. I concur having them over for dinner will help solidify relations." He glanced at his tablet. "Our sensor tactician, Teela Mezcal, was able to glean some data while on the Eagle Two. It appears Divinus does a rather robust trade. That we knew before. However, it also appears that there are some trading irregularities, bribes and undisclosed cargo. Considering the extensive amount of goods passing through Divinus, that is expected. What is unusual is an area below where your meetings were held is devoid of electronic signals. We believe that is where the royal interests are, which includes living areas and the administration."

"Is that a concern?" Regan asked. "It could just be a sign the royal family want to ensure their privacy."

"True, that is likely the reason. Because our negotiations are not concluded, it is something to keep in mind." He looked at Regan. "For this dinner, I believe we should include Charter of Conduct Officer Paul Thyssen. I will have a word with him stressing this is not the best time to push the Charter's agenda of a harmonized society. In the meantime, could you talk to our food and beverage manager, Diana Adoria? I would like her full attention in the meal's preparation, which will include appetizers and after dinner refreshments."

———

Diana looked up from her office chair at the approaching first officer, giving her a smile as she stood. "Good afternoon. What brings you here? Something regarding the dinner tomorrow for our guests?"

"Yes, Captain Elmwood wants to make sure everything is covered for the dinner, including appetizers and refreshments afterward."

"It won't be a problem. I've studied up on Divinus' food and culture. They enjoy using a lot of spices and herbs in their food. I will use a blend of their style of food with some of our traditional dishes. The challenge might be pairing the right wine with the food."

"I have no doubt you'll find the right wine for each food group."

"Thank you. I found something unusual. They grow a dark red berry that has a rather interesting characteristic. Basically, an over-the-top aphrodisiac. They take it only in small quantities due to its powerful effect. And no, I will not be serving it." She grinned. "I don't want to cause a problem with our dinner for our guests."

Morgan laughed. "Yes, and I'm glad you found out about it before including it in our dinner plans. Tell me, how things are going with Master Derik?"

Diana rolled her eyes. "How did I get involved with a man who thinks romance is an extra pair of cuffs?"

"Praxton males have a different view of relationships."

"No kidding. Master Derik has set up rules for me to follow but doesn't acknowledge he has to make any changes for himself. I'm not sure what to make of his various conditions other than I know he likes me. It seems he also wants to punish me. It's difficult to figure out if this is what I want."

"If you want a powerful male, Master Derik provides that. He will protect you and make you feel wanted. You just may not always agree with him."

"There lies the problem. I have a tendency to speak my mind. If we have a disagreement, it's me that ends up over his knee and getting a spanking."

"That sounds about right for a Praxton relationship." Morgan laughed.

"If it makes you feel any better, there are quite a few females getting their butts smacked."

"I don't know if that makes me feel any better, but I accept it is a way of life on board the Star Hawk. I better get back to working on the menu."

Morgan left, and Diana returned to working at her desk. She picked out three wines and a liqueur for the dinner, then studied desserts. Satisfied with the menu, she left her office to where Senior Technician Holston worked, finding him inspecting a pressure regulator.

"Master Derik, I have a request to make."

He looked at her, taking his time staring at her before meeting her eyes. "Yes, what is it, Diana?"

"I am in charge of catering the dinner with diplomats from the planet Divinus. My evening will be to ensure everything is perfect. I need to ask permission to leave my top on during that time, which will probably run past nine p.m."

"I see. If I am to grant your request, then I will require an additional obligation from you."

"What will that be?"

"I shall ask you to cook me dinner in your suite the following evening."

"Dinner?" She smiled. "Will you be requiring me to wear something in particular, or do anything special?"

"Of course. You will be nude, save for an appropriate use of cuffs and restraints."

"Of course, Master Derik. I will be pleased to prepare you dinner as you like it." Diana left, speculating on what type of dinner she would make for him.

Definitely not a vegetarian dish. He likes his meat. As for what I'll wear, that has been taken care of. I am getting used to being half-naked, so this isn't a big deal being naked and in cuffs. I wonder how Master Derik would enjoy being the one in cuffs and a collar. He would have to obey me instead. She smiled. *Well, that's never going to happen. Besides, I rather like things the way they are. There's something about wearing a collar, cuffs, and chains that makes me feel feminine and sexy.*

She returned to her workstation, going over the formal dinner menu one more time, making sure the wine and food paired well. She worked on the formulas for various wines and wished she had a wider selection to choose from. Satisfied with her choices, she ended the day by changing and going out for dinner by herself, choosing to be alone as she reviewed the dinner for Divinus.

[10]

SENIOR DIPLOMAT TIFFANY HARRIS took a glass from the tray. She watched the server carry the tray to the next guest and speculated what Elizabeth Harold, the Divinus Trade Authority official, thought of the servers' dress. Besides wearing the ship's uniform, they also wore a full complement of chains, including chains between their ankle cuffs. *She must think half the women are slaves on this ship.* Harris briefly watched a holographic quartet play classical music as she strolled over to Captain Elmwood.

"Captain."

"Ms. Harris. So far, it appears our pre-dinner social is going well. The Divinus Trade Authority group are enjoying the drinks and appetizers and seem to be in good spirits."

"That's true. I wonder if some good cheer is because of the what the servers are wearing. The men, at least, appreciate how they are presenting themselves."

"You're not jealous, are you? What you're wearing is very attractive too."

"Please. The diplomat uniform is practical, not interesting."

"It could be. You have the authority to tailor your uniform to something you feel will help in negotiations with other worlds. Simply put, you can have a uniform designed something more to your liking."

"That's something to keep in mind. Meanwhile, we still have women in a sexy uniform strolling around in chains. That's tough to top."

"Actually, that's the modest side of Praxton entertaining guests. On Praxton, during special events, nude women would lie on tables with food placed on them. They tie women with rope on poles at the entrance and in the foyer. Before you get upset, the women consider it an honour to be presented this way."

"An honour to be tied up naked? To each their own." She smiled. "Still, I understand the reasoning behind it. Tied up naked women would attract a lot of attention and add to the atmosphere."

"I'm glad you understand how Praxton culture works. Shall we converse with the Divinus delegation?"

"Yes, I suspect they may believe all the women on the Star Hawk enjoy walking around in a collar and chains."

The captain placed a hand on the small of her back and gently pressed her toward Elizabeth Harold.

Harris smiled at the Divinus trade representative. "Elizabeth, are you enjoying our social?"

"Yes, I find this different that our usual get togethers on Divinus. Mind you, I speak only about our government. The royal social events are very different."

"How are your social events conducted?"

"Our government social gatherings are more formal. The music is more subdued and less likely to use a holographic band. As you can see by my dress, people dress more conservatively." She gave a quick smile. "Not that I disapprove of how you and the servers are dressed. I think what the women and men are wearing add to the event."

"Thank you. I believe it is time for dinner. I'd love to continue to talk to you about Divinus and the differences you see on the Star Hawk."

Harris walked with the captain and Elizabeth to one of two U shaped tables with the open ends facing each other. Servers moved about, filling water glasses and bringing out the first course. She saw Diana Adoris, wearing a dark green dress, quietly walking around.

"Correct me if I'm wrong, but isn't Divinus governed by a monarchy?" Elmwood asked.

"Yes, that is true." Elizabeth nodded. "Divinus has distinct classes. The royal family and those living within its court, the government, which the monarchy appoints the ministers of different departments, the military, casuals and finally slaves. The casuals are those not employed by the government. Although some casuals do well financially, the majority live a meagre lifestyle."

"Would the slaves be part of the casuals?"

"No." Elizabeth sat, surprised Harris waited until the captain was seated first, and continued the conversation. "Some may be former slaves, but we use the majority of slaves in the government. Some of them live better than the casuals. We know that the Alliance worlds have outlawed slavery, but on the Rebel worlds, we accept it as part of our culture. The economy of many worlds depends on the use of slaves. Perhaps slavery is wrong, but many slaves are well adjusted to their condition and are not mistreated." Harris acknowledged a server as a plate was placed before her.

"As a planet that depends on trade, you must encounter many cultures." Harris asked.

"Yes, every planet is like an island of their own beliefs. What seems common and reasonable on some worlds would surprise you. For example, there is one planet where everyone wears a hat or head covering. The men wear hats and women a hairpiece. Some hats and hairpieces can be elaborate. It shocks them to see others without a head covering of some sort. On your ship, I notice the women wear a collar. Collars aren't uncommon, of course, but collars as part of a ship's uniform is surprising."

Harris waited until they removed the first course, and the next one placed in front of her. "The Star Hawk follows the Praxton culture. Initially we tried a blend of the Alliance and Praxton ways but later adopted the Praxton way of doing things."

"That makes sense. Praxton is a former Rebel world and has a powerful influence on other worlds. It seems the Alliance worlds have found that out as well. I noticed you don't wear a collar. Is that by choice or that the Alliance diplomats aren't allowed to?"

"I guess it's by choice. I could wear a collar but never even thought about it before. There are some other Praxton customs I don't follow on the ship." She looked across the table at Elmwood, who was listening, but didn't show any facial expression.

"May I ask what they are?"

"Generally, women defer to men on the ship. For example, men will sit at a table first and start eating first. I don't always follow that custom. I guess I'm seen as a rebel that way."

"Not a rebel." Elmwood chuckled. "Just someone who has their own set of rules. We're lucky to have her on board as we meet new worlds."

Harris was glad when the conversation shifted to various trades Divinus did with other worlds. She touched her neck. *I may be the only woman not wearing a collar on the Star Hawk. Maybe I should modify my uniform closer to the ship's uniform and add a collar. If I'm going to be on this ship for a long time, maybe I need to align myself more with the rest of the crew. Maybe I could finally find a friend or two.*

The dinner ended, and they moved back to an open area, enjoying after-dinner drinks. Harris listened as Paul Thyssen, the Charter of Conduct Officer, introduced himself to Elizabeth Harold.

"It's wonderful to meet you as well. Tell me what your role is on the Star Hawk."

Thyssen licked his lips and took a quick drink. His hand shook momentarily. "My role is more of a consultation. As I'm sure you're aware, the Charter of Conduct rules are complex and sometimes require expert interpretation. The Star Hawk follows many of the Praxton traditions, but we want them still to align with the objectives of the Charter."

"Forgive me for being blunt, but wasn't the Charter of Conduct Office the driving force to invade Praxton?" Elizabeth tilted her head. "Now you're here to ensure the Charter rules are being adhered to?"

Thyssen stuttered as he tried to answer. "Well, yes, perhaps to a point. I mean, the Charter wasn't the only reason Praxton was, was, was confronted. There were...complex issues. At the end, Praxton has become a welcomed member of the Alliance worlds."

"So how does the Charter of Conduct Officer view women wearing collars and deferring to men on the Star Hawk? Isn't there some conflict there with the Charter?" Elizabeth looked amused at Thyssen's discomfort.

Elmwood joined their group, placing a hand on Thyssen's shoulder. "Paul and I have had discussions on that very subject. As it turns out, there is flexibility on how to follow many of the Charter rules. What it comes down to acceptance of a way of doing things. Individuals may not always agree with some rules we have, but for the sake of a smooth-running ship, they will follow them. Paul has offered his viewpoint on several issues, and I take them into consideration."

"The Praxton lifestyle fits within the Charter rules," Tiffany Harris added. "Divinus has some unique laws and rules. The Alliance worlds, and the Charter of Conduct Office, respects them. If Divinus wants to increase relations with the Alliance worlds, we will not try to force change on how you do things. Our primary objective is to protect Alliance world citizens and property."

"Very good." Elizabeth made eye contact with her. "There was apprehension dealing with Alliance worlds knowing the history of the Charter of Conduct Office. For the time being, we will accept there isn't any wish to force us to follow the Charter. The memory of what happened to Praxton is still fresh."

"I understand. Can we accept times have changed, and this is a new beginning for relations between Divinus and the Alliance worlds?"

"Yes, we can." She lifted her glass. "To new relationships."

<hr>

Harris made her way to her room, carrying her shoes after she stepped out of the elevator. *That was some after-dinner talk. Poor Paul must have felt he was being ambushed. Good thing the captain arrived to smooth out the talks. The last thing they need is for the Charter to frighten off potential trade partners. Hopefully, Divinus and other planets won't see the Charter as a threat to their autonomy anymore.*

She dropped her shoes at the door and poured herself a glass of wine. From her dining room, she could see into her living room, and her bedroom door at the far side. She sipped her wine, pleased how her first planetary trade agreement went. *We stopped the pirates from using Divinus as a place to take Alliance citizens and goods, and increased trade to the Alliance worlds. Providing the prince signs the agreement and Elizabeth said that isn't likely a problem.*

Her mobile chirped, and she answered.

"Tiffany, this Elizabeth. I have just received word from Prince Francis that he will sign the agreement. There is a formality in we request you must travel to Divinus and meet him. There will be a dinner and a celebration. Will you be able to attend tomorrow?"

"That's wonderful news. And yes, I would be honoured to meet him."

[11]

TIFFANY HARRIS TRAVELLED with only a pilot on the Falcon One shuttle. She wasn't certain just what type of meeting she would have with the prince and carried several options regarding clothing. Elizabeth Harold greeted her as she exited from the shuttle and arranged for her luggage taken to her suite. They stepped into a private elevator operated by a royal guardsman.

"Perhaps you can advise me on what I should wear, and do, when I meet Prince Francis."

"Of course. This afternoon, you will meet him for a formal meeting where you will sign the trade agreements with him. This won't take long, and you can wear your diplomat's uniform. You can retire to your suite and rest until dinner. I suggest you wear a formal dress. After dinner, you'll have another break to relax. Next is the grand celebration.

"Just so you know, this will be my first invitation to a grand celebration, so I'm nervous about this as well. Wear an evening dress. There will be entertainment, drinking, dancing and it will last until morning."

"That sounds like quite a party."

They stepped out of the elevator and Elizabeth led the way to Tiffany's suite. "Here you go. I need to inform you your mobile doesn't work here. It's part of the security for the royal family that outside devices do not work."

"Then how can I communicate with my ship?"

"In your room there is a device you may use. It goes through an operator who will connect you to your ship." She lowered her voice. "I'm sorry, but the royal family has had its share of scandals and now restricts all outgoing messages. The prince caused some of those scandals."

"Should I be worried?"

Elizabeth stepped into the room. "I don't believe so. He has an eye for the ladies and has four wives. You may find his attention a little strong if he finds you attractive. Prince Francis is handsome and is used to having things his way."

After Elizabeth left, Tiffany inspected the extensive suite. It featured a sitting room plus a large bedroom that also included an armchair, a desk and a walk-in closet. The bed, she decided, was large enough for three people. She freshened up in the bathroom that had both a steam shower and a soaker tub. Various scented oils were available along with soft hidden lights for a quiet time in the bath. *Maybe I can stay here a couple of days.* She contacted the Star Hawk using the room's communicator, a square block sitting on a table in the sitting room.

"Put me through to the Star Hawk, First Officer Morgan Regan."

A male voice responded. "One moment while I authorize the communication."

Tiffany waited and Morgan responded. "Hi, Tiffany. Is everything okay? You're not using your communicator."

"Yes, I'm fine. Security protocols prevent me from using my mobile, so I have to use this device. It's being monitored, just so you know."

"All right, but this is rather unusual."

"I agree. It seems there will be a big party tonight. They call it a grand celebration, and I'm going to guess I won't be getting up early tomorrow. I may not be communicating much until I leave for the shuttle."

"Okay. Enjoy the party."

[12]

Diana checked the vegetables, and the baked potatoes once more. She was satisfied how they looked. The pot roast was nearing perfection and would be by the time they were ready to eat. She returned to the living room where Derik waited, drinking a glass of cabernet sauvignon.

"Dinner will be ready in fifteen minutes, exactly, if it pleases Master Derik." She picked up her own glass of wine and kneeled on the floor in front of where he rested in an armchair.

"That sounds perfect to me."

Diana looked up at him, remaining relaxed as he gazed at her nude form. Not quite nude, for she added the usual Praxton accessories such as cuffs and chains. The gold-coloured metal wrist cuffs had a thin chain between them, and another chain went from the centre of the wrist chain to one around her waist. Her ankle cuffs, and the chain between them, matched the wrist cuffs. Her final set of jewellery was gold nipple clips in the shape of a starburst. The cuffs and chains made her feel a more helpless, but paradoxically, a little less naked. At first, she was apprehensive at the prospect of cooking dinner for him in the nude, but as the evening progressed, she became more comfortable. She had showered in front of him previously in the beginning of their relationship, but their relationship had taken a downturn since then. This was a chance to reverse that difficult time. "I'm sure you'll enjoy what I've prepared. Would you like more wine?"

He took a longer sip from his glass. "Yes, please. I enjoy the sight of you moving around, even if it is only to refill my glass."

She rose smoothly to her feet, smiling. "I confess I enjoy you watching me. Having said that, perhaps we need to balance the sheet a little. I would like to see you naked as well."

"All in good time. Praxton customs rule here."

"Those Praxton rules mean you hold all the cards." She sauntered into the kitchen, checking the food. She called out, "Dinner is ready, Master Derik." Diana placed portions on two plates and carried them to the dining room.

"I hope this is to your satisfaction, Master Derik."

"I know it will be fantastic. I'm looking forward to the first bite."

Diana sat and waited for Derik to take the first bite. She watched him as his fork took a piece of meat. He chewed, smiled and proclaimed, "Exceptional."

Diana released her breath and reached for her own fork. She had allowed enough length of the chains, so she wasn't hindered in eating. The chains restricted her movements, and she was still eating when Derik finished. "Would you like another helping, Master Derik?"

"No, thank you. That was very nice. I shall wait for you and enjoy the wine."

Diana continued to eat, watching him watching her. She felt a renewed flush of arousal and warmth penetrating her core. She finished her plate and stood, taking both plates back to the kitchen, and returned with a bottle of wine.

She refilled his glass. "I have prepared dessert, but I thought we could relax first."

"Of course. Shall we retire to the living room?"

Diana followed him to the living room, where once more she kneeled in front of him. This time, he chose the couch.

He swirled the red wine in his glass as he eyed her. "You look most tempting."

Diana lowered her head for a moment, then looked back at him. "What do you want to do to me?" She smiled. "With theses cuffs and chains, I believe I'm at your mercy."

"Tell me, Diana, do you like it when I'm in control like this?"

"Yes."

"Then why do you resist surrendering to me?"

"What I want is difficult to explain. Yes, I want you to be strong and in control. But I want my feelings to be considered and respected, in particular I am from an Alliance world background."

"Okay, you said that before. But I'd prefer it if we were to move forward in our relationship and give me time to understand your Alliance ways."

"I'm sure you prefer it that way, but no. I want you to do it my way."

He took a drink of his wine and appeared to ponder the situation. "Okay, so no sex until I figure your Alliance ways."

"The same holds true for me as well."

"That makes me feel better." He grinned. "Now, did you say something about dessert?"

She laughed. "Apple crumble with ice cream." She stood. "I will serve it with coffee."

Ten minutes later, Diana raised her eyebrows as Derik finished his dessert. "You ate that fast. Would you like a second helping, Master Derik?"

He grinned. "It was very tasty, but I best not." He patted his stomach. "I need to make sure I don't have to change my belt size."

"I don't believe you have to worry about your weight. You're a big man and can carry a few kilos without it showing."

"Thanks, but I know you take care in how you look, and I should do the same." He finished his coffee.

"Would you like a drink? Perhaps you would like to retire to the living room."

"Yes, perhaps a small pour of a single-malt would be nice."

Diana went to the kitchen, poured the whisky into a tumbler and went to the living room where Derik sat in the armchair. She passed the glass to him and kneeled in front of him.

"Is there anything else I can get for you, Master Derik?"

He stared at the naked form in front of him. "There's something I want from you."

"Master Derik, I would love to give that to you as well. But I need my conditions met first."

"You are making it rather frustrating for me."

"I'm feeling rather frustrated too, but I'm not giving in." She smiled. "I'm forced to rely on my own devices until we can fully enjoy each other's company."

"It is rather ironic that if we were on an Alliance world, I would have you in bed right now. However, your insistence I show you some Alliance customs is preventing what we both want."

"Yes, but you knew what I wanted for some time now. I think if you truly want me, you need to make the effort."

"I will. Perhaps after I finish my drink, we can call it a night. Seeing a lovely naked woman and not being able to do anything about it is torture. Pleasant torture, but it needs to be come to an end."

"I understand, Master Derik."

He finished his whisky. "If I didn't know any better, one would believe you're enjoying sitting naked in front of me, knowing I can't do a thing abut it."

"Oh, Master Derik, I wouldn't dream of teasing you." She gave him a warm smile.

He stood. "Next time I shall give you a much-needed spanking."

She glanced at the strain at the fly of his pants, the semi-open weave showing the impression behind it. "If you feel it's necessary, Master Derik." Diana rose to her feet, moving with him to the door.

He paused with the door partially open, giving her a long, deep kiss. One hand slowly slid along her rib cage before they broke apart.

"Until tomorrow. I'll be here in the morning to escort you to work."

"I look forward to it."

Diana watched him walk down the hallway. A few crew members observed her at the open doorway. She ignored their stares. She was getting used to nudity on the Star Hawk.

———

Tiffany checked her appearance in the bedroom viewscreen. She wished the diplomate uniform was more stylish, and compared to the Star Hawk's military uniforms, it looked conservative. She sighed and wondered what a new uniform for herself should look like.

There was a knock on the door, and when she opened it Elizabeth Harold was standing there, waiting for her.

"Are you ready? It is important to be punctual when meeting royalty."

"Yes, I am." She noticed Elizabeth was wearing the same style of uniform she had seen on her before, but this was newer and fitted better. She had also had her hair fixed up and added makeup.

"Then let's make our way to where the documents will be signed. By the way, we will do the signatures on actual paper, and you will receive a copy."

"Paper? I haven't signed anything on paper before." She paused. "I don't have a pen or a writing instrument."

"No worries. One will be provided. Paper is rare, but royalty uses it on important documents. It's a tradition from long ago. The king has a royal department of paper makers who know the ancient art of turning wood fibers into paper."

"I'm looking forward to seeing this paper document."

They used an elevator to go down two floors. Once again, an elevator operator was present. A room with two guards posted at the entrance waited at the end of a hallway. They entered and met with several uniformed officials. At the end of the room, the prince sat behind a wood table. On the table rested several sheets of white paper with black text on them.

As Tiffany approached the table, Prince Francis stood. He stepped around the table to greet her, extending a hand.

She shook his hand, looking up at the bearded man. Tiffany took a deep breath, feeling intimidated by him and the surroundings.

"It is my honour to meet someone as lovely as yourself. You make me glad for this opportunity to sign a formal agreement with the Alliance worlds."

"Thank you, your highness. I wish to extend our thanks for your involvement in the trade agreement. It is a privilege to have met you."

The paper, Tiffany noted, was not perfectly smooth. It had a texture to it, and she wasn't sure if that was intentional, or a characteristic of how paper was made. She calmed herself enough to sign the documents without shaking her hand. The prince also signed along with two other officials as witnesses.

It surprised Tiffany when one copy she signed was placed in a heavy paper folder and inserted in a slim black leather attaché binder, along with the pen she used to sign the documents.

The prince presented the leather binder to her, bowing and extending it toward her.

A few minutes later, Tiffany left with Elizabeth. She held the leather binder close to her face, breathing in its aroma.

"This is real leather."

"Yes, it's a special gift from the prince. He wants to make a positive impression on you."

"It's very nice, but I can only guess what the ship's Charter of Conduct Officer will say about having an animal skin."

"Since it's not illegal here, he shouldn't say anything. It would be insulting to refuse it."

Tiffany returned to her room, clutching the attaché case. *I'm not giving this up without a fight.*

She placed a call via the same square device to the ship, informing them the contract was signed, mentioning it was done on actual paper, but not the leather case. She had a few hours to relax before dinner and made use of the tub.

She smelled the scent of the various oils, deciding on one in a blue glass container. She added the oil to the hot water and slipped into the tub.

"Room service, lower the lights and play soft music. Contemporary." The lights dimmed and music filtered in from hidden speakers. She closed her eyes, immersed in the comfort of water and the feeling of isolation. Her thoughts drifted to the signing of the agreement. She was shocked at putting her name on actual paper, remembering that was how documents were first produced and read. With humans living on nearly three hundred worlds, the only way they could send documents was digitally. Regardless, the Charter of Conduct Office had a section on environment, restricting the use of wood for either a construction material or refined into paper. While wood products and paper could still be purchased, the costs were high because of the reduced availability of wood. Paper products had almost completely disappeared.

Tiffany smiled at the thought of showing the paper and the leather attaché case to Paul Thyssen, the Charter of Conduct Officer. *He'll probably stutter something about it being illegal, and then give in because the paper is a legal document, and the attaché is a gift. I'll bet he can't resist touching either of them.*

Her thoughts changed to the prince, recalling his height, a handsome face, wearing a well-trimmed beard and his charming manner. *A woman could get used to being around a man like that.*

She decided her bath time was over and stepped out of the tub. She put on a silk robe and made her way to the sitting room. "Room service, could you send me tea?"

"Yes, Ms. Harris. The tea will arrive in approximately six minutes."

The bath was nice, but I feel isolated in this room. The communication to the ship is restricted and not private. But since I don't have a choice, I might as well enjoy it.

The knock on the door was followed by a voice announcing it was room service with her tea. Tiffany opened it to a pretty, short hair brunette behind a cart draped in a white cloth and holding several plates.

"Oh, I just asked for tea." She looked at the ceramic tea pot, the cup and saucer, a plate of small cookies and another with pastries.

"We thought you may enjoy a small bite with the tea." She pushed the cart into the room and poured the steaming tea into the cup. "Would you like me to add cream, sweetener, or lemon to your tea?"

Tiffany declined and looked at what the server was wearing. At first glance, it appeared to be a traditionally styled maid uniform, but she noticed the short skirt had a slit on one side to reveal bare skin high up the leg. The long sleeve, thin white top was loose until it reached the waist where it was snug. Around the server's neck was a white collar, appearing to be made of ceramic. There was a small padlock at the front of the collar latched to a chrome ring.

"Do you mind me asking if you are a slave?"

The girl smiled. "Yes, I am. The royal family purchased me to help with household duties."

"Does it bother you to know you are a slave?"

"Not at all. I consider myself fortunate to be working where I am. I'm treated well."

"But you can't leave."

"Why would I want to?" She shrugged. "Where would I go? I'm happy here."

"Fair enough." Her comment piqued Tiffany's curiosity. "Do most of the slaves here feel that way?"

"I think so. It depends on the owner, of course."

"What would happen if you took off your collar and ran away?"

She held out her left hand. An elaborate design was tattooed on the back. "Anyone who sees this tattoo would know I'm a slave. I wouldn't get away very long. I would also be punished for attempting to run away. But, like I said, I don't want to leave here."

Tiffany thanked her and went to her tea and tried one of the cookies. It was better than she expected and tried a pastry. After eating, she decided she needed to get ready for dinner.

[13]

Teela Mezcal and Mitch Gallow sat in one of the drinking lounges, this one near the men's living quarters. As usual, Mitch picked up Teela from the women's quarters, standing just outside of the common room doorway while she informed the senior female she was going out. Teela carried her shoes to the entrance and gave him a kiss.

She wondered how many of the semi-nude females he saw at the entranceway, knowing several of them made a point of walking over to have a look at him. A few of the women had seen him before and gave him a smile and a wave.

Teela carried the end of her leash, looped around her left wrist with the other end attached to her collar. She had expected he would take the leash from her, but instead, he held her hand.

"Let's go upstairs for a drink. I want to show you my quarters, but let's relax with a drink and a bite to eat first."

"That sounds wonderful. I'm looking forward to seeing your quarters." *Where I hope we can finally have some sex. Darn Yellow Standby has interfered with our alone time. The fact I was responsible for one of the Yellow Standby situations may lead to getting discipline from him. I hope.*

The lounge was busy, and Teela saw it had more men than women sitting around the tables. The conversation and laughter were loud. The women were all sitting with men and looked to be couples. One woman was topless, something Teela had noticed was becoming more prevalent. On Praxton, they considered female nudity normal. The Star Hawk was following the Praxton norms in behaviour and social customs, and as a result, women were taking advantage of not always being dressed.

Gallow ordered drinks and a small food platter from the female server. He glanced at a table where a woman sat topless, her shirt hanging on the back of the chair. "Is that something that appeals to you?"

"Sometimes it does, I have to admit. But it has to be on the right circumstances, like when I'm with you. I wouldn't do it when I'm alone."

"I understand. From what I can see, the women in your common area wear little clothing."

"Yeah, clothing is definitely optional. It took me a while to get used to that." Teela grinned. She looked up at an approaching dark-skinned man, medium height but with a muscular chest. He carried a glass of gold-coloured beer.

"Hey, Mitch."

"Al, trust you to be in here drinking."

"You know where to find me."

After Gallow introduced of Teel and Al to each other, Al smiled.

"So, this is the pretty woman you've been yapping about," Al said. "No wonder you didn't want to show her to us sooner. You wanted to keep her for yourself."

"I didn't want to give her the wrong impression by having her talking to you."

Al laughed. "What a thing to say after I saved your ass on Praxton."

"That's a faulty memory you have there. It was me keeping you safe."

Teela listened to the two men kibitz, smiling at the banter. Finally, Al turned serious.

"I best not overstay my welcome. Teela, it was great to meet you. As far as Mitch is concerned, don't you worry none about him. He's first class and will always treat you right."

"It was great to meet you as well."

After Al left, Gallow commented, "He's my best bud. We served together on Praxton. When he said he was going to apply to be on the Star Hawk, it took little convincing for me to do the same."

"So, in a way, he's responsible for us meeting. I'm glad he did."

"Me too. I'll bet right now he's wondering if you have a friend you can introduce him to."

Teela laughed. "I doubt very much he has trouble meeting women."

"Maybe that's true. But I think he's looking for someone special and you're special."

Teela blushed. *I wonder what they said about me when I wasn't there.*

After they finished their drinks, Gallow took her hand again and escorted her out of the lounge.

"Come, I want to show you my quarters now."

Teela noticed the common area for the men was smaller than for the women. The seating area was more functional, and it appeared to be less of an area for the men to socialize. She paid little attention to the empty area, going with Gallow to his room, one of eight by the common area.

She followed him to his room, removing her shoes as soon as she entered. His room was larger than hers, featuring a small sitting area with his own viewscreen for watching videos. A small combination fridge and stove sat in the corner. Teela looked around the seating area, seeing the bedroom past a wall. She saw a door at another wall at the side of the sitting room she suspected went to the washroom.

"This is a lot bigger than my room. That's hardly fair."

"The women have a larger common area. Maybe that balances it out."

"I don't think so, but I guess the Praxton custom is that women like to socialize more with each other than men."

"True. Men like to go to the bar to socialize. A large common area would be a waste." He went to the box shaped fridge and brought out two containers. He opened them before handing one to her.

"Thanks." She wandered to the bedroom, noting there was a door built into the wall that slid out. It didn't surprise her how neat the bedroom was, including the blanket corners done perfectly on the bed. The bed was wider than her own, although the same length. The closet was the same size, but the desk was longer, covering most of the length of one wall. She complimented him on his bedroom and went to sit on the loveseat that faced the viewscreen. She took a drink from the premixed cocktail. "I like your place. You can stay inside here and watch movies. My room pretty much only a bedroom and a shower. I have to hang around the common room for anything other than sleeping."

"Does that mean you've made a few friends?" He sat next to her.

"I have. There were two groups of us. Those who were originally from Praxton, and those of us from the Alliance worlds. That was at the beginning. Afterward the senior female, Narcel Cannith, laid down the law, and we all were had to be careful with her new rules. I suppose that made us closer as a group. Anyway, we all get along."

"I understand some females became best friends."

Teela laughed. "Some of them did, all right. Not me. I'm strictly into men."

"Good to know." Gallow leaned into her, kissing her on the lips. He broke away and returned for a long kiss.

Teela lifted her chin, giving Gallow an opportunity to kiss her neck. She felt a hand on her stomach that eased upward. She closed her eyes as the kisses continued and the hand cupped her breast over her top. She was content to allow him to kiss and touch her, moaning as an encouragement to continue. Teela knew enough about Praxton customs on what would come next, and she took the initiative to advance their relationship. She leaned forward, placing her drink on a small table. She took in a deep breath and rolled over his lap, crossing her wrists at the top of her head on the couch.

The first few smacks were soft and on top of her skirt. She waited as he increased the strength of his strikes. He paused to massage her cheeks and to lift her skirt. The spanking resumed, alternating between her cheeks and became more intense.

Teela took in deep breaths, sometimes enjoying the spanking and other times finding the pain too strong. She gave out only small groans, refusing to cry out.

"I'm going to smack you harder now. Ready?"

"Yes, Master Mitch. Thank you, Master Mitch." She squeezed her hands into fists as his hand came down on her ass. She kicked her feet and twisted her hips. A cry escaped her lips.

"Your ass is a beautiful red." Gallow stroked her skin.

She tried to twist around to look. "It sure feels sore and red."

"I was wondering when I would get a chance to spank you. It was worth the wait."

"It feels so good. Thank you, Master Mitch." She raised herself up, kneeling on the cushion on the loveseat. Teela took off her top. "I would like to please you now, Master Mitch." She slid on to the floor, placing herself between his legs. He didn't move as she worked open his fly and eased out his swelling cock. Her jaw dropped open as she stared at the thick shaft.

She leaned forward and licked his member before placing her lips around the head. Teela eased her mouth down over his erection, allowing it to slide deeper inside her. She paused once to ready herself and took in the entire length, lifted her head and repeated the motion. Teela rested a moment and raised her mouth to circle around the head, working her tongue around it.

Hands pressed on her shoulders, and she looked up.

"I'm not complaining. What you're doing is great." He gasped. "I want you on top of me."

"Are you sure?"

"Better move quick. I'm ready to come."

Teela climbed on top of him, impaling herself on his shaft. She used her legs to bounce on him, closing her eyes and lifting her chin. Hands squeezed her breasts. His body stiffened and he let out a long groan as she collapsed on his chest.

A minute passed before Teela rolled off Gallow. She laughed. "My ass was on fire, and it made everything much more sensitive."

"In that case, I need to give you a spanking more often."

"I won't argue with you on that."

"I'm hungry. Let's get something to eat."

Teela put on her clothes and went with Gallow to one of the dining rooms. It amused her by how fast he ate. "Wow, you really must have been hungry."

"I had to recoup my energy. It takes work to do a good spanking."

"You gave me a good paddling. I look forward to showing the girls how well you spanked me."

"You're going to show them your red ass?"

"Of course. It's something to brag about." She grinned. "The Praxton females let others know about their spankings. They also show off whip marks and rope impressions. It's a different culture they have."

"So if I was to whip you, you'd show that off too?"

Teela looked down at the table, flipped her hair back. "If you decide to whip me, I would show those off too."

Gallow took a drink of his beer. "I would like to whip you sometime."

"That is your choice, Master Mitch."

"But would you like to be whipped?" He frowned. "I'm talking about having your hands restrained above your head and your back being flogged."

She took a long breath. "Yes, I would like that, as long as it didn't hurt too much."

"Good. I'm going to inform my commanding officer that I would like to have shared accommodations with you." He peered at her. "Are you wanting this too?"

"Yes, Master Mitch. I want you as my guardian."

"I expect obedience from you. There will be discipline, as well."

"I understand and agree to this."

"Good," he said. "I best take you back to your quarters before it gets too late."

"Yes, Master Mitch." She stood and walked with him to the exit doors.

Teela was feeling excited as they walked down the hallway, holding hands.

"I believe I should establish control over you now rather than just waiting for when we're allowed to share quarters together."

"Of course, Master Mitch. What did you have in mind?"

"I think you need to have a leash with you at all times. When we're together, I want to have you leashed. That can be with a collar or wrist."

"Okay. I will always have a leash with me."

"I know this may sound unusual to you, but I like the thought of you wearing a chain belt, or something like it, with a chain that goes between your legs," he said. "I wouldn't require you to wear it often, but it would represent my control over you when I'm not around."

"I've never worn one before. But if it pleases you, I will. I understand you need to have control over me even when you're not around."

"Good. I'm positive the ship's stores carry a few different chain styles. Pick out one that you would like to wear."

They arrived at the women's quarters. "I will do as you instruct me." She put her arms around his neck and gave him a kiss. "See you tomorrow."

She strode into the common room, smiling. Five women looked up at her entrance.

A brunette, Aureo Greason, called out from where she was sitting, "What are you looking so happy about?"

"Just a very, very good evening." She turned around and lifted her skirt, receiving cheers from the others in the common room.

Aureo laughed. "Wow, did the rest of the evening go as well as the spanking?"

"It sure did. Master Mitch is going to request that we receive shared accommodation. He wants to be my guardian." Teela accepted the congratulations, deciding to have another drink with them as she related how her evening went.

Narcel Cannith, the senior female for their group, asked, "So, do you remember when I told you I would make you act like a proper female and that you may even thank me for it?"

"You were right." Teela nodded. "I'm glad you forced me to behave."

"And are you glad I made you take the fille d'affichage lessons? I understand you will perform on stage soon."

"Yes, I'm looking forward to that. I enjoy working through the routines." She sat on one of the lounge chairs next to Tess. She saw Tess, an Alliance female who quickly embraced the Praxton culture, had Julia sit on the floor by her side. Julia was nude, except for a full set of wrist and ankle cuffs with a long chain between them. Tess held the leash that went from Julia's collar.

Tess grabbed her hand and gave her a kiss on the cheek. "Congratulations. I think Master Mitch and you make a great looking couple. Julia and I have asked for shared accommodations too, so maybe we'll end up in the same area later."

Teela recalled how Julia at first resisted Tess's advances, but slowly gave in to the strong-willed woman. Part of the seduction included spankings and the use of the flogger. It was the only time Teela saw the flogger used in the common room. The common room also had restraint hooks in a wall, but they had not used them so far. The sight of them, along with the flogger, had a powerful influence of the behaviour among the women. "Thanks. It's good, Julia, that you're going to have shared accommodations. Your one room must be a little cramped."

"It is. The closet space is an issue and there's only one table for putting on makeup. Julia would like to go to her room to change and get ready for the day, but I make her wait until I'm done first. I don't want her to get used to going back to her room. That's now off limits for her." Tess stroked Julia's hair. "I still have her in a training mode."

Teela looked at Julia, who appeared content to lean against Tess. Her early rebellion to being controlled by Tess seemed to have disappeared. Two other women in her group had formed a relationship as well, but it appeared to be on equal footing.

Tess yawned. "I'm going to bed. See you in the morning." She stood and made her way to her room. Julia rose as well, following behind her.

"Julia sure is compliant."

"So far. I think Julia is more amused than enticed by Tess's desire to control her."

Teela glanced over at Karla sitting next to her. "You mean Julia is just pretending to be submissive to Tess?"

"Maybe not entirely. I think she likes the attention and Tess is her best option right now. That may change if she catches the attention of one of the officers. She craves powerful people."

"A lot of women do."

"I suppose so." Karla placed her hand on Teela's arm. "Your man certainly acts powerful, and I see how you act submissive to him."

"It's not an act. I like him when he's in control."

"Sorry, I didn't mean to sound that you were pretending. A few women do pretend to act submissive with men. I guess it's expected with this Praxton culture."

"It is. But I honestly feel obedient to him. Maybe because of the collar and cuffs, but I want to obey him. I'm not pretending."

"Okay. I can see the attraction for him. Some men just have that aura about them." She laughed. "Do you think Master Mitch would like to have more than one female?"

"I'm all that he needs." Teela laughed and stood. "Good night."

[14]

TIFFANY HARRIS SLIPPED on the grey and blue pattern dress. The dress featured an uneven hemline, rising from just above her knee on her left to mid-thigh on her right. The front had a conservative square neckline, while the back was cut much deeper, to the small of her back. She added a necklace and a bracelet before putting on high-heeled shoes, thankful that Praxton had perfected the method of making such footwear comfortable. She checked the time, realizing she had plenty of time before she had to leave for dinner. The meal was a lot later than she was used to. The room's communicator chirped.

"Tiffany, this is Elizabeth Harold. We have some time before the dinner, and I was wondering if you would like to share a drink first?"

"That would be great. I'm just waiting for when I have to leave."

"My room is close to yours. I'll be there in a few minutes."

Shortly later, Tiffany opened the door to Elizabeth, who carried a bottle of white wine.

"Please come in." She looked at the bright yellow dress Elizabeth was wearing. The short dress bared her shoulders and had a scooped neck.

"I'm nervous about this dinner, and thought if you were as well, maybe a drink would help relax us. I love your dress." Elizabeth gave a smile.

"Thank you. You look so different out of your uniform. Very nice."

Tiffany poured the wine into glasses and sat with Elizabeth on the couch. "Do you get to go to many dinners where the prince is in attendance?"

"Oh, no. I saw the prince once at a ceremony for the military, but there were over a hundred officers in attendance. This will be my first time in the royal dining hall and my first grand celebration. I'm so looking forward to it, but I'm also nervous."

"I'm nervous too. I'm think this wine will help. How did you end up going into the military as a career?"

"My parents are in the military, so that became my career choice," said Elizabeth. "On Divinus, we have social groups of royalty, military, government, casuals and slaves. People almost always marry within their social group, and they expect their offspring to follow that path."

"Does that mean, for example, casuals can't join the military?"

"In rare cases, they can. It would require a special promotion by the authorities. Sometimes slaves, or their children, can be moved up to be a casual."

"I hadn't thought they would allow slaves to have children," said Tiffany.

"Yes, although they require permission to have a relationship and to have children. I know the Alliance worlds don't approve of the use of slaves, but it works on our world. Slaves here are not mistreated, and live a comfortable, if restricted, life."

"I understand Divinus has their social structure, and that includes the use of slaves. It seems strange from where I come from, but every world has their own way of doing things."

"I hope someday we won't require slaves, but that is still far into the future. Shall we head to dinner?"

The dining room was a large, circular room. Entrance was through a door-less foyer. A rectangular table sat in the middle of the room, covered with a dark blue tablecloth as clusters of servants placed plates and utensils in position.

When Tiffany and Elizabeth entered the room, they were escorted to the table by a tall male servant. They sat next to each other, and Tiffany looked at the departing servant, admiring the cut of the blue and black uniform.

"He's rather tall."

"Anyone employed by the royal family needs to be above average in intelligence, looks and, with men, height."

A woman servant placed glasses of sparkling wine in front of them. She noticed the women's uniform, while the same colour as the men, was styled differently. Where the men's uniform was stiff looking, appearing like a tuxedo, the women's, were loose. The top was a peasant style, and the skirt was full length, at least at the back. The front of the skirt was open by an inverted U-shaped slit rising mid way up the thighs.

"That's quite a skirt the servants wear."

"The prince has an eye for the ladies and likes them presented in attractive attire."

"Mission accomplished."

Tiffany took a sip from her wine, observing the seats at the table were now filled, except for the head of the table, where an elaborate chair waited.

A few minutes later, the prince entered.

Tiffany, along with the others at the table, stood as Prince Francis made long strides to the table. He wore a decorative uniform with a vest, slash, and medals on the jacket. She saw the confident look in his steel-blue eyes, the chiselled chin and the well-trimmed beard. She stopped breathing for several seconds.

The prince made his way to the head of the table, picked up a glass of wine, and smiled. "Thank you for joining me for this dinner. We are here to celebrate, not just a written agreement with the Alliance worlds, but also the human interaction among people from diverse backgrounds. We all came from the planet Earth hundreds of years ago. We have a common heritage, a shared ancestry, and a belief we need to work together to ensure peace in the galaxy. I say to everyone present; this is a beginning of a new relationship from all of us that used to call Earth our home." He raised his glass to cheers from the guests, and a toast before sitting.

Tiffany whispered to Elizabeth, "Nice speech."

"He is an impressive speaker. Some of his speeches can be rather long but are always interesting."

"I just like hearing his voice."

Elizabeth laughed. "Yeah, that's just one of his qualities. There are a lot of women who love to spend time with him."

They served the prince first, but soon all the other guests received their first course. After the first course, additional plates and drinks were efficiently placed down and taken away. Tiffany observed that while the food on her plate looked identical to Elizabeth's, the men had different proportions on their plates.

"How come the men have different food than we do?"

"It's a Divinus custom. It is believed men require different nutrition than women, or at least prefer a different type of food. Our plate has more vegetables while the men have more meat. It depends on the situation on what they serve. Sometimes the food is identical, although the men usually have a larger portion. I'm not saying it is fair, but it is practical. Some men are pretty big and would require more substance."

"Okay, I was just curious." Tiffany finished the main course and received a glass of sparkling muscat wine when the plate was removed. She tasted the sweet, musky wine, declaring, "This is lovely."

"It is nice. I suppose it's meant to prepare us for dessert."

A few minutes later the dessert arrived, a crystal bowl of white and red swirls.

Tiffany tasted the cold mixture, the rich cream blending with a slight bitterness of red berries. "What is this called? It's delicious."

"The Emperor's Delight." She smiled. "We call those red berries calidi. As far as I know, they're only grown on Divinus."

"Really? Well, they are tasty." She looked over at one man's dessert, noting the crystal bowl had white and blue swirls. "The men have a different dessert."

"I suppose they feel men prefer a different dessert."

A woman bent between Tiffany and Elizabeth, speaking to Tiffany in a quiet voice. "Pardon the interruption, but Prince Francis would like to meet you after dinner. Perhaps Ms. Harold could introduce you formally to the prince."

Tiffany agreed, and after the woman left, whispered to Elizabeth, "I get to speak to the prince. This will be exciting."

Elizabeth cautioned her, "Yes, but be careful. Prince Francis has been rumoured to take advantage of his position."

Tiffany, along with Elizabeth, received a dessert wine. As the guests left the dining room, Elizabeth escorted Tiffany to where the prince shook hands and spoke a few words to departing guests.

"Your highness, Prince Francis, this is Senior Diplomat Tiffany Harris of the Alliance Worlds. You met her at the signing of the trade document with the Alliance worlds."

Tiffany was nervous as she met his piercing gaze and extended her hand to shake his. "Thank you for your invitation. The dinner was wonderful."

"The pleasure is all mine, I assure you." He took her hand and kissed the back of it, holding it afterward as he talked. "From what I understand, you did a marvelous job representing the Alliance World's interest while recognizing Divinus's own requirements. The Alliance worlds should be extremely pleased to have such a dedicated, intelligent envoy working on their behalf. A woman as lovely as yourself has no doubt attracted much attention at the Alliance Worlds government."

Tiffany blushed, glancing down at where the prince was using both hands to hold her one. "Thank you, but the negotiations were done by a team, not just myself."

"Ah, another of your qualities must be modesty." He peered at her. "Two things. One, I shall have you moved to a proper suite. Your present accommodation is not suitable for someone of your stature. And two, I insist we have a dance together at this evening's grand celebration."

Tiffany stuttered out a thank you. Shortly later, a woman servant led her to the new suite. Tiffany felt lost as they turned down a corridor and then another. The servant opened one door of a double set and ushered Tiffany inside. "This is your suite. Is there anything I can do to make you comfortable?"

Tiffany looked around the front room of the suite, seeing a seating area, a bar, several doors at a far wall. "No, this is beyond what I expected. I need my belongings brought here."

"Of course. I'll take care of that right away."

"Thank you." She looked at the name tag on the uniform. "Louise."

Tiffany walked around the suite, impressed by its size and amenities.

The washroom featured a clear glass soaker tub and a large shower in a glass enclosure with several shower heads.

Louise returned with Tiffany's suitcase, placing it on a stand and opening it for her.

"Thank you. May I ask you if this dress is appropriate for the grand celebration?" She held up her dark blue dress and twisted it around.

"It is, except it is rather, if you don't mind me saying so, conservative."

"Oh. Well, it's what I brought with me, and I guess I have little choice now."

"I can help you with that. I'll just have the royal tailor help us restyle the dress to something more appropriate for the grand celebration."

Tiffany thanked her and contacted the Star Hawk after she left.

"Room service, connect me with the Star Hawk."

"One moment."

Half a minute later, Tiffany spoke to Janice Madison, the communication officer.

"Hi, I'm just checking in before the grand celebration. From what I understand, it can be an all-night party, so I may need time before I call for a ride back to Star Hawk."

"No worries. Take your time and enjoy the festivities. What is Prince Francis like?"

"He's gorgeous, well spoken, and has charisma. It's too bad I'll be leaving soon."

"For all the hard work you did to get this agreement signed, you deserve some play time, said Janice. "We will talk to you tomorrow and you can tell me all the details of the grand celebration."

Tiffany said goodbye and had a nap while her dress was being redesigned.

I may need a rest if this party is anything like its name.

━━━

Tiffany Harris stretched after waking from her nap. She went to the shower and enjoyed the pulsating water for a few minutes before preparing for the evening. She checked her makeup, hair and nails, deciding she was as ready as she could be. Tiffany found a silk-like robe in the closet. The robe was transparent except for the woven flowered pattern.

"Room service, please contact Elizabeth Harold."

Shortly later, Elizabeth answered.

"Hi, are you getting ready for the grand celebration?"

"Yes, I'm waiting for my dress to be returned. The tailor is making modifications to it after I was told it was too conservative. I was wondering if you would like to join me for a drink? I'm nervous about this party."

"So am I. I must ask permission to join you first, since you moved to the royal floor. I don't think that'll be a problem."

"Great. I could use some company."

Tiffany listened to music and enjoyed a glass of white wine when a servant opened the door, admitting Elizabeth.

"Wow, pretty fancy suite you got."

"I wouldn't call it cozy." Tiffany poured her a glass of wine. She saw Elizabeth wore her uniform and carried a garment bag. "You're planning to change here, I assume."

"I didn't want to wear my new dress too soon. It's like most grand celebration dresses, too revealing to wear just anywhere."

They chatted, comparing stories of the Star Hawk and the life on Divinus. Tiffany thought the military on Divinus was not unlike the Star Hawk's crew, but other aspects of Divinus was very different.

"It seems like your royalty has a great deal of power without many restrictions. That seems a little unfair."

"Perhaps, but the king and his family rule as if by divine right. Whatever they do is considered above the law and should not be questioned."

The door chime sounded, and three female servants entered, one carrying a white box.

"Senior Diplomat Harris, we have your dress ready."

"Excellent. Please put it on the table." She pointed to a short, circular table in the centre of the common room.

The servant holding the box lifted her chin slightly. "Forgive me, but our instructions were to assist you in preparing for the dress. Shall we proceed to the bedroom?"

Tiffany nodded and gave Elizabeth a questioning look as she walked to the bedroom.

The servant carrying the box approached Tiffany. "Do you require assistance in removing your robe?"

"No." She slipped off the robe, tossing it on the bed. She stood as the servant opened the box. Tiffany saw her blue dress, along matching shoes and a smaller box containing two jars and a brush.

"We need to prepare you for tonight's grand celebration." The servant opened a jar, revealing a pale-yellow cream. The two other servants used their fingers to massage the cream on her skin, starting at her shoulders.

Tiffany felt embarrassed by the application of the cream as Elizabeth watched from the bedroom door with an amused expression. She felt like telling them she could apply the cream herself, especially when her breasts were massaged by the servants, but thought that would break a royal protocol.

The second jar contained silver and blue glitter, and the brush was used to apply it to her skin.

"Your dress, Ms. Harris." The servant held the dress open near the floor and Tiffany stepped into it.

Where's the back of the dress?

A strap at the back of her neck fastened the dress. A servant helped her with her shoes, immediately giving her height. She looked into the viewscreen, seeing the front of the dress had a scooped neck and the sides cut away to show her ribcage and the sides of her breasts. That, she considered, was acceptable for a special occasion such as the grand celebration. It was the back of the dress that shocked her. The short dress showed off her legs, but the back was completely bare, exposing her from her neck to half her ass.

"Am I supposed to wear this?" Tiffany was used to the revealing uniforms on the Star Hawk, but this would be a major departure from the conservative attire of the diplomatic corps she was used to.

"Of course, Ms. Harris. It was specifically designed for you by the royal tailor. It is perfect for you." The servant picked up the box. "When you are ready to go, please contact room service. They will provide an escort to the ballroom. Enjoy the party."

Elizabeth walked into the bedroom and around her. "Wow, I like it. Very nice."

"Really? Half my cheeks are showing."

"But it looks good. This is acceptable for the grand celebration."

"Okay, as if I have a choice. What are you wearing?"

"I'll show you." Elizabeth took off her clothes, standing nude as she opened the garment bag. She took out a red dress with streaks of imbedded orange and put it on.

Tiffany looked at the floor length dress. There was a wide cut out on the left side from above her hip to the floor. A pale red mesh went from her neck to her waist, showing off her breasts. The back of the dress had a circular red mesh between her should blades.

"That is a beautiful dress."

"Thank you. See, your dress isn't so outrageous. Just a different style of exposure." Elizabeth smoothed down her dress with her hands.

"Will all the women dress like this?" Her fingertips grazed the back of her dress, feeling where the top of her cheeks were exposed.

"Yes, there will be dresses that will expose a lot more."

"I think I need another drink before we leave."

Tiffany sat carefully, holding her dress hemline up so the rest of her cheeks didn't slide out. It also meant even more exposure of her legs. She saw Elizabeth wasn't concerned that the dress fell away on her left side when she sat, baring her up to her ribcage. "I guess our dresses weren't meant for sitting."

"No, just standing, walking and dancing." She laughed. "Let's drink up and leave for the ballroom."

Tiffany contacted the room service and shortly later, two guards arrived. Both men were tall and dressed in crisp uniforms. They walked in silence, the guard showing little inclination to speak. After a few turns down the wide hallways, they arrived at the ballroom. The expansive circular room was decorated with chandeliers, gold and silver trimmings, dark stone flooring and walls covered with stain glass mosaics.

Tables were on a raised platform around the perimeter, with seating only on the outside edge. Each table accommodated eight chairs with a space between the tables.

The room was already filling with guests, and another guard escorted

Elizabeth and herself to one of the tables. Tiffany saw that while the men wore formal suits and tuxedos, the women wore dresses with little coverage. She saw some women were topless or wearing only partial coverage. She was glad to sit with Elizabeth as she watched servants quickly bring each guest a drink. "You're right about what the women wear here. I don't feel so undressed now."

"I think events like this are so women can wear dresses that they wouldn't dare wear anywhere else."

"True, a lot of exposure here. I noticed a lot of women wear collars. Does that mean they are slaves?"

"No, the collars are considered a fashion accessory here. While they have a ring attached to the collar, most of them aren't locked. They don't mean the same thing as the Praxton collars, although one can assume the women who wear them have a submissive attitude."

She saw the men and women received different drinks. The men received a tumbler of a dark liquid while they gave the women a flute style of glass containing a red liqueur. She took a sip, identifying the taste as calidi. "They do like giving women calidi, don't they?"

"Yes, it is a traditional beverage for women."

The room filled with guests, leaving only the head table vacant. A sound of horned instruments announced Prince Francis and his entourage of four wives and two women slaves. The wives wore identical skirts except each was a different colour of bright red, green, yellow and orange. Their outfits consisted of a cape that reached the middle of their back, two long strips of a thin cloth that hung from a decorative metal belt around the hips at the front and the back. The wives wore an abundance of jewellery of different styles, such as nipple clips, necklaces, wrist bands and hair pieces. Each wife also wore a collar of a distinct style. The slaves wore a short blue wrap around their hips, a pair of nipple clips joined by a chain and a wide, dark-blue collar. The slaves each sat at the far end of the table. Prince Francis sat in the middle, flanked by two wives on each side.

A quiet filled the room. Two men and two women entered the room, going to the middle and facing the head table. The men wore dark suits and the women black dresses. A chime sounded and everyone, save for the head table, stood. The four sang, accompanied by unseen string instruments.

Tiffany listened to the Royal Anthem, not sure about the words describing the royal family as doing God's work, and their power was unlimited. The song ended, and the guest sat again.

"That was quite the lyrics in the anthem. Do you believe they rule because of God?"

"No, but the royal family can do what they want. If they break the law, then the law has to be amended. One never challenges the royal family on any matter."

Food quickly appeared at each table as dozens of servants moved to bring each course. Wine was poured and Tiffany indulged in the first course, a fruit salad. The lights dimmed and classical music played from hidden speakers as she watched as two men entered the ballroom, going to the centre to begin the performance. They wore old clothes and sat in the middle by a pile of wood that suddenly appeared by use of a holographic projection. The men tried to start a fire and for a moment, an orange glow could be seen in the wood pile. Thunder rolled and rain, another holographic projection came down and extinguished the fire. The rain was also represented by the appearance of eight naked women, whose bodies gleamed as if wet. They danced around the men and the wood.

Elizabeth commented, "This is one of our famous musicals called The Rain and the Fire. The rain tries to stop the fire, but the fire fights back. The men are unaware of the battle between the two sides."

Tiffany watched another group of women enter. She saw they were also nude, but with holographic paint that gave the impression of fire dancing on their skin. They danced around the wood, trying to bring fire into the wood. It became a battle between the two groups, with occasional pushing and wrestling between the groups as they danced.

A bowl of soup was placed in front of Tiffany, giving off a spicy aroma. "That's a rather erotic dance. I know they're supposed to be fighting, but they way they're rubbing their bodies together, it seems they're more friends than enemies."

"I think a man must have written the play. You're right. That's a lot of hugging."

A nude woman entered, glowing with a yellow light. She spread her arms around her. The women dressed as rain slowed down and curled up on the floor. The fire women now danced freely around the wood pile and flames curled around the wood. The two men warmed their hands to the fire as the music ended. Applause followed, and the dancers took a bow before departing.

"That was interesting."

"Yes, a common theme of many plays that there are forces we cannot see. That includes spirits. Our dominant religion has fifty-six gods that rule our lives. So the play uses a rain god, a fire god and the sun god. Well, actually goddesses, hence the nude women."

"Are there male gods?"

"Yes, but we're less likely to see them dance around."

Tiffany started on the main course as more dancers enter the room. The dancers were paired, four men and women. The men wore blue pants with black shoes and the women loose fitting blue short dresses and were barefoot. As they danced, the women were frequently lifted into the air, their skirts sliding up to their hips. The fast-paced music made for quick and sudden movements, including the women being held up-side-down. Their arms dropped as their legs locked around the neck of the male dancers. The men spun around as the women's dresses floated up and off their arms, leaving them only in their panties. The men returned the women to their feet, and they continued to dance, exchanging partners. The music slowed, and each man dropped to his knees in front of a woman, reaching up and pulled down her panties. The women bent at their waist over the shoulder of the man in front of them. The men stood, each carrying a woman on their shoulder as the music ended.

"More nude women. It seems to be a common theme for these dances."

"Prince Francis likes those styles of dances. He enjoys looking at the female form." Elizabeth lowered her voice. "I've heard that if a group wants to perform in front of the prince, then it would be wise to include naked women."

Dessert arrived, and the entertainment was simply a ten-piece orchestra that sat in a semicircle facing the head table. Tiffany noticed the dessert, although a dark chocolate in colour and flavour, also had a hint of the calidi berry in it. *I don't know if it's watching those dancers, but I'm definitely feeling aroused. Coupled with the drinks, I better be careful I don't do anything I'll regret in the morning.*

After the desserts were finished, Prince Francis made an announcement, thanking everyone for attending and those who provided the entertainment.

"But I would be remiss if I didn't make a special mention to the person responsible for the reason of our grand celebration. Senior Diplomate Tiffany Harris of the Alliance Worlds worked hard to provide a trade agreement between our two great governments. Please, let us give Ms. Harris a warm welcome."

Tiffany stood as the applause filled the ballroom. *I hope he wasn't expecting me to give a speech.*

His speech also signalled the end of the dinner portion, and the guests filtered to the open floor. Servants moved high-top circular tables to the lower floor and guests gathered around the tables. Tiffany talked to several officials and answered questions about the Alliance Worlds. Servants carried trays of drinks and Tiffany choose to follow the Divinus tradition of women picking the long-stemmed glassware while the men picked the tumblers. She wondered how many people were observing her from her back and seeing how bare she was. She resisted the temptation to check how her dress was positioned on her body, trusting she wasn't showing more than many other dresses in the room. Elizabeth joined her, introducing her to others.

Tiffany saw that some dresses had a cape or shawl that covered a bare top. She commented to Elizabeth. "Do those women plan to remove their top later?"

"Yes. As the evening progresses, those tops will come off. Eventually, some ladies will be nude as they dance." She gave a smile. "You'll be pressured to remove your dress, just giving you a warning."

"How about you? Are you planning to take off your dress?"

"I didn't wear any underwear. If the right guy is dancing with me, I just might." She laughed nervously.

Tiffany took another glass from a passing servant. "This is a very decadent party."

The music changed its tempo, and several couples danced. Tiffany stepped away from the dancefloor, defined by lights that gave the floor a green pattern. A tall, dark-haired man in a military uniform approached and asked her to dance. She accepted, pleased he was a smooth dancer that helped her adjust to the music and dance style. She felt his hand on her waist, and he seemed satisfied to leave it there and not venture lower. He danced with her a second time before taking her back to where she stood before.

"I would love to dance with you more, but one of my duties is to make sure every lady has at least one dance. I hope we can meet again."

Elizabeth returned from a dance and joined her at the table. "One nice thing is that they have extra guards available, so every lady gets to dance as much as she wants."

"I think that's great. We're not wearing these dresses to stand by the tables."

Two guards approached them, requesting a dance. Tiffany placed her glass on a table and entered the dance area. She found the new dance partner a little more adventurous than the first guard. His hand slid down to her exposed cheeks and up to the middle of her back, repeating the motion as they moved around the dance floor. Tiffany saw that several women had removed their tops and wore only skirts. Prince Francis was dancing with one of his wives, who had removed her cape.

After two dances, the guard escorted her back to the table. She saw Elizabeth dancing with an older gentleman in a dark suit. His hand was on her ass, through the opening of the side of her dress.

"May I have this dance with you?"

Tiffany looked at the middle-aged man. He was about her height, with a slim build. "I would be happy to."

He was an excellent dancer, and Tiffany enjoyed being spun around in a circle. Several times, he pulled her close in his arms and bent her backward. The next dance was slow, and he held her tight. It didn't surprise her when he took advantage of their close quarters to feel her bare skin, briefly touching the side of her breast.

Tiffany returned to where her drink was at a table after thanking him for the dances. Across the floor she saw a slim redhead, wearing only her high-heels and a see-through skirt dance with a distinguished man. She was laughing, obviously enjoying the attention she was receiving. Elizabeth came into view, the male dancer with his hand still under her dress. *Different rules for dancing here.*

A servant approached her.

"Prince Francis would like to dance with you. Please follow me."

Can't he ask me himself? Tiffany followed the servant to where a cluster of people stood near the head table.

The prince spotted her and walked toward her, grinning. "I do hope you are enjoying the grand celebration."

"Yes, I am."

"Wonderful." He took one hand of hers into each one of his own. "The food and entertainment were all satisfactory?"

"Both were very good."

"Good, otherwise the head chef would scrub floors tomorrow." He laughed at his joke. "Please, I wish to dance with you."

She walked with him to the dance floor, people moving to the side and giving them a large area of the dance floor to themselves.

"You are a lovely dancer. Tell me, do all Alliance women dance as well as you? Or are you just an exceptionally adapt at moving to the music?"

"I'm not that good. I'm just trying to follow you."

They moved around the dance floor, danced a second dance and then a third.

"I think your dress looks fantastic on you."

"Thank you, your tailor was the one who altered my dress."

His hand went to the top of her back and traced a path down, resting on the top of her bare cheeks. "It would be nice if the dress went even lower."

"If it went any lower, then I would be wearing just a strip of cloth at the front." *If it wasn't for the prince, I would move his hand back up. I don't want to cause any problems just after we signed the trade agreement.*

He whispered in her ear. "I should think it would be most pleasant to dance with you with your dress removed." He kissed her cheek as his hand floated above her bare skin. His hand moved down under the fabric of the skirt, his fingers pressing against her ass. Prince Francis lowered his head and kissed her on the lips.

Tiffany hesitated and kissed him back. After a few more dance steps, he kissed her again, his mouth lingering on her lips. She closed her eyes and leaned her head against his chest, enjoying his light touches on her back. His hand moved to her side, grazing her breast before returning down to her ass again. He repeated the motion. He kissed her again, this time a hand went over her breast, teasing the nipple until it became hard.

Tiffany looked around and saw several couples watching the prince and her dance. There were several topless women dancing, including the wives of the prince. Two of the wives were dancing with each other. She took a deep breath, feeling powerless to stop the prince from doing what he wanted.

The music increased its tempo, giving Tiffany space from Prince Francis. She saw the determined look in his eyes. *He wants me. What should I do? He is very handsome, and Elizabeth told me that he gets what he wants. What would happen if I were to refuse him? Would he resend the treaty?*

He moved around her, and she let him watch her dance from behind her. She saw Elizabeth was facing away from her dance partner. The tall man in a suit was undoing the back of her dress, allowing it to drop from her shoulders. A few dance steps later, it fell to the floor. Elizabeth picked it up, carrying it under her arm as she danced.

The song ended and a slower piece began.

"How about if we continue our dance in a more secluded area?"

"Where would that be?"

"My private suite. Come with me." He took her hand and led her out of the dancefloor.

"Wait, I want to talk to my friend, Elizabeth." She looked around and saw Elizabeth. She gave her a wave.

Elizabeth left her dance partner and Tiffany met her. "What's up?"

"Um, the prince has invited me to his suite. I don't want to leave you here by yourself."

"You are lucky, but I thought he liked you. Go. I'm enjoying myself and can find plenty of dance partners."

Tiffany looked at Prince Francis. "Could you arrange for Elizabeth to stay in my suite if she needs to tonight? She left her clothes in my room, so it would be good if she could return there."

"Of course." He signaled for a servant to approach. "Ms. Elizabeth Harold will stay in Ms. Harris' room tonight. Have one of the royal guardsmen attend to her needs and escort her to the room when the evening is done."

After the servant hurried off, Tiffany thanked him. "I don't want Elizabeth to get into any difficulties."

"Do not worry. A royal guardsman will ensure her safety."

Elizabeth gave Tiffany a hug, whispering, "Be careful."

"I'll be fine." She gave Elizabeth a kiss on the lips. "I hope we can get together before I leave tomorrow."

Tiffany held the prince's arm, and a short distance later, they arrived at an elevator. Her heart pounded in her ears. A guard opened the doors and rode with them to a lower floor, opening to a large, well-appointed room.

"This is part of my quarters." He spoke to the room, ordering it to provide romantic music, then began to dance with her again, kissing and touching her.

Tiffany moaned as they finished a long kiss. She clung to his neck as he undid the top strap of her dress. *Why am I behaving this way? I should be finding a way out of this, but I really don't want to. He's hot, sexy and has me on fire.* "My dress is going to fall off."

"Yes, it will. I want you naked."

Tiffany sighed and separated herself from him enough the dress fell. When it reached her hips, he pushed it down. She stepped out of the dress. "Okay, so you now have me naked. But you're still dressed."

He stopped dancing, cupped her breast and kissed her.

Tiffany felt light-headed as a wave of warmth covered her body. They kissed, they danced, and he fondled her. She couldn't resist him. Her skin was on fire to his touches. His hardness pressed against her, and she reached down to rub the outline of his erection.

Tiffany leaned back her head as he kissed her neck, moving lower. She continued to bend backward as his lips traced a path to her breasts. Her knees buckled as he sucked on her nipples.

He whispered in her ear. "What do you want?"

"I want your cock." Tiffany went to her knees. She opened the fly of his pants and pulled out the stiff cock, licking the shaft.

"I won't last much longer if you continue to do that."

"That's okay." She put her mouth over the head, working her tongue over it.

Prince Francis lifted her by her shoulders. "I have a better place for us to do this."

He carried her in his arms to a massive bedroom and gently placed her on a circular bed.

She propped herself up by her elbow and watched Prince Francis remove his clothing. He stepped to her, his erection moving toward her face. She kissed the large member and looked up at him.

"Do you want me to finish you now?"

"No, I want to make sure you're pleased as well. As a prince, I have a reputation to uphold."

She fell back on her back, aware of him kissing and touching her body, doing what he wanted. She gasped and spread her legs. Her last thoughts before she cried out were of him grunting with pleasure as he pounded inside her.

MORGAN STOOD at the door to Captain Elmwood's suite. She took a deep breath. It was five minutes to her appointed time to meet him. He had already informed her she would be stripped naked and whipped as punishment for seeing him naked. That occurred on the planet Proelium, where he was naked and whipped after being captured by a conservative religious order. Praxton social customs considered the viewing of an undressed male by a female, who was not her guardian, against the law and required punishment. Morgan knew his decision to discipline her was based on an opportunity to show he was interested in pursuing her to become her guardian.

She pressed the door chime, and the door opened, revealing Elmwood.

"Please come in. I thought we could have a drink first before we start."

"Thank you, I could use a drink. I'm nervous about this." She removed her shoes.

"Good, if you were bored, then I would be concerned." Elmwood passed her a dark-coloured liquid. "Rum." He sat on the couch.

Morgan followed him, kneeling on floor. "Thank you for the drink, Master Julius."

"I have arranged for dinner to be brought here at eighteen hundred. That will give me two hours to punish you. To be clear, my intention is not to make you suffer, but rather to stimulate you. As I told you earlier, I want to be your guardian. This discipline session will indicate how I will treat you."

"That sounds good to me, Master Julius." She finished her drink, the liquid warming her.

"Undress."

Morgan rose, removed her top and skirt, standing nude in front of him with her arms folded at the elbows behind her back. "I am ready for my punishment, Master Julius."

He took her by the elbow to a wall where hooks were inserted above her head. He faced her to the wall and secured a wrist cuff to each hook.

Morgan took quick breaths as she listened to the swishing sound of a flogger. Then he struck. The lashes grazed her back, and he slowly moved downward until he reached her knees.

He increased the intensity of the lashes, striking quickly in a back-and-forth pattern. Morgan grunted from the repeated blows. There was a pause, and she heard him step closer to her. He began to spank her, the palm of his hand making a loud slapping sound and hurting much more than the whip.

She gave out a muffled cry, but the spanking continued. She knew he would stop if she asked him to but refused to give in to the pain. *I can take this. I deserve this.*

He stopped, breathing hard. "I will return later."

She hung by her wrists, waiting. Although her arms were getting tired, her weight was supported by her legs. She heard him take another drink and waited.

Elmwood returned, smacking her ass again several times.

"Okay, now to whip your front." He released her wrists and turned her around. Her wrist cuffs were reattached above her, and, to her surprise, her legs spread apart to hooks on the wall. She felt her weight pull on her arms as she wiggled on the four hooks. This time she faced the room and saw he had removed his jacket. His face looked flushed as he held the flogger.

He started slowly on her, increasing the pressure of the flogger as he moved up and down on her body. Only near her groin did he ease up, as he thoroughly whipped her front. Her breasts received the most attention, and she occasionally closed her eyes at the strikes. She gasped when he used a hand to squeeze a breast.

"Your skin feels hot."

"Yes, Master Julius. I feel very warm."

He reached between her legs. "I can tell." His hand remained there, pressing upward.

"Yes, Master Julius. I feel very turned on."

"Your skin has hundreds of red stripes on it."

"I hope that pleases you, Master Julius."

He stepped away and looked at her. "I think I'll have another drink."

Morgan sagged in her bounds, feeling exhausted, sore and extremely aroused. She watched him enjoy another rum as she took deep breaths. She groaned as she tried to flex her tired limbs.

Elmwood finished his drink and walked to in front of her. "You looked tired."

"I am, Master Julius."

"Then you shall rest." He undid her wrist and ankle cuffs from the wall hooks, taking her by the arm upstairs to the guest bedroom.

"Into the cage you go."

Morgan dropped to her knees and crawled into the rectangular cage, laying on her side on the cushioned floor with her legs curled up. She closed her eyes, hearing the door locked behind her. She didn't sleep but drifted in the twilight zone between sleep and being awake. There wasn't anything she could do but rest, but she stroked her skin, feeling the warm areas where the whip struck. She was pleased with herself that she didn't ask him to stop or cry out. She rolled onto her back with her knees up, waiting. She felt the first press of hunger reach her. She sighed, pushing her feet against the cage bars. *Nothing I can do until he comes and gets me. She placed a hand between her legs and quickly withdrew it. Damn, I'm sensitive there. I wonder what Master Julius would say if he caught me masturbating?* She grinned at the thought. She spread her knees and rested her arms across her chest. *Okay, the thrill of being caged is over, Master Julius. Please come and get me.*

Morgan rolled onto her side again, wondering if she should call out, when Elmwood entered the room. He bent down by the cage.

"Have you learned your lesson about looking at undressed males?" He gave her a smile.

"I guess I shouldn't say it was worth it." She grinned. Then in a different tone, she relied. "Yes, Master Julius, I have learned my lesson."

He opened the cage door. "Dinner is ready. Come with me."

Morgan followed him downstairs to the dining room, where two plates were set. She waited for him to sit down first. "This looks delicious. I'm starving."

He took a bite. "Then eat up. I can order more food."

"Oh, no. If I'm going to be naked in front of you, I will not eat like a bear coming out of hibernation."

After they finished eating, she kneeled on a cushion on the floor near the armchair where he sat. She held a glass of sparkling wine in her hand and looked up at him. "Master Julius, thank you for showing me how you will discipline me. I hope you will become my guardian soon. I would very much like to please you."

"I understand. Our circumstances are a little different from the rest of the personnel on the ship. I have already received a few requests for couples wanting to share rooms. I have told every one of them there is a waiting period of five weeks after such a request will be granted. The reason is that we want to avoid a quick pairing of people, only to find a few weeks later they are not compatible.

"The role of a woman and her guardian should not be taken lightly. I remind men once you agree to be a guardian, you cannot simply change your mind. Under Praxton rules, a guardian remains her guardian until the female has found another guardian. Obviously, the rules on the Star Hawk are going to be altered. But I do not want only short-term romances on this ship. That will lead to problems."

"I understand, Master Julius. If I interpret what you are saying correctly, then you don't want us to rush into a relationship of you being my guardian after telling others they cannot do so."

"Exactly. I want others to know I am pursuing you with the purpose of being your guardian. After a period, I hope you will accept me as such."

"You know I will."

"I like to believe so. When I become your guardian, I assure you it will be a grand party."

"I know what those parties entitles." Morgan blushed. "Myself being nude and whipped in front of our friends."

"Yes, you'll get all the attention." He laughed.

Diana woke to soft music playing above her from unseen speakers. Light gradually filled her room in a pale yellow. In a few minutes, the music would increase in volume and the light would become brighter. She yawned, stretched like a cat, and reached to undo her ankle cuff. In the weeks she had been on the Star Hawk, the custom of women always sleeping in the nude with an ankle cuff attached to the foot of the bed had changed from being odd into a habit she followed without a thought.

Her movements became more hurried. She went downstairs from her bedroom to the kitchen, making a cup of coffee she would drink as she prepared for the day. Yesterday, Derik Holton had told her he would have breakfast in her room. That meant he would arrive early enough to watch her shower. His requirements also meant she had to serve him breakfast naked. Last night, she organized her makeup and how she would prepare herself for his viewing.

She set the shower so it would only spray her below the shoulders, allowing her to fix her hair and makeup ahead of time. The eye makeup took the longest. Current fashion was for exaggerated lines extending past the eyes and fine sparkles on the eyelid. She added bright red lipstick and checked the time. It was eight minutes to seven o'clock. *I have enough time for a half cup of coffee before he arrives.* She smiled to herself, knowing he would arrive exactly at seven o'clock.

Diana sat on the edge of her bed, sipping her coffee. Unlike the last time when Derik showed up for breakfast, she kept her bedroom wall facing the lower level living room transparent. She saw him enter her suite and look up at her. Without a smile or a wave, he entered the kitchen, returning with a cup of coffee. She waited until he sat in an armchair before proceeding to the shower.

The warm water sprayed her as she used a sponge to soap her body. She followed the suggestions for Praxton female showering, slowly pivoting around as she washed. Diana kept one foot slightly raised, twisting her hips to an unheard melody. She washed slower than usual, letting him observe the soapy water rinse off her gleaming skin.

Diana turned off the water and turned on the dryer mode. The warm, dry air dried off her skin. She sauntered to her makeup table and applied body cream. She continued her slow movements, glancing to see his reaction. He was leaning forward in his chair as Diana placed one leg on the cushioned stool in front of the table and rubbed cream on the smooth skin. She changed legs, changing position so she faced him.

She stood, massaging the oily cream on her stomach and up over her breasts. He dropped his coffee cup.

Diana finished with the body cream and sat on the stool to apply a special makeup for her nipples. They designed the cream to enhance the colour and stimulate her nipples, although she knew they were already sensitive to the touch.

She put on a wide, black collar, hearing the lock at the back click into place. The wrist and ankle cuffs matched the collar in style. Between the pairs of cuffs, she added silver chains. The chains weren't long or delicate but made a statement she was under control. She took a deep breath and made her way downstairs.

Holton had cleaned up the coffee spill, standing as she walked across the living room.

"Thank you."

"Don't thank me yet, Master Derik. I haven't made your breakfast." She gave him a grin as she went past him.

She prepared the pancakes, scrambled eggs and sausages. As she flipped a pancake, she saw him standing in the doorway. "Please sit at the table, Master Derik. I'll have breakfast ready for you in a minute."

She carried the plates to the table, noticing he looked flushed. "I hope you're hungry."

"It looks great." He stared at his plate. "I was hungry when I arrived, but I feel distracted right now."

"Master Derik, I understand what you're saying, but we need to eat, and I must get ready for the day."

Diana ate her breakfast after waiting for Holton to begin first. After she finished eating, she made him another cup of coffee and went upstairs to dress. She quickly put on the clothes she had decided on the night before and returned downstairs. She matched the bright blue skirt with a soft yellow top. Under the top, she wore a pair of nipple clips with a dangling diamond. She returned downstairs, putting on a pair of pale-yellow high heels. She handed Holton a short leash, which he attached to her wrist cuffs.

"You look very nice in your cuffs and collar. I do like the chain between your cuffs."

"I know you do. That's why I put them on."

"Is that the only reason you wear them? Do you like wearing them as well?"

"I like the collar. I don't mind the chain between my wrist cuffs, but I'm less comfortable with the ankle cuffs and chains."

"But you wore them, anyway."

"Yes, because you would likely spank me if I didn't. Our current arrangement gives you the right to discipline me if I do anything that displeases you. If my wearing cuffs and chains makes you happy, then I shall comply."

"Thank you for your indulgence to my wants. I noticed you're wearing shorter skirts."

"I am. The shorter shirts are something I don't mind. It took a while for me to get used to the fashions on board the Star Hawk."

"May I ask if you're wearing panties?"

"I am. I know our preference is for me to leave them off, but I need some modesty for when I sit down with this skirt."

"I understand."

They reached her office. "I will see you later, Diana. Perhaps we can have lunch together."

"That would be nice, Master Derik." Diana focused on the formulas for the creation of a soup base. She studied the different components, adding more protein strings to the mixture. The graphs changed on her monitor, and she frowned at the new data. *That would taste rather bland.* She typed in a command to the computer, adding a spice and a fat molecule. The three-dimensional graph changed. *That looks promising. Let's see what that tastes like.* She ordered the computer to produce a test sample at the kitchen.

She went down the half flight of stairs to where the food processing tanks were located. At the end of the room was a kitchen. She noticed several technicians checking the tanks and the pipes among them, all colour coded according to use. The technicians were junior members of the food processing department, and she had met most of them.

Diana went behind the counter and poured a sample of the chicken soup base into a cup. She first breathed in the vapours of the steaming liquid. Satisfied, she used a spoon to taste the mixture. *Not bad at all. Very close to what it should be.*

She looked over and recognized a junior technician. "Chiela, can I ask you to try this chicken soup base?"

"Sure." The redhead woman with blonde streaks approached kitchen counter.

Diana watched Chiela rest her tablet on the counter. She poured another cup of the soup and placed it in front of Chiela.

"This is good." She used the spoon to take more. "I like the seasoning in it."

"Great. We use this base a lot, so I want it to be good."

"It is." She paused, looked uncertain for a moment. "Ms. Diana, I noticed how Master Derik and yourself interact. Even though Master Derik wants to be your guardian, you refuse to give in easily. I really admire your strength in resisting him and establishing what you want in a relationship."

"Thank you, but I'm only acting as most Alliance women would."

"Maybe that's the reason, but I would like to get advice from you on how to handle a problem I have."

"Of course," said Diana. "What is it?"

"Can we go someplace private to talk?"

"Sure. Let's go to a lounge." Diana walked with Chiela to a lounge normally used by non-executive crew. Chiela wasn't permitted in an executive lounge, so Diana agreed to go to a lounge Chiela normally used. They picked a table near a wall, and each sat with a coffee.

Diana looked around, noticing the lounge design was much like the executive lounges, except it was larger and table service wasn't provided. The table and chairs were of a different quality, but still comfortable. "What's the problem you're having?"

"It's a situation with Master Collin, another technician. Do you remember meeting him?"

"Yes. He's the tall, slim man. Dark hair and a thin mustache."

"That's him. Master Collin is showing great interest in me. I like him, but I don't want him to be my guardian. I really don't want any guardian at this time. I'm enjoying being single and free right now, but even if I chose to have a guardian, Master Collin is not one I would agree to have."

"Have you told him you're not interested?"

"Not exactly. Our group, the food quality technicians, hang around together. So there's flirting and teasing going on between all of us. I've had sex with a couple of them. Nothing serious. Master Collin wants me to give him a blowjob, but I've told him no. But he keeps asking me."

"I thought men were supposed to leave women alone after they were refused. At least that's my understanding of the Praxton culture."

"It is, except we all hang around together and his request comes more along the line of teasing. I would like to give him a blowjob." She gave a smile. "But with Master Collin, I think he would try to dominate me afterward and make our friendship uncomfortable. Ms. Diana, how can I give him a blowjob without him thinking I want him to be my guardian? You really know how to handle males. How did you get Master Derik to change how he approaches you?"

Diana tried to keep her face looking neutral. *You want to give him a blowjob and then go back to just being friends? How does that work?* "First thing. You're an independent woman. You shouldn't feel any obligation to perform oral sex for him."

"It isn't an obligation, I feel. I want to give him a blowjob." She shrugged. "It's something I enjoy doing. I just don't want him to think he could then dominate me and give me orders."

"Oh, well then." *Praxton women are different.* Diana paused to consider her answer. "Chiela, if you have sex with him, whether it's a blowjob or one of mutual satisfaction, he will become closer to you. You can't avoid that. My advice is to not to give in to his wants. You have to just tell him you're not interested."

"I guess you're right. I don't want to hurt his feelings. We work together and hang around with others after work."

"It would hurt his feelings even more if you give in to him for that blowjob and then say no to him. Chiela, consider your own feelings in this. If you give in to him, he'll be happy, but you'll be in a difficult spot."

"That's true. Thanks, Ms. Diana. You've helped me decide." She frowned. "It won't be easy to say to him I'm not interested, but as you said, it's better this way."

Diana returned to her office, checking again the chemicals in the chicken soup base. She saw Derik enter her office, and she immediately stood, holding her hands together in front of her. "Hello, Master Derik."

"Hello, Diana. Would you like to go for lunch?"

"Yes, that would be nice." She shut off the three-dimensional monitor and met him at the doorway, handing him the leash attached to the wrist cuff. She didn't ask him which lounge they would go to, understanding the decision was his and she would find out soon enough. He didn't choose the closest lounge, but they walked to another lounge usually used for formal meals.

He guided her to a table near a wall, hooking the end of her leash at the top of the chair. The viewscreen that covered the wall gave the impression of looking out pane glass to a sea with sailboats moving with a wind.

"This is nice. I love the water and the seashore."

"I arranged for the viewscreen to show this scene. I read more on your biography, and you mentioned how you enjoyed the ocean. I think it's because you love open spaces rather than confined areas."

"My claustrophobia." She laughed. "Yes, that's true."

The server arrived, and he ordered for both of them.

Diana paid attention to what he ordered for her. A green salad and a bowl of clam chowder, along with garlic toast. He included a glass of chardonnay for her. The chardonnay style was lightly oaked, and she approved how it would match the soup.

"This is a more elaborate lunch than normal, Master Derik. Is there a special reason for this?" She took a drink of her wine.

"My attempt to romance you the Alliance way. I studied what you like, and I hope I found the right wine for your clam chowder. I'm paying attention to your wants, Diana." He raised his own glass of wine to her and took a drink.

"Thank you. The chardonnay is perfect with the clam chowder. The chardonnay helps to pick up the creaminess of the soup." She took a sip of the soup.

"Good. I want to take you out for dinner tonight."

"That would be nice." She watched his eyes, looking for a clue of what he may be planning for dinner.

"I'll be at your door at seven. May I suggest you wear a dress?"

"I will do so." *Ah, so it will be a formal occasion.*

"Afterward, I would like to take you to my quarters. You haven't been there yet, and I believe it's time I showed you hospitality as well." He finished his soup and began to eat the salad.

"That would be nice." *This is a big step on his part. Does he have something else planned?*

After lunch, Derik escorted her back to her office. He held her leash attached to her wrist close, allowing for a quiet conversation.

"Master Derik, thank you for taking me to lunch. I truly appreciate your effort to know me better."

"Diana, I am determined to win you over by using Alliance and Praxton customs. For the dinner tonight, I plan to use both. I believe it will make for an interesting night."

[16]

TIFFANY WOKE UP ALONE. Her mouth felt dry as she lifted her head. Memories of the previous night came back to her, and a smile came to her lips. She slid off the bed and looked around. *This bedroom is bigger than my ship's quarters.*

"Good afternoon, Ms. Harris. Can I get you anything?"

Afternoon? How long did I sleep? She looked at the slave girl kneeling by the side of the bed, wearing only a collar.

"Something to drink." She responded. "Which door goes to the washroom? And where is Prince Francis?"

The slim, dark-skinned slave rose to her feet in a fluid motion. She had short, black hair, small breasts and perfect skin. "I will show you to your washroom."

"There's more than one washroom?"

"Yes, Ms. Harris. One is for Prince Francis and the other for guests. Prince Francis is doing business but will return shortly. He instructed me to look after your needs."

Tiffany looked around in the washroom, seeing a large sunken tub and a glass-enclosed shower with two shower heads. *Something to drink and then a long shower.*

When she left the washroom, she saw a cart holding water, juice and tea. There was also a plate with biscuits and a jar of blue spread.

"Is there anything else I may get for you?" The slave girl was kneeling by the cart.

"I would like to contact my ship and Elizabeth Harold."

"I'm very sorry, but you need permission from Prince Francis to use the communication service."

"All right, I'll ask him when he returns. After my breakfast, I'm going to have a shower. Can I get something to wear afterward?"

"I am sorry, but I may not do so without permission from Prince Francis."

"I'm to stay naked until he says I can have clothes?" She sighed. "I'm too tired to complain right now." She finished the tea, the juice and two biscuits.

"Do you wish more tea?"

"No, thank you. I need the shower to clear my head."

"Do you wish for me to join you in the shower?"

"I think I can wash myself."

"Very good, Ms. Harris. Is there anything else I can do for you?"

"No, other than permission to call my ship and get some clothing."

Tiffany went to the washroom and turned on the water. She stepped inside and turned around in the water, seeing the slave girl kneeling at the washroom entrance watching her. *Okay, this is a little unnerving. I know Praxton women are used to being watched as they shower, but this is a new experience for me.*

After she finished showering, Tiffany turned on the warm air dryer. She stepped out of the shower and the slave girl used a soft towel to absorb any remaining water drops on her.

They returned to the bedroom and Tiffany sat on the bed. "Is there anything I can do while we wait for Prince Francis to return?"

"I could give you a massage."

"No, I'd fall asleep again. Am I allowed to leave the bedroom?"

"No, we would need permission from Prince Francis to do so."

"In other words, I'm a prisoner here. A naked one at that."

"Oh, no, Ms. Harris. You are a special guest of Prince Francis."

"I fail to see the distinction." She saw the troubled look on the slave girl. "What is your name?"

"Colina, Ms. Harris."

"You look very young, Colina. Were you always a slave for Prince Francis?"

"I am older than I look, Ms. Harris. Prince Francis chose me from other slaves that applied to work for the royal family. I was very fortunate he picked me to be a slave for him. Prince Francis is a very kind owner. He never hits or causes pain to his slaves."

"Does he treat his wives well?"

"Oh, yes, Ms. Harris. Prince Francis is most generous to them."

"He never hits or loses his temper with them?"

"Never." Colina paused and gave a smile. "He spanks them, but not as a punishment. The wives appreciate his firm hand."

"I'll bet they do. And here is our prince." Tiffany stood and crossed her arms, watching him as he approached the bed. He wore a dark blue military-style uniform with a white shirt. A red sash was visible underneath the jacket, going from his shoulder to his waist.

"Hello, Tiffany, how are you feeling this afternoon?"

"I would feel better if I could put some clothes on, talk to my ship and perhaps walk around outside this bedroom."

"My humble apologizes. I neglected to tell Colina you could have something to wear. Some rooms outside the bedroom are sensitive areas. I'm sure you understand." He looked at Colina. "Please fetch a skirt and top for Ms. Harris."

"Thank you. I want to talk to my ship and to Elizabeth Harold."

"Of course. We limit the communication on the royal floors to certain people for security reasons. I will open a channel for you now." He pressed a button on the wall. "Room service, establish a link to the spaceship Star Hawk."

"The link is now open."

Prince Francis stepped back and gestured for Tiffany to continue the conversation.

"Star Hawk, this is Senior Diplomate Tiffany Harris."

"Go ahead, this is Communication Officer Janice Madison."

"I attended the grand celebration last night and woke up a bit late. I believe it'll take me this afternoon to sort out things, and I'm scheduled to meet Prince Francis later as well."

"Very good. I'll inform Captain Elmwood you still have negotiations to do."

Tiffany sighed a relief. *I'm glad I don't have to explain about needing more negotiations after the agreement was signed.*

"Do you wish to speak with Elizabeth now?"

"Yes, please."

Prince Francis ordered a voice communication to Elizabeth Harold.

"Hello, Elizabeth?" She called out to open air.

"Tiffany! I'm so glad to hear from you."

"Are you all right?" Tiffany heard stress in Elizabeth's voice.

"I'm good. But I have a problem."

"How so?"

"I don't have any clothes. I woke up naked and all my clothes are gone. Your clothes as well. I can't get room service to help me. I'm stuck here until I can get something to wear," Elizabeth said.

"Clothes seem to disappear around here." She gave the prince a hard look. "Look, I'll get Prince Francis to help. I'll call you back later."

Tiffany turned to Prince Francis. "You heard. Elizabeth doesn't have any clothes. What is going on here? I woke up with nothing to wear and now Elizabeth has the same problem."

"I will find out what happened and will make sure your friend gets clothes to wear." He went over to her to kiss her on the lips.

"No." She stepped back. "Not now. Help Elizabeth first."

"Very well, I will be back soon."

She watched him leave, letting out a sigh. *Damn, he looks good.*

Colina returned, carrying a brown and gold trimmed skirt and a matching bra top. The material was light and semi-transparent. "I hope you find these acceptable, Ms. Harris."

"Thank you. I'm sure they'll be fine." She put on the long, flowing skirt and tied the string belt. "Do you ever wear clothes?"

"No, Ms. Harris, not often. Prince Francis prefers the slaves to be nude, but occasionally I'm allowed to wear a skirt. I am quite used to being naked."

Tiffany to put on her top and looked down, seeing her breasts were partially visible. *It's better than nothing.*

———

Prince Francis returned. "I investigated the situation regarding your suite and Elizabeth Harold's lack of clothing. The servants assumed you would not be returning to your suite and sent your clothing and personal items to the space shuttle that is to transport you back to Star Hawk. Ms. Harold's clothing was sent to be cleaned. I trust you understand that no harm was intended and simply a case the servants did what they thought was appropriate."

"All right. Are you getting clothes for Elizabeth?"

"Yes. I have sent a dress for her to wear, and I invited her to join us for lunch. I hope that is acceptable to you."

"It is. Can I go for a walk now?"

"Of course. I will be honoured to escort you."

Tiffany walked next to Prince Francis as he showed her part of the royal apartments. The high ceilings, wall decorations, furnishings and view of the outside impressed her.

"This is all exquisite." She noticed servants were everywhere, cleaning or carrying items, and guards, who were standing at attention at the doorways. She saw two naked slaves as well, kneeling on cushions in a room.

"Why do you keep your slaves naked?"

"I enjoy the sight of a naked woman. It also helps to distinguish them as slaves. Are you offended they are naked?"

"No, it doesn't bother me. I am getting used to the Praxton culture on the Star Hawk and there is a lot of female nudity present."

They arrived in a small dining room where a rectangular table was being prepared with a fresh tablecloth and the floor swept for invisible dust. The room also contained a bay window area, with a small table with chairs.

"Shall we enjoy the view while we wait for Ms. Harold?"

"That would be nice." She sat and looked out at the green countryside. She noticed there wasn't a barrier to the outside other than a force-field, making it easy to see detail.

"I can remove the force-field if you like, but it is quite windy today." He reached across the table for her hand.

"This is fine." She squeezed his hand, wondering how she had fallen for him so quickly.

"I want you to stay the night."

"I can't. I need to return to the Star Hawk."

"Just one more day won't cause a problem. I would like to hear more about the Alliance Worlds perspective on how to eliminate illegal slave trading."

"Oh, so you want me to tell the Star Hawk to wait while I converse with you about slave trading? I don't think they'll believe that. As much as I want to spend more time with you, my duty calls for me to return. I hope you understand."

"I do. I shall warn you. I'll do everything I can to get you to stay tonight."

Tiffany laughed. "Fair warning." She looked past Prince Francis and saw Elizabeth approach, wearing a tight yellow dress that reached the floor with a slit starting at her waist. The fabric was light enough to show she was likely without underwear. A guard walked closely with her, giving the impression she wasn't free of his control. Like herself, Elizabeth was barefoot.

"Elizabeth! Are you all right?" She quickly rose to meet her.

"I'm fine." She spread out her arms. "I had all morning to bathe and put on makeup. Once I was told I was getting a dress and wasn't a prisoner, it was quite a relaxing morning."

Tiffany gave her a hug. "You look great."

"So do you." She spoke to Prince Francis. "Thank you for your help. The room service wouldn't help me, and the guard outside the suite wasn't very informative either."

"I'm sorry to hear of your difficulties, Ms. Harold. I hope our lunch will make it up to you."

Tiffany sat with the others at the dining table, then looked at the various plates containing foods. "There's enough food here for three meals, let alone lunch."

"Please, choose whatever you wish. After your morning difficulties, I want to make sure you have a pleasant lunch."

Elizabeth took a small portion of food. "This dress shows everything. I don't think I'll overindulge, but everything looks so good." She asked Prince Francis. "I was informed I don't have to report for work as I'll be a guest of the Prince Francis. How long will I be a guest here?"

"Do not worry about your return to work. I assure you there will be plenty of time for work later. I'm trying to convince Ms. Harris to stay for dinner and the night."

"That would be wonderful."

"Yes, but she is resisting my invitation."

Tiffany smiled. "I'll consider it, but no promises."

They served the meal with white wine, followed by red liqueur for the women and a gold-coloured liquor for the prince.

Tiffany tasted the sweet liqueur. "I detect calidi. Is it used in all drinks served to women?"

Elizabeth answered. "It is a very common drink for women at social events. It is believed it makes women warmer and more receptive suggestions by gentlemen."

Tiffany looked upward. "Yeah, another way of saying it's an aphrodisiac. I suppose if someone is told they have taken an aphrodisiac, even if doesn't have a physical effect, the power of suggestion is there." *Although it sure worked last night.*

"Ms. Harold, would you be staying with us for dinner? It will be on the later side, but I assure you it will be worthwhile the wait." Prince Francis touched her arm as he asked.

"I would be happy to."

The prince motioned with his hand for a guard to approach. "Please escort Ms. Harold to a guest room. She will be staying for dinner, so ask the royal tailor to design an appropriate dress for her."

"Yes, sir. Understood, sir." The guard waited for Elizabeth to rise and led her out of the dining room.

Prince Francis stood. "Shall we continue our walk?"

"Yes. So, was inviting Elizabeth to dinner part of your plan to keep me here longer?"

"It is. I might hold her ransom until you agree to stay the night."

"Prince Francis, have you no scruples?" She laughed.

"I have principles, but I do what I can to get what I want. And I want you to stay longer."

They walked down a hallway with one wall showing the outside. They passed guards and servants as they strolled. He kept one arm around her waist, occasionally sliding it down to squeeze her ass.

"Prince Francis, you already have four wives. Why do you want or need me?"

"As a prince, I am expected to have several wives. It would be odd if I had only one. I love each wife very much, but there is room for me to still seek a beautiful, desirable woman such as yourself." He stopped to kiss her deeply. "Love cannot be too full. It cannot be blocked." He kissed her again, pressing her against a wall as he kissed her. A hand covered a breast.

Tiffany moaned.

"I know another way to ensure you will stay the night."

"What is that?" She felt like she was out of breath.

"Hold your hands in front of you."

Tiffany lifted her hands together and watched as he slipped off his belt and used the thick leather to wrap around her wrists, securing the loose end. "Hey." She smiled.

"Now you are captured and have to stay."

"Really? This is a solution?"

"It is. Do you see a problem with it?"

She held up her hands. "Where do I start?"

He kissed her. "This also has another advantage."

"Which is?"

He smacked her ass twice. "You can't defend yourself from getting a spanking."

"That is an advantage for you, all right."

They continued their walk. "Are you seriously going to keep me tied until I agree to staying overnight?"

"I am."

"Okay, let me speak to the Star Hawk."

Moments later she spoke to Janice Madison. "I have been invited to dinner with Prince Francis and I thought it would be best I accepted. My understanding the dinner is served late and I may end up staying the night."

"Understood. Business relationships can be a serious matter."

Tiffany ended the call and thought she could hear a touch of humour in her voice. *Yeah, business relationship.*

"Okay, I'll shall stay the night."

"You see, I can be persuasive."

"I know." She held up her hands. "Can you undo these now?"

"Do you mind leaving them tied a while longer? I find the sight of your wrists tied together intriguing." He took her elbow and began to walk.

"What will the servants and guards think seeing me tied like this?"

"Their job is not to observe such things. If, for example, I was to put you over my knee and spank you, they would not see it."

"Let us not go there and find out."

"I think you would enjoy being spanked."

"You can speculate on that as much as you want. Where are we going?"

"This hallway leads to another view, this one of the Mountains of Tellamore. I thought we could sit, have a drink and enjoy the view."

The viewing area was in another bay area, also with a small table with chairs. They sat and a servant immediately approached and took his order for drinks. Tiffany looked out at the snow-capped mountains with a green curtain covering the lower regions.

"Very nice, Prince Francis."

A tall glass of white wine was set in front of her, and he received a tumbler of a gold liquid.

"Can you drink your wine with your wrists tied?"

"Yes, I have seen women on the Star Hawk eat dinner with their wrists cuffed together. I can drink this way." She used both hands to hold the glass and took a sip. "How long are you planning to keep my wrists tied together?"

"I won't be asking you to eat dinner that way." He chuckled. "I plan to leave them on until you ask me to untie them."

"You asked me to stay overnight. Will that be in your bed, or will I have room of my own?"

"My bed, but I can arrange for you to have a room for yourself as well."

"Perhaps I can get something different to wear for the dinner tonight."

"If you wish. I can ask the tailor to make something to your liking."

"Okay. Now I would like to rest up before dinner."

"Of course." He stepped around the table and took her by the elbow, leading back from the direction they came.

"Will your wives be there at dinner?"

"Yes, I would like you to meet them."

That may be an interesting meeting. I'm having an affair with a man with four wives. I doubt there's any way that will be anything but awkward. She looked down at her tied wrists. *Why did I give in so easily to him? He has a way of getting what he wants.*

———

Prince Frances took Tiffany to a circular area that contained soft chairs, floor cushions, soft carpeting and low lights. Two wives were relaxing on cushions, conversing over drinks. Each wore just a skirt and watched Prince Francis and Tiffany enter.

"Ah, Ebba, Alice, this is Tiffany Harris. She will stay the night in one of the extra rooms. You will have a chance to talk with her at dinner." He led Tiffany through one of the seven doors that faced the curved wall.

He opened the decorative door. "This is actually a room reserved for my wives but is presently unoccupied."

"Very nice." The large, square room held a bed big enough for three people.

"I believe you'll find the room adequate for your needs. I will send in a slave to make sure your needs are attended to."

"Aren't you forgetting something?" She held up her hands. "Also, another kiss would be nice."

"My apologies." Prince Francis untied her wrists and gave her a long kiss. "We'll see you later."

As soon as Prince Francis left, a slave entered. She was blonde, long haired and heavier than Colina.

"Hello, Ms. Harris. I am Allula. How may I assist you?"

"I need something to wear for dinner tonight. Can you arrange for a dress for me?"

"Yes, I will have an assortment of garments brought in for you to choose from."

"Thank you. I'm going to rest now."

"Of course, Ms. Harris. Would you like me to undress you?"

I guess I'm not supposed to sleep in street clothes. "No, I can manage just fine." Tiffany waited until Allula left and undressed. She slipped under the silk-like covering and ordered the room to lower the lights. *At least it listened to that command.*

———

Diana finished work early, deciding she needed extra time to prepare for dinner. When she returned to her suite, she contacted Khloe Levit.

"Hi, I have a big date tonight with Master Derik that will end in his quarters. I was wondering if you have any pointers for my dinner with him. I don't want to make a mistake."

"Of course. I'll come over and help you out with a few details."

Diana opened her door to Khloe, who was carrying a dress on her arm.

"Thank you for coming over."

"I'm happy to do so. I bought you a dress I have. We're close to same size and this dress will fit most females."

Diana held up the dress. "Where's the other half?"

"You'll look beautiful in it. Now let's have a glass of wine and I'll go through a few things with you."

Diana poured two glasses of sauvignon blanc and sat with Khloe. "Am I in for a surprise for some Praxton custom I don't know about?"

"I think you're aware of the Praxton customs. If this is a more formal dinner with him, then he may use more dominance on you. In formal settings, the female is usually on a leash. Sometimes her wrist cuffs are joined prior to eating. I recommend you wear a wider collar and cuffs."

"I have a wide collar and matching cuffs I can wear. Anything different with the chains?"

"No, just make sure each cuff has a chain attached to it. And a chain between the nipple clips. You should have more body makeup, including patterns and markings."

"It's going to take a while to get ready."

"Except for dressing. One dress and you're done. I'll help you with the makeup. It'll be fun."

Diana sat on the cushioned bench naked as Khloe used a brush on her back to paint thick red lines. The straight and curved lines produced an abstract image of a famous web-leafed desert Praxton plant. The rest of the makeup was soft and skin toned. She added rose-coloured nipple clips in the shape of a daisy. A thin chain draped between the clips.

"That looks great. Now put on the dress and we can add the cuffs and chains."

Diana stood and slipped on the dress over her head. The dark blue beaded dress was mid thigh in length. The front had two strips from the waist that circled behind her neck, while the back featured only thin strings criss-crossing that reached around to the front strips. She added wrist cuffs while Khloe added her ankle cuffs. The cuffs matched her wide, black collar that restricted her head movement.

"I hope I can eat with this collar on."

"Small bites." Khloe laughed as she added a chain belt around her waist. "Now let's get those chains attached."

Diana looked at herself in the full-length viewscreen. Gold chains stood out in front of the blue dress, reaching from the waist belt to the ankle and wrist cuffs.

"You look very nice."

"Thank you. I really like the drawing you did. You're a bit of an artist."

"Just something I learned to do. I think we have time for one more glass of wine before Master Derik arrives."

After Khloe left, Diana waited a short time before Derik arrived.

"Master Derik, you're right on time as usual." She saw him holding what appeared to be flowers. "Are those for me?" It surprised her to see flowers, knowing they were not typically grown on a military ship.

"Yes. I understand flowers are a traditional gift for Alliance females." He handed the flowers to her. "They actually made these of fabric and molded to resemble flowers. A scent has been added to them. I hope you like them."

"They're lovely. Thank you very much." She took the brightly coloured imitation flowers and placed them on a table in the living room. "I must order a vase for them. They look and smell so real."

After Diana slipped on blue stilettoes, Derik attached a short leash to her wrist cuff and led her to the same lounge they went to for lunch.

"Your dress looks lovely on you."

"Thank you. I borrowed it from Khloe. She helped me get ready."

"I approve. Your collar looks especially interesting."

"I was saving it for a special occasion. I believe this evening counts as one."

"I hope it does for both of us."

The lounge had changed the wall to show old white buildings with blue trim. Narrow streets followed twists and turns toward a wharf. The evening sun cast a yellow glow on the buildings. Their table gave a view as if they were on the rooftop of a two-story building.

After they sat, Derik ordered wine and a cheese fondue to start.

"This is very relaxing." Diana listened to the soft music played with a background of birds that flew around the wharf.

"It is nice. I hope the rest of the evening will be to your enjoyment."

"Why, Master Derik, if I didn't know any better, I would say you were trying to seduce me."

"I have plans for you."

Diana looked at his grin. *I can guess what those plans are too.*

The Greek salad was followed by fish served with onions and tomatoes. It impressed Diana how the chef used the right amount of spices on the cod.

"I am stuffed. That was a delicious meal." Diana took a drink of her sauvignon blanc.

"It was very good. Normally I prefer red meat, but I have to admit the fish is something I would like to have again." He signaled the server, and despite Diana's protest, ordered dessert.

The revani, a sweet cake, arrived at their table. A glass of muscat wine was added, and Diana found she had room for the small dessert.

After coffee, Derik escorted her, using a leash attached to her wrist. She followed him along the familiar route until they turned off on another corridor. She licked her lips, feeling nervous as they approached his suite. After he opened the door, she followed him inside, taking off her shoes.

"I will get us a glass of liqueur to relax with. Please make yourself comfortable." Derik removed her leash.

Diana looked around the two-level suite. The living room was larger than her own suite, but the kitchen was smaller. The upper level showed there were two bedrooms. She saw a cushion near an armchair and moved the cushion in front of the chair. She kneeled on the cushion as she waited for him.

Derik handed her a glass of the tea-coloured liquid and sat in the armchair. "I had expected you would sit on the couch."

"I'm in your suite and should follow Praxton customs. You have tried hard to follow Alliance customs, and I should try to follow Praxton customs when I'm with you. I don't mind kneeling in front of you. The cushion is quite comfortable."

He didn't speak as he studied her, taking a sip from his glass.

"Is something wrong, Master Derik?"

"No, nothing. It seems to me I have achieved a perfect moment right now and don't wish to disturb it by speaking." He smiled. "I'm thinking when we first met… I could not have envisioned that this would happen."

"That you have finally tamed the disobedient Alliance female?" She grinned.

"I have no illusions I have tamed you. You are of strong character and will always do what you want to do. Still, I treasure this moment of tranquility between us. I hope it lasts a while longer."

They finished their drink and Diana looked at the couch. "Master Derik, there is an Alliance custom I think you may enjoy. Let's sit on the couch together."

"All right." He held out his hand to her and they sat on the couch, side by side.

She curled under his arm, resting her head on his chest. "I enjoy close contact with you like this." She undid buttons on his shirt, placing her hand on his chest.

"It is nice." His hand traced a pattern on her bare back. "Would you like to spend the night here in the second bedroom? They design it for a Praxton female."

"I might be late for work if I slept here."

"True, but neither of us have to start work exactly on time."

"Okay, I think it would be okay if I stayed the night in a separate bed."

"Good," said Derik. "I'll even make coffee in the morning for you."

"No breakfast?" She laughed.

He took her by her hand upstairs to the guest bedroom. He didn't leave her, but helped her undress.

Well, he has seen me naked before. She watched him remove her chains and helped her take off her dress. He removed her ankle cuffs and waited until she removed her collar. "I don't think I can sleep with this on."

"No worries. No collar is required in bedrooms." He joined her wrist cuffs together at her front.

"Hey, is this a new custom?"

"No, I think it'll help you feel a bit more under my control." He guided her to the bed. After attaching an ankle cuff to her, he covered her with the blanket, planting a kiss on her lips. "I will see you in the morning."

"Goodnight, Master Derik."

Diana closed her eyes, but sleep didn't come. The wrist cuffs were on her mind, and his words of being under his control haunted her. *I can't sleep feeling like this.*

She sat up and undid the ankle cuff. *Time to assert some Alliance customs.* Diana made her way to his bedroom, her eyes making out his form in the bed. She slipped under the covers.

"Master Derik, on Alliance worlds, when a gentleman invites a lady to stay overnight, it rarely means leaving her alone in a guest room." She kissed him as her hands slid down his bare skin. She grabbed his thickening penis, holding it as it swelled.

He rolled on top of her, placing her cuffed wrists above her head. He kissed her on the mouth and lowered his head. Derik kissed her neck and moved down, stopping at her breasts.

Diana moaned as he sucked on her nipples, giving small bites as one hand explored between her legs. He continued to kiss and fondle her, working on every inch of her body. Derik rolled her on her side and gave her several strikes on her ass. He pushed her onto her stomach, kissed her back and massaged her. He smacked her ass again.

"You like being spanked."

"Hmm."

"How about being spanked in front of others?" He continued to spank her.

"Yes, if Master Derik desires to do so."

"I'm talking about your desires."

"Yes, I would enjoy that."

He smacked her ass again and rolled her onto her back. His erection was pressed against her stomach and he slid up, rubbing it on her breasts.

Diana felt helpless with her wrists cuffed together. She tried to arch her back and placed her hands on his head, not able to return his touches. "Please, Master Derik, you have me on the edge."

He took his cock and placed it on her mouth.

Her tongue reached out, licking at the long shaft. She wondered if she was to give him oral sex and that would be the conclusion to the lovemaking. Instead, he pulled away, resting on top of her, and pressed his cock against her swollen clitoris. He pushed inside her, and she gasped. She lifted her knees, wrapping her legs around him. *You're not going anywhere now.*

She came, and he continued to thrust inside her. Suddenly, she felt his muscles tighten and he let out a long, low growl.

A minute passed, and he rolled off her. "That was worth the wait."

She laughed and kissed his chest. She placed her head on his stomach, occasionally kissing his skin as he stroked her hair.

She felt tired, ready to sleep, but knew there was something missing. "Master Derik, would you please attach my ankle cuff? I won't sleep well without it on."

"Of course."

She felt him gently attach the ankle cuff, cover her with the blanket, and place an arm over her. She sighed and drifted off to sleep.

[17]

AFTER TIFFANY WOKE up from her nap, she went to the washroom that held an oversized shower with transparent walls and a soaker tub. The soaker tub looked like two tubs joined together and was designed for two people facing each other. *That would be a rather interesting way to talk to someone.* She exited the washroom and Allula showed her the walk-in closet where a dozen dresses and skirts hung.

"I can get you more, but this is the most usual style worn to dinner by the wives."

"I am not his wife."

"I am sorry. I did not mean to offend. This is one of the rooms reserved for his wives."

"No offense taken." She took out a red dress and held it up. The lacey material was long with a single shoulder strap on the right side. The left side was bare along the top. "I don't know about this one. Lovely colour, but I don't know about leaving my left boob exposed." She went through several other dresses and settled on a yellow two-piece dress. The top was short, with long sleeves. It was held together at the front by three thin gold chains, exposing her bosom in the middle. The long skirt portion sat low on her hips with slits on both sides that went up to gold belt.

"You look very pretty, Ms. Harris."

"Thank you. Is this appropriate for the dinner? Do I need anything else? Shoes?"

"Some wives add jewellery and body decorations. Shoes are not worn by women inside Prince Francis' quarters."

"Okay. I don't have jewellery to wear, but perhaps you can help with the body decorations."

Tiffany stood as Allula applied glittering paint to her skin. She made thin brush strokes of different colours to show an abstract figure of a woman reclining. She also adjusted the belt of the skirt so it sat lower.

"It is expected to show off some of your cheeks, Ms. Harris."

"It feels like it is ready to fall off."

"I suggest, Ms. Harris, that you walk carefully."

Prince Francis entered the room. "You look radiant, Tiffany. Are you ready for dinner?"

"Yes. Allula helped me get ready." She looked at the slave girl, seeing she was kneeling on the floor with her head bowed.

"That is good to hear." He held up his arm for Tiffany.

"I am nervous about this dinner." She took his arm. "You have me staying in one of the rooms reserved for wives. I hope they don't get the wrong impression. I'm not moving in here."

"There's no reason to be nervous. It will delight my wives to meet you."

They entered a large dining room. The table appeared to be able to hold a dozen guests. Tiffany saw the four wives were already seated. Elizabeth Harold sat between two wives, looking anxious. Servants stood waiting at the far wall and two guards stood at the entrance. At each corner of the table, a slave girl kneeled. The wives stood and clasped their hands in front of them.

Prince Francis took Tiffany by the hand to the head of the table. "My dear wives, this is Tiffany Harris. She is visiting us from the Alliance World's spaceship, the Star Hawk. Tiffany, this is Ebba, Alice, Anette and Cecilie."

Tiffany sat next to Prince Francis. She saw the wives wore light fabric dresses. Two were topless, and all wore several pieces of jewellery. One had several necklaces that helped cover up her breasts. Body paint and nipple jewellery helped to distract skin exposure. Elizabeth wore a green ribbon that spiraled around her with a sheer mesh between the fabric. The green covered one breast but left the other exposed.

Servants quickly placed plates in front of each guest. The first course was a soup, and Tiffany watched to know when to eat.

"Don't be so nervous. Just think of this as a family dinner."

She glanced at Prince Francis. "Yes, but this is a royal family dinner with me being observed by four wives wondering what I'm doing here."

"You are my guest. Drink some wine and worry not what others think. I think you're wonderful, beautiful and intelligent." He leaned over and kissed her on the cheek.

After the salad was served, five entertainers entered the room, three women and two men. One man played a string instrument while the other used a flute. The three women wore identical dresses but of different colours. The green, blue and red dresses had long strips of cloth hanging down from their neckline and held at their waist by a gold belt. Underneath the dress, a gold bodice and panties could be seen as they moved. The men wore loose, colourful pants and black vests.

The woman in the red dress danced seductively, moving from the men and the other two women, who sang as the men played.

Another course arrived as the entertainment carried on, moving from a slow ballad to a fast-paced dance song. As the dancer in the red dress moved from behind the men to the front of the other women, each singer pulled at a strip of cloth off her. The dancer twisted and turned as the red fabric fell to the floor. Near the end of the song, she was wearing only her belt and underwear. The third song was slow and included the men singing as well.

The dancer continued her movements, occasionally dropping to her knees. The blue dressed singer undid the back of the bodice and it fell to floor. The dancer carried on, moving around the group. When she passed the singer in the green dress, she removed her belt. The dancer moved between the two female singers. She raised her hands in the air as the other women undid the sides of her panties, leaving her nude to finish her dance.

It was the end of the entertainment, and the diners gave a small applause.

"You do like your women entertainers naked," Tiffany commented.

"It is one luxury I have as part of the royal family. If an entertainer wishes to perform in front of me, then there's a criterion to be met. Not all performances must include naked women, but it is something my entertainment manager considers strongly. She understands my taste. Did you enjoy the show?"

"Yes, it was good. The music was excellent and the dancer, even if she lost her clothes, was good as well."

They finished the meal with a calidi influenced dessert and a port. Tiffany carried her port to where the wives and Elizabeth were standing near an open area by the table. She first gave Elizabeth a hug and a kiss on the cheek, joining in with the others in light conversation. She was pleased the wives didn't show any resentment to her, although she could tell they were appraising her as a partner for Prince Francis.

"How are you doing, Elizabeth? You look lovely in that dress."

"Thank you. I'm good and enjoying my time here. By the way, I was told I won't be leaving the royal floors for some time. I have my room and a guard follows me wherever I go. Other than that, I am enjoying my time here."

"You sure you're okay? I can talk to Prince Francis."

"Please don't. This is good. I like this pampered lifestyle. I even have my own slave and she's very nice to talk to."

"All right." Tiffany said goodbye to the wives and walked with Prince Francis. "I understand you have taken over from your father as head of the royal family. Do you have any siblings?"

"Yes, several. My father had several wives as well. So, I have numerous brothers and sisters. I am the oldest son and hence first in line to be king."

"Do you have older sisters?"

"Yes, one half-sister is older."

"Isn't she in line as head of the royal family?"

"She thought so and made a fuss when I was made first in line. I took care of her challenge."

"How so?"

"I confine her to her own suite. She has several slaves and servants to tend to her needs. Because she is royal, she doesn't want to be seen as a slave so I also restricted her to wearing only skirts, so therefore she doesn't leave her suite."

"Isn't that being mean?"

"No, she has to respect the king's wishes. She didn't and there are consequences. I could have had her whipped, but I showed mercy. She is behaving now, and I may grant her additional freedom in the future. Does that worry you how I treated my half-sister?"

"No, unless you are planning to do that to me."

"Which? Confining you or the whipping?" He grinned.

"Prince Francis, would you really whip a diplomat from the Alliance Worlds? That would not be good for relations."

"True. But what about a spanking?" He reached over and smacked her ass.

Tiffany laughed. "That would depend on circumstances."

He smacked her ass again. "And what would those circumstances be?" He continued to pepper her ass with minor hits.

She moved her hands behind her to block him. "I don't know of any right now." She tried to dance away from his hands and giggled.

Prince Francis teased her with more hits, moving past her hands. "As a prince, perhaps it is me that decides if you receive a spanking." His hand continued to smack her bottom as she walked backward in front of him.

"You're going to pull I'm the prince card on me?"

He grabbed one of her wrists behind her back in each hand. "I just might." He kissed her until her mouth opened.

Tiffany moaned and relaxed her arms.

Prince Francis folded her arms at her elbows, holding them in place with one hand. He kissed her again. His other hand hit her ass several times, alternating between sides.

She lifted her head to kiss at his neck, gasping as he spanked her. A warmth spread to her groin.

"Tell me if you want me to stop."

"Don't stop." She leaned against him, the blows increasing in strength.

"I understand on Praxton, spanking is common. Do you ever get spanked on the Star Hawk?"

"No." *I wish.* Her ass burned.

"That is too bad. I shall have to make up for your lack of spanking." He rubbed her cheeks, squeezing them.

Tiffany took rapid, deep breaths. *I'm getting spanked where guards and servants can see me, and I don't care.*

The spanking resumed and shortly later, Tiffany cried out.

"Do you want me to stop?"

"Yes."

"Ten more hits first."

Tiffany counted twelve more strikes, tears running from her eyes.

"Now, we go to my bed where I will take care of you." He took off her skirt and her top.

Tiffany looked behind her at her red cheeks, touching them lightly. "They're so sore." She took his arm as he carried her skirt and top in the other hand. She noticed the guards standing at intervals along the hallway didn't change their straight forward look. Tiffany was glad when they reached his bedroom and went to the bed, sitting on the mattress. She watched on her hands and knees as he undressed, his erection full.

"Do you need another spanking?"

"No, Prince Francis."

"Will you obey me?"

"Yes, Prince Francis."

He went to a table and lifted out a velvet box. He carried the box to her and opened it, revealing a collar similar to what his wives wear. "Since you are a special guest here, it is appropriate for you to wear a collar." He waited as she lifted it out of the box.

"I don't know about wearing this collar."

"It would please me if you did."

"Very well, Prince Francis." Tiffany put the collar around her neck and heard a click as it locked.

He climbed on top of her, kissing and touching her body. He squeezed her breasts as her fingers dug into his back.

Her ass hurt from being pressed on the bed by his weight. "Please, now, come inside me."

He slid inside her wet pussy and rode her. She came and cried out, but he continued his movements of rapid pumping. She lifted her hands above her head, exhausted. He finally finished and rolled off her.

After a minute, she twisted and put her head on his chest. She felt him stroking her hair. She sighed. *I've been spanked, collared and screwed. What a wonderful night.*

———

Diana woke to the soft lights in Derik's bedroom. She yawned and looked around through half-open eyes. Derik wasn't in the bed, and moments later she recognized the sound of a shower. She pushed the blanket off her and reached for the cuff holding her ankle. She struggled briefly to undo the cuff with her wrists joined, then made her way to his shower.

A muscular chest gleamed under soap and water, his thick arms scrubbing at his lean stomach. She took a deep breath and entered the doorless shower, passing between the curved glass entrance.

"Good morning." She gave him a kiss. "I guess I slept in."

"Only a bit." He kissed the top of her head.

Diana kissed his chest and left a trail of kisses as she dropped to her knees. *This is going to be different with my wrists cuffed together.* She fondled his shaft and testicles with her fingers, running her tongue on his cock as it swelled. Her hands pulled on his shaft, and she parted her lips to take in the head. Her tongue played with the head as her fingers stroked his balls. Slowly, she pressed forward, taking his erection deep inside her. She pulled back and pressed inward again, repeating the motion slowly as her fingers worked on him. His hands pressed at the back of her head. Her face rested against his firm stomach for several moments before she could pull away. She gasped for air as water poured down her.

She licked the length of his erection and placed her mouth over it, pushing it inside her quickly. She felt him stiffen and knew he was ready to come. Once more, she pulled back and plunged on him. He exploded inside her and she tried to swallow as much as she could before lifting her head off him. A second wave sprayed over her as he leaned back against the shower wall, moaning.

Diana grinned up at him. "Did I please you, Master Derik?"

He took another gulp of air before replying. "Don't be a brat." He grinned at her.

Diana finished showering with him after he undid her wrist cuffs. While he dressed, she put on her collar and made coffee for them.

"Thank you for making coffee and staying naked."

"You're welcome. I'm used to being naked around you."

"Yesterday and this morning, we took a significant step forward in our relationship. I hope we can continue to make progress."

"Do you want me to proclaim you are now my guardian? I'm ready to do so if that's what you want."

"I want that. Praxton customs require I show my control over you publicly and I believe I have done so."

She finished her coffee. "I best get dressed." She went upstairs, putting on the dress from the night before, and added the chains and cuffs. When she went downstairs, Derik was waiting for her. He undid the chain between her wrist cuffs and stepped behind her, joining her wrist cuffs behind her back with the chain. He attached the leash to a wrist cuff.

"I'll escort you to your suite so you can change."

Diana went with Derik along the corridor. She received a few glances from others, deciding it was more to do with wearing an evening dress than having her hands cuffed behind her back. *Still, it must make for an interesting sight. Anyone seeing us will know he now owns me.*

They arrived at her suite, and he undid her wrist cuffs. "I'll wait here and escort you to your office. No panties."

"Yes, Master Derik."

Diana studied her closet, deciding on a black pleated skirt. It was short, but she believed the loose fabric would give her better coverage while sitting than a tight skirt. She added a pair of blue nipple clips that matched her earrings and added a white, sleeveless blouse. She changed her collar and cuffs to narrow metal ones. The gold collar and cuffs had a padded interior and fitted snugly.

She went downstairs where Derik stood and appraised her. "Lovely. You look beautiful."

"Thank you." She waited as Derik removed the chain between her wrist cuffs and joined them together. He undid the buttons on the front of her blouse except the bottom two.

"I'll escort you to work." He added a leash to her wrist cuffs.

Diana walked with him. "May I ask how often you plan to escort me this way?"

"Not much longer. I believe I've shown others you are under my control now."

Diana was silent until they reached her office. She gave him a quick kiss when he removed the leash. She held up her wrists. "Can you undo these now?"

"No. They will stay joined. I'll be back to take you to lunch."

Diana gave him an exasperated look. "Yes, Master Derik."

After he left, Diana began work, finding she could adapt to hands cuffed together, although it was slower to work through the various chemical formulas using the keyboard.

"Hello." Khloe entered her office. She was smiling as she approached her desk. "I heard you were being escorted this morning while wearing an evening dress. Can I assume good news is in order?"

Diana held up her wrists cuffed together. "If one ignores this development, then yes." She gave a grin. "It seems Master Derik has decided on restrictions for me to follow."

"That's splendid news. Tell me about what happened last night."

Diana related the events, including the flowers, dinner and going to his place. "I agreed to stay overnight in the guest bedroom, but I couldn't sleep. I decided it was time to make things happen. I went to his bed." She smiled. "It was great."

"Did you please him first?"

"No, he satisfied me first."

"Wow, that's not the Praxton custom at all."

"Yes, well, I pleased him in the shower in the morning."

Khloe laughed. "A great way to start the morning, especially for him."

"So, what can I expect from him now? Besides the cuffed wrists."

"Likely a few spankings. Maybe public nudity. Praxton customs mean he has to show he is in complete control of you."

"Fun times." Diana frowned. "He unbuttoned my blouse this morning, so I guess that should have indicated what's going to happen."

"Remember, if he tells you to do something, just do it. Arguing or showing any reluctance to his commands would likely mean discipline." Khloe stepped around the desk and gave her a kiss on her cheek. "I'm thrilled for you. You've adjusted really well to the Praxton way of doing things. I'll see you later."

Diana watched her leave and went back to work. She made a few changes to a caramel sauce and went to the kitchen to check the test sample. She wasn't surprised to see Chiela and said hello to her.

"How are you doing today, Chiela?"

"Great. I have thought about our conversation about Master Collin, and I believe I've found a solution."

"Really? What is that?"

"I don't want to encourage him, as you know, but I found out his birthday is in three weeks' time. I figure I can give him a blowjob as a birthday present, but that wouldn't mean I would accept him as my guardian."

Diana thought about what Chiela said. "You're sure that the blowjob wouldn't mean more than a birthday present?"

"Yeah, I'll make it clear to him." She pointed at Diana's wrists. "Did Master Derik do that?"

"Yes, he's giving me orders and adding restrictions on me."

"That's great." She grinned. "Is he your guardian now?"

"In all but name. I'm not happy having my wrists cuffed together, but that's his choice."

"I can't wait to see what else he may do to you."

Diana laughed. "I'm not so eager to learn that. Want to try some caramel sauce?"

Chiela quickly accepted and approved of the flavour. "I'm happy for you. Master Derik will make a great guardian. I think he'll be strict, but I can tell he really likes you."

"I'm sure he does. I just wish he would show me by wine and roses."

Chiela covered her mouth as she giggled. "You're funny with your Alliance views."

Diana returned to her workstation, occasionally grumbling at errors caused by her joined wrists as she typed in new commands. She looked up and saw Derik. She quickly stood.

"Master Derik."

"It's time for lunch." He attached a leash to her wrist cuffs.

"Master Derik, am I supposed to eat with my writs cuffed together?"

"No, I'll release them so you can eat. If we were going for drinks, I would leave them cuffed together."

Diana sat with Derik at a table where he separated her wrist cuffs. Before their lunch order was taken, Morgan and Janice joined them. The server arrived and Derik ordered lunch for Diana and himself. Morgan and Janice didn't react to Derik ordering for her and gave their own requests.

The conversation centred around the mission of the trade agreement with the planet Divinus.

"I believe our diplomat, Tiffany Harris, is enjoying the company of Prince Francis. They supposedly did a special celebration of the trade agreement." Janice spoke.

Morgan added, "Tiffany did an outstanding job in working out the trade agreement. Divinus is a destination place for the pirates, and the agreement effectively puts an end to Alliance citizens being sold as slaves there." She looked at Diana. "That was a wonderful dinner you planned for our guests from Divinus. I hope we have more of those in the future."

"Thank you. I really enjoyed working out the meal and the wine pairing."

The table talk continued on the excitement of visiting new worlds, and Diana found the time pass quickly.

"Diana, it's time I take you back to work."

Diana stood and looked at Derik. She hesitated and held her hands in front of her. He joined her wrist cuffs and attached a leash to a cuff. She saw Morgan and Janice watch as he led away her from the table. *I guess now they know he has taken control of me.*

When they arrived at her office, he removed the leash, keeping her wrists cuffed together. "I'll see you later." He gave her a smile.

"Yes, Master Derik." He has something else planned.

Work for Diana comprised trying to design a new spice sauce. She made several trips to the kitchen, finding the right flavour elusive. She finally decided on increasing the onion taste and reducing one of the peppers.

Derik approached her at her workstation. "How was your afternoon?"

"Frustrating. I was designing a new sauce for tacos and chili but had trouble discerning some flavours. After tasting several variants of the new sauce, I lost some of my tastebuds. I'll try again tomorrow. How was your day?"

"Good. No major issues." He shrugged. "I have to keep a close watch on the junior technicians as they have a tendency to prioritize social activities over work."

"They are young."

"Yes. The work isn't difficult, so the junior technicians have extra time. My concern is they may do something that would result in a reprimand on their personnel file. I can cover small indiscretions, but I informed them don't do anything that could damage their careers." He attached a leash to her wrist cuffs.

She went to her suite with him. "May I ask if we're doing anything tonight?"

"You will stay in your suite tonight."

"I cannot go out?"

"No. You will be nude from the minute we arrive. I will come by later this evening to share a drink with you, but you're confined to your suite until tomorrow morning."

"And I have to be naked?" Her voice changed in pitch.

"Yes, and if I hear any objections, I can add to that condition as well."

"No, sir, no objections."

Diana entered her suite and after Derik released her wrist cuffs, went upstairs while Derik waited downstairs. She removed her clothes, leaving on her collar and cuffs but with without chains. She tried to keep the annoyance from showing on her face as she returned downstairs.

"You looked beautiful even when you're angry with me."

"If you say so, Master Derik."

"I will return here later this evening."

Diana watched him leave, glaring at the closed door. *I need a drink.* She decided on rye whisky, enjoying the warmth it gave her. After her second sip, she called Khloe.

"Khloe, I have a situation."

"Something with Master Derik?"

"Yes. He has ordered me to stay in my suite this evening. Naked."

"Oh! That's good news."

"How is that good news?"

"It's a Praxton thing males do. Master Derik is telling you how much he wants you and to be your guardian."

"Yeah, by keeping me naked in my suite."

Khloe laughed. "I wish a male would order me stay naked in my room. I think it's really nice he likes you so much."

"Thanks, but all I can do is sit around here until he comes by later."

"So, you're going to have dinner in your suite?"

"No choice. Fortunately, I have a good kitchen with lots of food."

"How about I join you for dinner and drinks?"

"I'm naked."

"I've seen lots of naked females," said Khloe. "Honestly, it really isn't a big deal."

"All right. Dinner for two it is."

Diana finished her drink and thought about what she would make for dinner. She programmed the food synthesizer when Khloe arrived at her door. Diana used her voice command to open the door, meeting her in the living room.

"Sorry, I was programming our dinner menu. Thanks for coming over and sorry about my state of undress."

"Don't apologize. They allow Praxton females to be nude in their own home. In fact, it's encouraged." She took off her uniform top. "See, nudity is nothing to worry about, at least on Praxton."

"Thanks. Can I offer you a drink? I'm drinking whisky."

"Gin and tonic please." She sat in a chair and waited for Diana to hand her the drink. "Look, if you were another female, Master Derik would have likely made you go to dinner in the nude. Maybe even spank you in a lounge. He's showing you he respects your Alliance background by having you naked in the privacy of your suite."

"Oh, I hadn't thought of it in that way."

"He is trying to accommodate your Alliance ways. Now he still may give you a public spanking, but I know he is being sensitive to your comfort levels. On Praxton, we believe a female should be punished publicly before the guardian will accept her. A measure of humiliation is accepted by her, so everyone knows he is in control."

"I guess I should be thankful for the flowers he gave me." She pointed to the fabric flowers in the vase.

"Those are pretty. See, he is trying."

"You're right. I just have trouble figuring this Praxton culture." I still may be spanked publicly?

"There are a lot of nuances to learn. What smells so good?"

"French onion soup, pot roast, roasted potatoes, vegetables." She smiled. "Apple pie for dessert."

"This is better than going to the lounge for dinner. I think you're my best friend now."

Diana laughed. "So, I can buy your friendship."

"Food and drinks are the way to my heart. And a good spanking from the right male."

Diana grinned at Khloe's joke. "Let's sit in the living room." She led the way from the dining area to the living room, refilling the cocktail glasses first. The conversation was a maze of subjects, from Praxton and Alliance customs to how the Star Hawk was venturing into new territories as they visited the Rebel worlds.

"What time is Master Derik going to come by?"

"He didn't say, just some time this evening. He's always punctual about his time, and I suspect he'll show up exactly at seven, or eight, or half past the hour. That way he'll still arrive exactly on time, even if he didn't state what time he would be here."

"It seems you understand Master Derik well. That's good, a female should know her guardian's habits."

"I have little choice in understanding him. It is that or get spanked."

Khloe told Diana about some other discipline measures Praxton males have used and her own experiences. "What Master Derik is doing is very mild."

The door chime sounded and Diana opened the door to Master Derik.

"Hello, Diana, Khloe."

Khloe stood. "Hello, Master Derik." She put on her top. "I was just ready to leave." As she went by Diana, she whispered, "It's exactly eight o'clock."

"How was your evening, Diana?"

"It went very well. Khloe was kind to keep me company. We had dinner and talked a lot. How was your evening?"

"A bit boring, actually. I missed you."

"That was by your choice."

"It was, but it was necessary to do this."

"By Praxton customs." She frowned. "I will obey you, even though I don't fully understand the reasons behind Praxton traditions."

"I appreciate what you said. I try to accommodate your Alliance background." He gave her a kiss. "Are you still angry?"

"No, Master Derik." She returned his kiss.

"Would you object to my coming over for breakfast tomorrow morning?"

"That would be fine." I'll wear what I have on now.

"That would be great. Until tomorrow." He kissed her goodnight.

[18]

DIANA RINSED the soapy water off her body. She took her time in the shower, knowing Derik Holton was watching her from below. The first time she showered with him watching her, she tried to act as if he wasn't there, but deliberately used slow movements to wash herself and used an excess of soap. Now she felt more relaxed as she showered, and even waved at him from the glass wall.

After she finished her shower, she added her collar and went downstairs. She gave him a kiss and went to the kitchen to make their breakfast. She heard him call out.

"I really look forward to watching you shower. It is not only erotic but also very relaxing. It's a wonderful start to my day."

"Thank you. I'm glad you enjoy it." Diana carried two plates to the dining room. "Breakfast is served."

Holton sat and began to eat, pausing to compliment her on the food. "A heavenly start to the day."

Diana was pleased he enjoyed the breakfast, but he seemed to be in an unusually good mood. She cleared the table and went upstairs to dress. She put extra effort on her makeup and choose a bright red skirt she knew he liked on her. After adding a white top and appropriate number of cuffs and chains, she returned downstairs. She waited as he added a leash to her wrist cuff and followed him to her office.

"I'll return to take you for lunch."

"Thank you, Master Derik. I look forward to it."

Diana busied herself with working on starch formulas for noodles. She went to the lower level to test the new product and saw a few technicians inviting them to sample the noodles.

"I'm hoping they have better texture and don't taste like soft cardboard."

Chiela commented, "Actually, these taste pretty good. I'll start ordering pasta again if you use this."

Diana returned to her office once she was sure of the combination. She sent a formula change request to Holton's office and began to look at the formulas for wine, choosing a dry Riesling as one to work on.

Her efforts were interrupted by Holton.

"It's time for lunch." He held up a leash.

"That sounds good." She stood as he attached the leash to her wrist cuff. She detected a slight hesitation in his voice and noticed he was smiling. *Is he up to something?*

The dining lounge was busy, and they sat with several other members of the executive officers, including First Officer Morgan Regan, Captain Elmwood and Communication Officer Janice Madison. A few minutes later, Khloe Levit joined them giving Diana a warm smile.

"I like what you're wearing, Diana. Very pretty."

"Thanks." Diana ate her meal that Holton ordered for her. She felt she was being observed by everyone at the table. *Something is going on. Is he planning to give me a public spanking? That certainly is the Praxton way of doing things.*

After a longer than normal lunch, Holton escorted her back to her office. Waiting in her office were the technicians standing by her desk. Diana slowed her steps after Holton detached the leash from her wrist. She walked halfway to her desk and looked behind her to see what Holton was doing. Behind him, she saw the captain, Morgan, Janice and Khloe enter the office.

"Master Derik, what is going on?"

He dropped to one knee and stared at her. "Diana, you have done everything I asked to conform to the Praxton way. I feel humbled at your efforts to accommodate my wants. Now, as we move forward in our relationship, I want to do something that shows I respect your Alliance heritage." He opened his hand, showing a gold ring with a cluster of small diamonds. "Please, Diana, will you accept this ring?"

Diana's mouth opened, but words didn't materialize. Her eyes became wet as she extended shaking hands.

"Diana?"

"Yes," she whispered and wrapped her arms around his neck. "Yes, yes, yes!"

Her feet lifted off the floor as he stood. They kissed, and she heard the applause around her. After they broke apart, her left hand trembled as he pushed the ring on her finger. She was showing it off to the interested crew around her.

Khloe asked if that meant they were married.

"No, this is called an engagement ring. It means I have accepted his proposal to get married."

"Does he get a ring as well?"

"No, not now. When a couple gets married, the bride and the groom get a wedding ring. Only the woman gets an engagement ring."

"So, you get two rings?"

"Yes, but the wedding ring is usually less elaborate than the engagement ring."

"I think it looks beautiful. Maybe that's something guardians should give their females."

Diana accepted congratulations from the rest of the crew, including the captain. Morgan gave her a hug.

"This was a nice interruption, but we better get back to maintaining the Star Hawk."

Diana walked hand in hand with Holton to his office. "Thank you so much for the ring. I never expected you would do something like that for me."

"Diana, I love you and know how you value the Alliance way of doing things. I want you to know I respect your Alliance heritage, just as you have shown respect for the Praxton way of life."

They stopped at his office. "I may have to work later than normal today. I missed a portion of my workday this afternoon."

"Of course, Master Derik. I will go to your office after I finish work." She gave him a kiss. "I'll see you later."

Diana returned to her office. *I think I'll investigate various white wine varietals. That should be fun and I feel like having a few drinks.*

Diana investigated several wines, making notes on what needed to be improved on. After tasting a chardonnay, pinot gris, sauvignon blanc, semillon and a verdlho, she decided it was time to end her day.

Diana inputted her notes on the wine for later use and went to Holton's office.

"Master Derik, I see you are still hard at work."

"Yes, I must finish these reports before I call it a day. Did you wish to wait for me in a lounge?"

"No, I'll wait here for you." Diana saw a cushion on the floor, removed her shoes, and kneeled on it near his desk. She undid her top and removed it. She saw him look at her. "Is this too distracting for you, Master Derik?"

"No, not at all. It is a most pleasant sight."

"Would it be all right if I removed my skirt as well?"

"Please do."

Diana stood just enough to remove her skirt, kneeling just in her panties. "I will wait patiently for you, Master Derik."

She heard him sigh but decided against teasing him anymore.

A few minutes later, Vanessa entered the office.

"Master Derik, may I get you anything?" She stood with her hands behind her back.

"A coffee would be good. Diana, do you wish anything?"

"A coffee as well. Black."

After she left, Diana asked, "Does she often check on your needs?" She remembered the first time she met Vanessa. The cadet was kneeling by his desk as he worked, causing Diana to get upset.

"Yes, she often inquires on my needs. I know you don't like her kneeling near me, but I cannot stop her from doing what is considered normal Praxton behaviour."

"Very well. I understand Praxton customs better now. It doesn't bother me she is near you. Just as long as you know she has feelings for you."

"I try not to encourage her." He frowned. "I'm much her senior and I wouldn't take advantage of her."

"I know. I trust you on that."

Vanessa returned with the coffee, hesitated, and kneeled on the floor halfway between the door and the desk.

Diana pointed at another cushion near the desk. "Use that."

"Yes, thank you, Ms. Diana." She took off her shoes and kneeled. "May I take off my top, Ms. Diana?"

Diana nodded. "Yes, but only because I'm here."

"May I remove my skirt as well?"

"No, that may be too distracting for Master Derik."

She watched Holton work, apparently intent on the monitor in front of him. She had no doubt he had listened to and saw everything. *I'm almost naked and Vanessa is topless. Yet he acts like we're not here. I suspect he's having trouble concentrating.*

Holton finished his work. Diana stood and dressed. Vanessa merely picked up her shoes and top, carrying them out the door.

After they parted ways with Vanessa, Diana commented. "She's not shy, is she?"

Holton attached a leash to Diana's wrist. "Most Praxton women are comfortable with their bodies, but these younger females seem to find clothes a nuisance. I've had to tell more than one they need to be fully dressed at work. They are very casual about being covered up."

"Maybe they deserve a good spanking?" Diana grinned.

"It would more likely just encourage more of the same bad attitude." He smacked her bottom. "Besides, what would you say if you caught me spanking Vanessa?"

"I would say she deserved it and that I'd like to watch her spanking. But I would also be mad at you. If you want to spank someone, you have me."

"Very well. Just so you know you will be getting a spanking tonight. A damn good one."

"Don't I have to do something wrong before I get spanked?" she asked.

"I'll invent something."

"Well, that's a surprise."

———

"Has Senior Diplomat Harris contacted us?" asked Morgan.

"No, ma'am. Shall I try to contact her?"

She nodded. Tiffany has the right to stay as long as she wants but she was supposed to keep the ship apprised of her time there.

"Ma'am? They are saying their communication system is down for maintenance."

"What? So she can't call us?" Morgan didn't like this, and she knew Elmwood wouldn't either. "Did they say for how long?"

"They said it should only take a few hours but asked us to give it a day in case there is an issue."

"Then make sure we call in exactly twenty-four hours."

———

In the lounge Diana was approached by others wanting to see her ring and offer their congratulations. Holton ordered their food, pairing their steaks with a red wine.

"Does this merlot and cabernet sauvignon blend meet your approval?" asked Holton.

"Yes, it is an excellent choice. A classic Bordeaux blend."

"I wouldn't know that, but that's why we have you as our food and wine expert."

Diana smiled. Between bites of food, she looked at her ring. "You have really made my day. You must have put so much effort in learning about Alliance customs and then having a ring made."

"It was worth it to make you happy." He added the leash to her wrist. "I shall escort you to your suite."

"What happens at my suite? Am I confined there again?"

"Yes. You will be naked as well."

"Will you be coming in?"

"Yes, if you like. Perhaps for a drink."

Diana opened her door and removed her shoes. "Excuse me. I'll get undressed." She went upstairs and removed her clothing, adding wrist and ankle chains between her cuffs. She went downstairs, she went to the kitchen, returning with two glasses of port to the living room. Diana passed one glass to Holton, sitting in an armchair and kneeled in front of him. "May I ask how long you are going to order me to stay in my suite naked every night?"

"I haven't determined that yet. It is when I feel you will be obedient to my wishes."

"I thought I was doing that."

"Yes, but I want to be sure."

Diana refrained from frowning. "I understand, Master Derik."

"Good. I believe there is an Alliance custom of a wedding day. Is that an important day? Is it a celebration of some sort?"

"It is very important. A wedding day starts with the exchange of vows and wedding rings. Afterward, there is a reception that includes dinner and dancing. It usually lasts very late into the night. It's a formal affair."

"Oh. Can it be combined with a ceremony of my becoming your guardian?"

"No. A wedding takes up the whole day. Besides, I'll be wearing a wedding dress that I will not remove until it's time for bed."

"Really?"

"Yes, and that's final. I want my Alliance wedding."

"So be it. I won't argue with you on that. When should we have this wedding?"

"In a few months. It will take time to take care of all the details."

"A few months? Why does it take that long to plan a ceremony?"

"Yes, it takes that long. I won't be rushed on this."

Holton sighed. "Could we have the guardian ceremony ahead of the wedding, then?"

"No, I want the wedding first."

Holton put down his empty glass. "You do make life difficult."

Diana smiled. "Will you be staying the night?"

"I would like that." He stood. "Tell me about this custom of carrying a female over the threshold. What does that mean?"

"I'll explain it later. It's about romance."

He patted his lap. "Perhaps you can explain it to me as I give you a nice, long spanking."

Diana licked her lips. "When a man and a woman choose a place to live, it is traditional for the man to carry the woman through the doorway." She rested on his lap. His hand gave her cheek a quick slap.

"Carries her how? Over the shoulder?"

Diana felt a few more smacks on her ass. She laughed. "No, that's not romantic. In his, ow, arms."

"Hmm. Is she naked?" He massaged her ass.

"No. Well, I guess she could be. Usually, she is wearing a pretty dress." Her ass was beginning to get warm, and she wiggled on his lap, her hip nudging his erection.

"How about tied up? Maybe gagged?" His hand repeatedly struck hard on her ass.

"No! Think romance. Being tied up is not romantic."

"But it is sexy."

"True." She took in a deep breath. "Tell you what. Carry me over the threshold with me in a pretty dress and then you can tie me up to your heart's content." *Oh, that feels good.*

He massaged her cheeks. "That sounds like a deal to me. Naked and tied up."

Diana gasped. *Romance, Praxton style, has its merits too.*

▭

Tiffany's eyes fluttered open. *This has been a hell of a week.* Last night had been like the others where she ended the say in the prince's bed and she had to admit that she loved every minute of it. She turned over and saw the other half of the bed was empty once again. She used her arms to push to a sitting position and looked around, seeing a kneeling slave.

"Colina, where's Prince Francis?"

"He is now in washroom, Ms. Harris."

"In that case, I better get ready." She went to the guest washroom and a few minutes later turned on the shower, stepping around the curved, doorless shower entrance. She saw Colina was following her. "Colina, is there a slave helping Prince Francis wash?"

"Yes, Ms. Harris."

"Not on my watch." She hurried out of the guest washroom and to his washroom. The washroom was larger and more elaborate, but her attention went to where a slave was washing his back in the shower. Tiffany stepped into the shower, surprising the blonde slave girl.

"Out. I'll take over washing him." She grabbed the wash sponge.

Prince Francis turned around, smiling. "Good morning."

"Good morning. If you wanted company in the shower, you should have called me." She scrubbed his chest.

"I didn't want to wake you."

She continued to wash him, pushing away his hand when he attempted to take the sponge. "I'll be leaving in a few hours, and I want you to remember me." She washed down his arms and dropped to her knees, working on his legs.

"I won't be forgetting you."

She used the sponge and her hands to wash his balls and penis. Tiffany dropped the sponge and placed the stiffening cock into her mouth. She carefully held his testicles and slid her head along the shaft.

"Stand up and we can finish in the shower." He gasped.

She stopped and looked up at him. "No, I want you to come into my mouth." She resumed her efforts, pleased how hard he was. Tiffany increased her efforts, using her hands on his shaft and balls. She felt his body stiffen, and he grunted with exertion when the hot fluid surged into her mouth. She leaned back as the semen sprayed over her face.

He gasped and dropped to his knees to kiss her. "Perhaps I can wash you now."

Tiffany laughed. "Just a washing. I need to contact the Star Hawk. I'll bet they're wondering what happened to me."

Later, as she dressed, she wondered if she should come up with an excuse why she was reporting to the ship so late in the morning. *No point in lying. Janice has figured out I'm doing more than just business here.*

She saw Prince Francis standing, waiting for her. She gave him a smile. "Okay, let me contact the Star Hawk." She waited as he spoke.

"Room service, contact the spaceship Star Hawk." He gestured for Tiffany to continue.

A male voice responded, "Communication with the Star Hawk is not possible at this time. The spaceship had to leave to attend to an emergency in Alliance space. It may be gone for several days. I can inform you when it returns."

Tiffany's jaw dropped.

Prince Francis put his arm around her. "I'll send out an urgent communication to the ship and obtain more information. There's no reason to panic. The Star Hawk, I'm sure, needed to respond to a distress call. When that is cleared up, it can return for you."

"I suppose you're right and the Star Hawk will return soon. I guess they couldn't afford the time to wait for me."

"In the meantime, you will be my guest. I look forward to the time we can spend together. Shall we go for breakfast? I have invited Ms. Harold to join us."

Tiffany gave Elizabeth, who was wearing last night's dress, a warm hello when they met in a small dining area. "I guess I'll be here a few more days. The Star Hawk had to leave on an emergency call without me."

"That is unfortunate for you, but I'm glad you're here a bit longer."

Prince Francis, after finishing his meal, stood. "I have business to attend to. I'll find you ladies later." He gave Tiffany a kiss and hurried away.

"Come, I'll show you my suite. It's similar to one the wives have and we can get a change of clothes."

As they walked, Tiffany asked Elizabeth if she knew anything about Prince Francis' older sister. "I understand they keep her in a kind of house arrest."

"Well, first you have to understand the history of the royal family. The king at one time only had one wife, with oldest sibling taking over as king or queen as ruler. Then the king starting having more wives, which led to infighting among the many siblings. Usually, the oldest never lived long enough to be the ruler. To prevent that, the successor is appointed earlier in secret. The other siblings wouldn't know who the new successor was until the day of the appointment. Murder was eliminated, and the perpetrator of such an act would be placed in exile or executed."

They reached Tiffany's suite. Allula awaited them, kneeling near the entrance. "Good morning, Ms. Harris. Good morning, Ms. Harold. May I do anything for you?"

"Hello, Allula. No, we are fine."

"Oh, this is nice." Elizabeth wandered around the room, opening doors. "Clothes to wear, too." She continued to the washroom. "Wow, this makes me want to become one of his wives. That tub looks wonderful."

"It is unique. Want to take a bath together?"

"Sure."

Allula hurried to the washroom, turning on the water to the bathtub. "Ms. Harris, what type of oils or bath soap would you prefer?"

"Pick out anything. Not too much soap. I think we just want to soak and talk."

A few minutes later, Tiffany slid into the water with a scattering of soap on the surface, facing Elizabeth. Allula keeled next to the tub.

"Would you like me to wash you first, Ms. Harris? Or should I start with Ms. Harold?"

"Neither. We can wash ourselves. Could you get a pitcher of juice and three glasses, please?"

"Of course, Ms. Harris." Allula quickly rose and hurried out of the washroom.

"Now tell me more about the royal family," Tiffany requested.

"I told you the successor is appointed early, and in this case, they chose Prince Francis after King Louis and his wives agreed he was the best choice, bypassing his older half-sister. Princess Natalie was infuriated and started a campaign to change their minds. One of her acts was to discredit him by exposing his, let us say, his more adventurous side. She believed she was immune to his retaliation because he had not yet been granted full power. The transfer of power from the king to his successor takes over a year, with a lot of ceremonies and declarations. And, of course, grand celebrations."

"I do like those grand celebrations." Tiffany laughed.

"So do I. Prince Francis had enough of her antics. I believe he gave her one warning, which she ignored, and then he acted. He ordered her confined to her quarters, had a slave collar locked on her, reduced her wardrobe to four thin skirts and forbid her to communicate with anyone outside her quarters without his permission. Then, in front of all her servants and slaves, he had her spanked bare assed by a guard."

"He really humiliated her."

"One would think. He hired her servants and slaves and they would report if she said she should be ruler or said something bad about Prince Francis. If she behaved poorly, she would receive another spanking in front of her servants and slaves. She has had several severe spankings."

"You would think she would learn her lesson. I would think being spanked in front of everyone would stop her."

"There's more. Princess Natalie would have her freedom if she would sign a document agreeing he was the true ruler and to stop her claims, but she refuses to sign. Her spankings are done by the same guard. After the spanking, she always slaps his face and goes to the bedroom. It is rumoured he follows her there shortly later."

"Oh, so she enjoys those spankings."

"By one of those royal guards, who are always tall and good looking."

"I can see the appeal."

Allula returned with a tray. "Your refreshments, Ms. Harris. I hope you find it acceptable."

"I'm sure it will be fine. Pour three glasses. You will have one as well."

"Yes, Ms. Harris. Thank you, Ms. Harris."

Elizabeth tasted the drink. "This is tasty. I need something after last night. Too much wine." She took another sip. "One other thing, Prince Francis allows her to join in some family dinners. They are elaborate affairs with all the siblings attending. Princess Natalie turns down his offer to wear a dress for the occasion, arriving with just the skirt and a slave collar. Her escort is the same guard who spanks her. It causes quite a scene at the dinners, I'm told."

"I'm guessing Princess Natalie loves attention and drama."

"That she does."

"Are any of Prince Francis's wives pregnant?" asked Tiffany.

"No, not yet. Prince Francis will have seven wives. He will then decide which wife will have his first born, the likely successor to himself. So, he will take his time in that decision. After the first born, then he will allow the other wives to become pregnant."

"And here I thought choosing a name for a baby would be hard."

Tiffany suspected calidi mixed in with the juice. She was feeling aroused, enjoying the sight of Elizabeth's breasts as she shifted her position higher in the water. "I love this tub. I think I'll have one installed in my suite on the Star Hawk." She reached for her hand.

Elizabeth gripped her hand and leaned forward.

Tiffany bent forward and exchanged a long kiss with her, parted and returned for a longer, open mouth kiss. "I shall miss you when I go back to Star Hawk."

"We will have to meet occasionally for additional trade agreements, I hope."

"I hope so. I think this is enough tub time. Let's find something to wear."

"Do you wish a massage first, Ms. Harris?" Allula asked.

"No, I'm fine."

Elizabeth stepped into the closet, looking at the clothes. "Are you aware that the massage she's offering is more than just massaging your muscles? The slaves are versed in pleasing both men and women."

"Oh, I never thought of that." She pulled out a skirt. "This looks rather strange." She held it up. The belt was a thick, black cloth. The skirt material was of a heavy material of orange and vertical yellow stripes. The skirt was long, but only wrapped two-thirds around.

"That would look great on you." Elizabeth helped her put it on. "You see, you leave one leg uncovered front and back."

Tiffany laughed. "Yeah, including the side of my cheek." She shifted her hips and looked down at her bare leg. "I like it. I need to find a top to go with it."

"How about this?" Elizabeth held up a short yellow top with small holes dotted throughout the cloth.

"That will do." She put on the top. "I'm dressed. Half naked but dressed. Let's find something for you to wear."

Elizabeth tried on different skirts but ended up wearing a blue dress with two strips of fabric going from her shoulders and criss-crossing down her back to a skirt. The strips also went down her front, each covering the centre of her breasts.

Tiffany complimented her on her dress as they walked out of the bedroom.

"Thanks, but it's your dress."

"Those slaves must see and hear a lot. Isn't privacy a concern?"

"No. The slaves never repeat what they see or hear. If they did, they would lose their employment in the royal quarters immediately. Unless Prince Francis asks them. They are always loyal to the ruler."

They left the bedroom, walking along one hallway that provided a view of the outside. Tiffany understood the hallway actually made a complete journey around the building, although portions were only available to those with sufficient security clearance.

Elizabeth took her hand as they walked. "It's nice to spend time with you. Part of me is hoping you won't return to your ship and stay here. Prince Francis is quite taken with you, and I'm sure he'll find a position here for you."

"I think the position he wants for me is on my back."

Elizabeth giggled. "I can appreciate that thought." She leaned over and gave Tiffany a kiss on her cheek. "I'm not really bi-sexual. I much prefer men. But I'd like to sleep with you."

Tiffany walked a few steps more, looking out the window. "I'd like to sleep with you, too."

"If only I didn't have Prince Francis as competition."

Tiffany laughed. "Tell me more about him. Is he a good ruler?"

"Yes, King Louis was an excellent leader, and I believe Prince Francis will follow his leadership style. Prince Francis works hard. Every day, he meets with business leaders, social advocate leaders and military leaders, trying to improve life on Divinus. He carefully plans moves in politics and his personal life."

"So he is popular?"

"Yes, the military and civilians support him. He makes alliances with different leaders and is very good at getting them to agree on a plan of action. His wives are all daughters of powerful families. A general's daughter and business leaders' daughter, for example."

"They are also beautiful."

"They are, but there are a lot of beautiful women, especially with the gene-therapy drugs available. He also wants them to be smart, as he will ask them to help with negotiations. A pretty woman sitting at a table with businesspeople sometimes helps win an agreement."

"I can understand that. As long as she may speak her mind, that is a good way to negotiate."

"Yes, they are allowed to express themselves. He has used his wives in another way."

"In what way."

"He spanked one of his wives and sent a video of it to her mother, who was holding up an agreement for more compensation. He told her it would be released publicly in two days if she didn't agree to his conditions. The woman signed the next day."

"He likes to spank women."

"I suppose so. Most men do. Many women like being spanked. Few want their spanking being shown to everyone."

"That's true. On the Star Hawk, spankings are done rather openly. Praxton has a different culture regarding female discipline. Spankings are a regular occurrence and are not considered something only done in private."

"That would be interesting to be around. There's a dining area up ahead. Let's stop for a bite to eat."

Tiffany enjoyed the soup and salad, deciding it was as much as she wanted for lunch. Calidi berries were sprinkled in the salad, and she wondered about their effect they would have on her. She was already feeling aroused as she walked with Elizabeth.

"Tell me, Elizabeth, is there ever a call to improve the rights of the slaves on Divinus?"

"There isn't a strong movement to change things among the class of people. The slaves here are treated better than in the past and much better than on other worlds. By definition a slave has no rights, but on Divinus they enjoy certain freedoms."

"I assume very limited freedoms."

"Yes, but they're allowed an education and can improve their skill levels to a point where they are given greater autonomy in their lives. Occasionally, a slave's offspring can be promoted to civilian status." She took a drink of her wine. "My understanding the women on Praxton were treated as slaves just a few years ago until the invasion of the Alliance world forces. Perhaps the Alliance worlds shouldn't judge how slaves are treated in other worlds. One thing all the Rebel worlds are concerned about, if the Alliance worlds find fault with our way of life, will they attack and invade us?"

"The Alliance worlds would not do that. We only wish to establish trade and stop pirates from attacking our ships."

"I believe you, but understand not all Rebel worlds trust the Alliance worlds after their attack on Praxton."

"I see your point. But the Star Hawk has a larger contingent of Praxton citizens on board. I think with Praxton, women were not slaves but were suppressed. Slaves are common in human space. The difference on Praxton was a whole gender was denied the right to vote, have a financial account and to live alone. I believe Praxton women don't mind having a male as head of the household. What they wanted was the right to have their voice heard and the right to say they owned something. They now have that."

"Fair enough. Let's continue our walk."

Tiffany noticed Elizabeth made a point of changing the subject to less controversial subjects, talking about the differences in fashion between the royal, military, civilian and slave populations. "Each has a style of clothes. Military uniforms are practical, civilian clothes have their own fashion style, and the royal fashions are usually impractical."

"That's true. These clothes are short on coverage, for women anyway."

"I need to use the restroom." She led the way to a room that was more than just for the use of the toilet. A large stone counter contained various soaps, perfumes, makeup and hairbrushes. *What a restroom. There's even a shower in here. I guess living with the royal family has its perks.*

Elizabeth returned from the restroom. "If today's dinner is going to be anything like yesterday's, I think it would be wise to have a brief rest first."

"I agree. Now, are you using this just an excuse to get me into bed?"

"Could be." She laughed as she took Tiffany's hand.

[19]

Captain Elmwood stood staring at Communication Officer Janice Madison. "They said Senior Diplomat Tiffany Harris is not available to speak with us? We've already had to wait because of their maintenance. Did they give a reason, or when she could talk to us?"

"No, sir. Just that she would respond to us later."

"I suppose we should assume she's in a meeting. In one hour, send another request to speak with her. Check that, ask for a videoconference with her. I'm not entirely happy we've only had audio with her so far."

"Yes, sir. I'll inform you when the message is sent again."

"Good, I'll be in my office. General Howling will want an update, and I wish I could give her more information on what Diplomat Harris is doing."

⸻

General Noreen Howling frowned when Elmwood inform her of the status of Diplomat Harris. "This doesn't sound right at all. I cannot believe Diplomat Harris would not communicate why she is continuing to negotiate after they have signed the trade agreement. This is most irregular." She shifted her position behind her desk. "Captain Elmwood, if you have not heard from Diplomat Harris by twenty-four hundred, you have my

154

permission to use military force to discover her whereabouts and to ensure her safe return to the Star Hawk."

"Thank you, General Howling. I hope it won't be necessary to use military action, but I appreciate your support in using it if required."

"Move with caution, Captain Elmwood. This is one of our first engagements with a Rebel world and we don't want it to end in a conflict."

"Understood, General Howling."

Elmwood made his way back to the command centre. "Any communication from Diplomat Harris yet?"

Communication Officer Janice Madison swivelled in her chair to face him. "No, sir. Should I send another request to speak to her?"

"Let's switch our tack. Send a message marked urgent to General Edward McQuaid requesting a video call with myself."

"Aye, sir."

Elmwood paced around the command centre. He thought about what he knew of Tiffany Harris. Smart, professional, pretty, single and career driven. *I can't imagine her not following protocol regarding communicating with the ship. I hope this is just a problem with Divinus communication network.*

"Captain, General Edward McQuaid is available for a video communication."

"Send it to my console."

Elmwood sat and looked at the holographic image of General McQuaid. "General McQuaid, thank you for quickly responding to my request to speak with you."

"My pleasure, Captain Elmwood. How may I be of help to you?"

"We are concerned about the welfare of Alliance Worlds Senior Diplomat Tiffany Harris. We have not been in contact with her for two days now. This is not normal protocol, and we need her to contact the Star Hawk immediately."

"I'm surprised she hasn't contacted you. She is, of course, free to do as she wishes. She is our guest, and we wouldn't prevent her from contacting you. I will say this. If she is on the royal floors, they would restrict her to voice only. We restrict video communication for security reasons."

"That may well be, General McQuaid. But our request is the same. We want her to contact the Star Hawk immediately."

"I will look into the matter and speak to her of your request."

"Thank you. I will expect to hear from her within the hour."

Elmwood stood after ending the call, and Morgan approached him.

"There's something very wrong. Tiffany wouldn't fail to give an update. I believe we should do more than wait for a response."

"Such as?"

"We have a big military ship. Perhaps the Star Hawk could make things uncomfortable for Divinus by moving closer."

Elmwood appeared to consider her suggestion. "Put the ship on Yellow Alert. If we don't hear from General McQuaid or Diplomat Harris within an hour, we could face military action." He looked at Steermaster Nicole Redding. "Set a course for orbit around Divinus, at ten percent of the speed of light. Execute on my orders."

"Yes, sir."

"I'll be back in thirty minutes. Inform me if Diplomat Harris contacts us. I'm going to stretch my legs."

Elmwood walked between the control centre and his quarters, a short distance, and back again. He didn't like the thought of a military action, but knew if Harris didn't respond with a call, that might be his only option.

"Captain Elmwood."

He turned, seeing the tall, distinguished looking woman with dark features. Her collar was black with a series of chrome spikes projecting around the circumference. "Nallix Sorlity Tality Ellis. What brings you to this area?"

"The Yellow Standby. I'm curious what is going on." She smiled. "You remembered my full name." She placed a hand on his arm.

"You're an interesting woman. That makes it easier to remember details about you." He saw she wore a burnt orange dress. The dress was slim fitting and featured a triangle of bare midriff that showed part of a metallic tattoo.

"Thank you. Can you tell me about the Yellow Standby? It seems unusual after a trade agreement was recently signed with Divinus." She gave him a smile.

"After the trade agreement, our Senior Diplomat Tiffany Harris has gone missing, or rather, no longer communicating with us."

"What did the Divinus government say about that?"

"Not much. General McQuaid said he would look into it but assured me Ms. Harris was fine and not restricted from contacting us."

"Captain, I know you're in charge, but I have had a lot of experience in dealing with high-ranking officials. Would it be possible to see a recording of the general's conversation with you? I may provide you with more insight with what may be happening."

"I suppose it wouldn't hurt to have another set of eyes and ears on the situation. Follow me to my office. You can review the exchange there." He looked at Morgan. "You have command while we review the recordings."

Morgan watched the exchange between Elmwood and Nallix, frowning.

———

A few minutes later, Nallix Ellis watched the recording of General McQuaid. She watched the recording twice before commenting. "Captain, I believe General McQuaid is not telling you the complete truth. If you watch him, his hands fidget, his eyes move around, and he appears far from relaxed. He is hiding something about Ms. Harris."

"Ms. Harris is to contact us soon. If she doesn't, we will have to consider our options to rescue her."

"May I wait with you in the command centre? If she responds, I may be able to discern if she is telling us everything that transpired or if she is under duress."

"I think we can use your expertise in this."

They returned to the command centre and waited for a return call from Harris.

"What if she doesn't call back?" Nallix looked at Elmwood.

"Then we'll move past Yellow Standby. The Star Hawk is a military ship. We'll do what we must to protect our crew."

"Captain, we have a communication from Senior Diplomat Tiffany Harris." Communication Officer Madison reported.

"Video or just audio?"

"Audio only."

Elmwood scowled. "Let's hear what she has to say."

"Captain Elmwood, I apologize for not communicating with you earlier. I have been very busy with issues on the trade agreement that

157

Divinus was not clear on. We have resolved those issues. On a personal note, I have decided to remain on Divinus. Prince Francis and I have become very close, and I have accepted his proposal to become his wife. I understand this will become a surprise to you and it will necessitate the promotion of a new senior diplomat. However, my mind is made up in this matter and I must insist you do not attempt to change my mind or try to contact me again. Thank you for your understanding, and I wish you and the Star Hawk success in your journey."

Elmwood tried to ask a question, but the communication to Divinus had ended. He looked at Nallix. "What do you make of that?"

"That was very odd. Do you have earlier recordings of her I could listen to?"

"Of course." Elmwood thought about the statement he just heard from Harris. *There's something odd about it, besides her becoming engaged to Prince Francis.* He looked at Morgan. "What is your impression?"

"I don't believe Tiffany would have said a goodbye in that manner. It was her voice, but this would be an emotional decision for her. She didn't stumble over one word. We can listen to earlier recordings of her voice, but I'm telling you that wasn't her."

"I agree with you, but to avoid an incident we need to have more positive proof."

Nallix listened to several earlier recordings of the diplomat in Elmwood's office. Then she listened to the recent recording of Harris's transmission to the Star Hawk. Nallix twisted around in a chair. "I need someone who is proficient in analysing in electronic signals. There's a cadence in her voice I find unusual." She looked at Elmwood. "Did it sound like her to you?"

"It was her voice, but it didn't sound like her. I can't explain it. First Officer Regan is certain that wasn't her speaking."

"I agree. I listened to her earlier voice recordings. It sounds like her, but there's something different."

"Maybe it was because she was engaged to be married. I don't know."

"Get me an expert in digital signals and I'll get you some answers."

"All right."

Captain Elmwood introduced Nallix Ellis to Teela Mezcal. "Corporal Mezcal is one of our Sensor Readings Tacticians. I believe she can help you find what you are looking for in the digital signals."

Nallix first played back audio recordings from Diplomat Harris, including the last message. "To my ears, there is something odd how she speaks in the last message. There isn't anything I can put my finger on, but I'm certain that isn't her speaking."

"Do you believe someone is pretending to be her?" Elmwood asked. "I agree the technology is available to make an exact copy of anyone's voice. It is against the law in most regions, but Divinus does not follow Alliance worlds' laws. Is there a way we can determine if it is a fake copy of her voice?"

Teela looked at a monitor that showed the voice recording represented by a jumble of lines. She made a few adjustments to the three-dimensional representation of the recording. Coloured lines appeared at intervals. She made more adjustments, enlarging a segment of the recording. She used her index finger to point at the area in red. "Right there is a time delay, almost one-tenth of a millisecond. I believe what we're seeing here is a time delay generated by a software program to mimic Diplomat Harris' voice. A person is reading a script, or it could be an entirely digital source, but what is happening here is a delay in converting that sound." She looked at Nallix. "What you picked up is that slight delay between words. Some words are more premeditated than others. For example, mono-syllable words can be quickly converted compared to longer words."

"So, this is a fake voice purporting to be from Diplomate Harris?" asked Elmwood.

"Yes, sir. I'm certain of that."

He looked at Nallix. "Do you concur?"

"Yes, between General McQuaid's posture when responding to you, and Ms. Mezcal's analysis of this recording, I believe there is only one conclusion to draw. Diplomat Harris is being held against her will."

Elmwood nodded. "Thank you for your input." He left the room, hurrying to the command centre.

The two women looked at each other and followed him, stopping at the edge of the command centre entrance. They heard him announce over the ship's intercom. "Attention, all personnel, we are now on Red Alert. Repeat, we are now on Red Alert."

Teela heard the message repeat and saw the top portion of the walls change to red. She ran to her station, seeing others hurry to their destination.

Elmwood looked at Steermaster Nicole Redding. "In sixty seconds, move the Star Hawk one million kilometres closer to Divinus." He next spoke to Communication Officer Janice Madison. "Ms. Madison, please inform Divinus we request to speak with General McQuaid. Tell them it is urgent we talk to him."

Across the room, he saw Senior Weapons Officer Kelly Walling. "Are we prepared for battle, Mr. Walling?"

"Yes, sir. More than ready. Against these Divinus ships, I know we will prevail."

A minute later, a worried looking General McQuaid spoke on the video link. "Captain Elmwood, you have passed within the ten-million-kilometre zone without authorization. What is the meaning of this infraction?"

"General McQuaid, we are operating under the assumption Diplomat Tiffany Harris is being held against her will. We have moved only one-million kilometres to show we are willing to be reasonable while we wait to hear from her. In thirty minutes, we will advance another one-million kilometre. I strongly suggest you inform your fleet not to come any closer than one kilometre to the Star Hawk or we may view it as hostile intent."

"Captain Elmwood, please, cannot we first discuss this situation?"

"So far, our discussion has revealed deceit from Divinus. The last recording purported to be from Diplomat Harris was a fake, doctored to sound like her."

McQuaid rubbed his face. "Captain, I assure you I only relay the information given to me."

"I'm going under the assumption that information came from Prince Francis. I want to speak directly with King Louis. You have twenty-nine minutes until we advance again. Star Hawk out." Elmwood walked across to where Steermaster Redding sat at her console. "Move the Star Hawk another one-million kilometres in twenty-eight minutes."

"Yes, sir. The course is set."

"Kelly, are the Divinus ships staying away?"

"They are, captain. They're hovering around us like bees but at least one-kilometre away."

"Good. Let's hope a battle doesn't become necessary." Elmwood saw Nallix Ellis standing just inside the entrance of the command centre, watching him.

She stepped toward him. "You seemed to have the Divinus general looking uncomfortable. Do you believe he will comply with your request to speak to King Louis?"

"I wouldn't be doing this if I didn't. The general doesn't want to go into battle against us. His best option is to have King Louis to talk to us."

"General McQuaid wants to speak with you, captain." Communication Officer Janice Madison announced.

"Put him on the main screen. Let's hope he has something positive to say."

[20]

TIFFANY HARRIS WOKE up from a light slumber, holding the hand of Elizabeth Harrold's. They were both lying on their backs with a sheet up to their waist. "That was a nice rest."

"Yeah, the rest was good too." Elizabeth giggled.

"Come on, we only kissed a bit." Tiffany laughed in return.

"I know, but it was good lying next to another person you care about. It's been a long time between partners for me."

Allula stood at the foot of the bed. "Ms. Harris, please forgive me for the interruption, but your presence is requested. Ms. Harold is also requested to attend."

Tiffany wondered how long Allula was standing there and waiting for them to wake up. "Of course. Do I need to wear something special for this?"

"No, Ms. Harris. You may remain naked or wear something if you wish."

"I'll put on what I had on earlier." Tiffany picked up her skirt and top from the floor next to the bed. She saw Elizabeth putting on her dress, frowning as she adjusted the straps to cover her nipples. "Maybe you just leave the straps between your breasts. That's where they want to go, anyway."

162

"Maybe I should, but they help hold things in place while I walk."

Tiffany brushed her hair, checked her makeup, and followed Allula out to the common room. The four wives were already waiting, kneeling on pillows. Three were wearing skirts, and two of those were wearing tops. A fourth wife was nude. There were two vacant pillows, and Tiffany and Elizabeth quietly made their way to them. They kneeled with their hands on their laps.

A guard entered with two female servants behind him. "Ladies, Prince Francis has given each of you a gift. The expectation of accepting the gift is for you to wear the items within the gift box for dinner this evening." He bowed as the two servants stepped forward, each carrying a black wood box. They stopped at each kneeling woman and presented a box to them.

Tiffany opened the decorative box with an inlay of gold and diamonds. Inside, she saw a gold and diamond necklace, a gold waist chain, an anklet, a pair of nipple clips joined by delicate chains, and a diamond encrusted butt plug. She carefully touched the necklace and examined the nipple clips, joined by three chains of different lengths. Each clip was attached to a large, round gold disc with a diamond in the centre.

Tiffany looked at Elizabeth. "Wow, this is very expensive jewellery."

"I don't believe money is an object for Prince Francis."

"True. But this box alone is something I have never seen before. Actual wood. This is almost illegal on Alliance worlds." She stood after she saw the wives standing.

"We don't have such reservations of using wood on Divinus. Perhaps we can export wood as a trade item."

"That would be nice. It would likely need approval from the Charter of Conduct Office."

One wife, Alice, approached Tiffany. "Excuse me, but do you know the reason for the gifts from Prince Francis?"

"No, I don't. Is it normal to receive a gift from him?"

"We often receive small gifts such as rings or earrings. But this is something special, usually given when there is a special occasion."

Another wife, Anette, spoke, "We speculated perhaps Prince Francis was going to propose to you and you would become wife number five. He is spending a lot of time with you, and it makes sense that he would want to have a wife connected to the Alliance worlds."

"I don't think so. I don't know Prince Francis well enough to even consider being his wife."

The other wives clustered around her. Ebba touched her arm. "It is not always a question of love, or knowing someone, for marriage. I was told by my mother I had to accept Prince Francis' proposal for the good of our family and for Divinus. My family is in the construction business and my marriage ensures their success. Being married to Prince Francis is good. I do not consider it a hardship."

Alice added, "It would help the relationship between the Alliance worlds and Divinus if you were to marry Prince Francis. Besides, we all like you, and it would be great to have you in our group."

Tiffany remained silent at first at their suggestions of marriage. She looked at the group of wives around her and shook her head. "I'm sorry, I don't know what to say. I have just thought of my time here as part of my job as a diplomat."

"Maybe you should at least think about the possibility of living here as a wife of Prince Francis." Anette gave her a smile.

Tiffany returned to her room with Elizabeth. "I guess dressing is going to be easier to decide for this evening. One skirt and a lot of jewellery."

"That's true, although I'm not looking forward to that butt plug."

"It's not so bad to wear, but I usually like to be the one deciding if I wear one." Tiffany entered the closet, going through the various skirts. "This is unusual." She held a light-blue skirt with a green interior. The skirt, a common style in the closet, didn't reach around her waist. Along the open sides, a series of metal hooks were attached at intervals. "Is this skirt reversible?"

"No, put it on, and I'll show you." Elizabeth put on a long, bright yellow skirt with an open side.

Tiffany put on the skirt, liking the feel of the thin fabric.

"Those metal hooks can be attached to the belt." Elizabeth lifted middle part of the open side of the skirt, placing a hook into the belt. "You can do either the front or the back. It gives a nice look of the green over the blue."

"That's true, although it exposes my leg more."

"You'll be topless with jewellery. I doubt anyone will be looking at your leg."

"You're right." Tiffany put on the jewellery. "This is a lot of gold." She put on the necklace, the waist chain, and the anklet and finally the nipple clips, noting the discs covered her nipples.

Elizabeth held up the butt plug. "This may be the most expensive piece of jewellery I have with all these diamonds."

"Too bad no one will see it."

"Oh, I'm sure Prince Francis will see yours. It might make a spanking that much more interesting." She laughed.

Tiffany blushed as she went to the washroom. *How did I end up wearing almost nothing with rumours of being proposed to by Prince Francis? When will the Star Hawk return?*

Tiffany and Elizabeth joined the four wives in the common room. All the women wore only jewellery and a skirt. The skirts varied in length and colour, with a common theme of one side open. One wife wore a skirt similar to Tiffany's, with the yellow interior shown pinned up at the front, rather than the back.

Shortly later, six royal guardsmen arrived. Each attached a gold chain leash to the collar of a woman and escorted them down a long hallway. Servants stopped and stood as they went by.

Tiffany looked up at the guard as they followed one wife. "May I ask where we are going?"

"To the Blue Dining Room, Ms. Harris."

"What is so special about this room that I need an escort?"

"It is traditional, Ms. Harris, to have women secured on special occasions while entering the interior zone of the royal quarters."

"So, I'm not a prisoner?"

"No, Ms. Harris. Just a tradition. If you are uncomfortable with the leash, I can remove it."

"No, it's fine. I'm quite used to seeing women wearing a collar and leash. My first experience, though."

They reached the dining room, a round room with a deep blue tile along the walls. A curved, dark wood table faced the centre of the room. Only one part of the table was set with placemats.

Tiffany sat near the middle, with an empty chair next to her. On the other side of the empty chair, Elizabeth sat.

Ebba commented to her, "You're sitting next to Prince Francis. I suspect there may be an excellent reason for that." She lifted an eyebrow.

Prince Francis entered, wearing a loose-fitting blue shirt and brown pants. The pants and shirt were decorative with gold and silver threads along the heavy material. Hanging from his belt was a wooden handle with several strands of a leather-like material. He sat between Tiffany and Elizabeth after acknowledging his wives individually.

"I am pleased to see Elizabeth and yourself are wearing the gifts I sent earlier." He gave Tiffany a brief kiss on the lips.

"They are beautiful. Thank you, Prince Francis, for your gift."

Drinks were poured, and they carried on a light conversation. Servers presented the first course of a cold soup. After the servers departed, sixteen entertainers entered in a single file, alternating between a woman and a man. The men wore outfits similar to what Prince Francis wore, a colourful, loose shirt hanging over a pair of tan pants. Their boots were brown, pointed, and had a short wooden heel. At the side of the pants hung a multi-strand whip on a handle. The women's skirt and tops were loose and in bright colours. Unlike the men, they were barefoot.

Three men carried musical instruments: a pair of wooden drums, a string instrument and a flute.

Tiffany watched four men and four women stand near the far wall, arranging the musical instruments. In front of them, four pairs of men and women stood.

Prince Francis leaned over and whispered, "This is an ancient dance. It originated from the original settlers of Divinus. Our royal family can trace our roots to these settlers."

The music started with a man playing the drums with his hands, followed by the stringed instrument. The four women sang along with one male. The flute player joined in as four couples danced.

Tiffany thought the dancing was energetic and chaotic, with the men making a series of jumps and displays of athletic ability.

The next course appeared, and the music and dancing increased in intensity. Near the end of the song, each woman approached a man and removed his shirt, including those playing music. The pants were low slung, with the front lower than the back. The men looked too warm as they danced, their chests shiny with perspiration. The women danced around them, touching their chests and stomach with outstretched hands. They didn't keep to the same partner as they twisted about. As the music continued, each woman removed the top of another woman, leaving them topless.

Tiffany noticed the dancers were taking turns to perform in front of Prince Francis, and she admired the effort they put into their dance. It didn't surprise her when the women removed each other skirts and dance nude in front of the men, who displayed their strength by lifting the women in air for brief periods. The men circled the women and used their whips on them, lightly lashing as the dance increased in intensity.

The women fell to their knees while they were whipped front and back. They slowly fell on their backs with their arms above their heads.

Tiffany observed the female singers dropped to their knees to finish the last song. They received applause as the music ended. The men, including those playing music, each picked up a woman and placed her over their shoulder, carrying the limp body away.

"What do you think of the dance?" Prince Francis asked Tiffany.

"It was very interesting."

"How about the use of the whip?"

"It was unusual, but I know they're used on Praxton."

He placed his whip on the table. "I would like to use it on you. Not harshly, but to stimulate you. Does that worry you?"

She felt the strands of the whip. "No, but I think we need to know each other better before you use a whip on me."

"I see. But a spanking is okay?"

She laughed. "It depends on the circumstances."

"Perhaps a light spanking for you and your friend, Elizabeth, tonight."

"Are you suggesting a threesome?"

"I am. Because I want to find a way for you to want to stay here on Divinus. I need an intelligent woman to help me with future trade negotiations with the Alliance worlds. You're also beautiful and desirable. I would like you to stay on Divinus and become my wife."

Tiffany barely noticed her dessert being placed in front of her. Her heart was racing as she thought of his proposal. *A handsome, rich man wants to marry me. He also wants me to give up my career as a diplomat for the Star Hawk. And he wants to spank and whip me. Damn, this is tempting. Why would I refuse his offer? Why would I say yes?* "I need to think about this."

"Take your time. But please understand I can be very persuasive." He kissed her, pressing on her lips until she opened her mouth. "I want you, Tiffany. Please do not refuse me."

Tiffany gasped. "If I say yes, there are some conditions I'll insist on."

"Whatever you wish. You are the prize I wish to have at any cost."

[21]

"CAPTAIN ELMWOOD, you wished to speak with me?"

Elmwood looked at the tall figure. The holographic image displayed in the command centre showed King Louis wearing a dark blue uniform with a small cape over his shoulders. The bearded man stood among several servants, two nude kneeling women, and three other women wearing only a skirt and jewellery.

"Yes, King Louis, I wanted to talk to you about a serious situation we have concerning the Alliance worlds Senior Diplomat Tiffany Harris."

"I understand she is visiting Prince Francis. I believe she is negotiating a trade agreement between the Alliance worlds and Divinus."

"That much is true, King Louis. Unfortunately, we have not been able to contact her for several days. One message we received purporting to be her was a fake, that someone pretended to be her to have us believe she was all right."

His jaw dropped slightly. "Are you certain it was a fake?"

"Yes, our experts determined the message was done by electronic means and was not her voice."

"This is a very serious matter." He snapped his finger. "Guard, locate and bring Diplomat Harris here immediately. If there are any objections, inform them you are operating under my orders. Make haste." He looked back at Elmwood. "Please give me a few minutes to sort this out. I assure you I will contact you as soon as they bring me Diplomat Harris. I am hoping there's only a misunderstanding regarding her disappearance."

Elmwood ended the call and looked at Nallix Ellis. "What do you think? Was King Louis being honest?"

"Yes, I believe so. He appeared genuinely surprised at the possibility of a fake voice. There wasn't a sign of deceit."

"Then we shall wait for his next call."

━━━

Tiffany walked with Prince Francis and Elizabeth down the hallway, a hallway she knew led to his bedroom. Without speaking with Elizabeth, she had acknowledged that the three of them would spend the night together.

Prince Francis walked between the women with their arms around each other. "As Elizabeth knows, this dance has several variances to it. The women do not always end up naked, but the whip is always used. It is symbolic the man must do to ensure the woman stays loyal to him. The dance originated after men returned from battle and needed to restore order in his household."

"Of course, any excuse to have a woman at a man's mercy." Tiffany laughed. "How about if we get to use the whip on you instead?"

"No, that's not how things are done. I assure you, when you are both naked, you will appreciate the use of the whip applied with an even measure."

Elizabeth shifted her arm around Prince Francis, touching Tiffany's arm. "If we are to be naked while being whipped, then you must be naked too."

"I agree to those terms."

"Diplomat Harris!"

Tiffany turned to see a guard run to where they were standing.

"Yes?"

"You must come with me at once. King Louis commands it."

She gave a worried look to Prince Francis and Elizabeth and went with the guard.

The guard slowed down his long strides so Tiffany could keep up. She quickly became lost as they went through hallways and into an elevator. The guard refused to give her any details other than King Louis wanted her to appear before him as soon as possible.

She walked into a large room, seeing King Louis stand with his arms crossed as he peered at her. *Did I do something wrong?*

"Ms. Harris, I would like to inquire if you're feeling all right."

"Yes, I am, thank you. Why do you ask, King Louis?"

"The captain of the Star Hawk is concerned about you. He said he hasn't heard from you in a while and was worried something may have happened to you."

"No, I'm fine."

"That is good to hear. Please stand next to me while I contact the Star Hawk."

Tiffany walked over to King Louis, receiving curious looks from the surrounding women. A few seconds later, she saw the holographic image of Captain Elmwood and a few crew members near him. She resisted the temptation of using her arms to cover her top, instead placing her hands behind her back. "Captain Elmwood, sir."

"Diplomat Harris, we are concerned about your well-being."

"I am fine, sir. I see you have returned from the emergency situation."

"Returned from the emergency? I don't understand. We have never left the Coelum star system. We haven't heard from you for over two days and were becoming concerned about your well-being."

Tiffany saw Prince Francis enter the room, hurrying toward her. "Captain, I'm afraid I was lied to. I was told the Star Hawk had to leave to attend to an emergency. I would like to return to the Star hawk immediately."

"I can send a shuttle to Divinus. It will be there in three hours."

King Louis interjected. "Captain, there is a delicate situation between the Star Hawk and our military ships. I propose we transport Diplomat Harris on the royal shuttle to your ship. It will be faster and safer."

"Agreed. I will inform our weapons officer to allow your shuttle to dock with the Star Hawk."

The transmission ended and Prince Francis stood with his arms spread apart. "Please, Tiffany, I am sorry for my deception. I only wanted to spend more time with you."

"You can save your breath. I don't want to hear your apology right now."

She turned to King Louis. "May I have an escort? I would like to say goodbye to the wives of Prince Francis and to Elizabeth Harold. After that I would to use your shuttle to return to the Star Hawk."

"Of course." He signalled a royal guard to escort Tiffany and raised his voice. "Francis, I want to have a talk with you. Now."

━━━

Tiffany rushed back to her bedroom. The wives and Elizabeth were waiting for her. She took a deep breath and explained she would leave for the Star Hawk. "Prince Francis lied to me when he said the Star Hawk had left for an emergency. The ship had not left at all. I'm leaving now. I don't want to see him or say goodbye to him. I'm so angry." Her expression softened. "But it was wonderful to meet all of you, and I will miss you." She gave each wife a hug and gave Elizabeth a kiss as well.

Elizabeth handed her the wood box the jewellery came in. "Please stay in contact with us. I'm sure there will be more trade items to discuss in the future."

"There will be." She gave Elizabeth another hug and left with the royal guard.

After a journey of elevators and hallways, she arrived at the royal shuttle, an oversized shuttle containing luxury seating and amenities. She entered the shuttle when she saw Prince Francis run to the shuttle doors.

"Please, Tiffany, allow me to say goodbye to you." He panted out the words.

"You deserve a slap on the face for lying to me."

"Yes, I do. But if this is to be the last time we see each other, could we not depart with a kiss instead? I know I was wrong, but my heart made me do something desperate."

She stared at him for several seconds. "This is a kiss goodbye. Make no mistake, you have not won me over." She kissed him and broke away with her eyes wet.

She stepped away from him as the shuttle doors closed. A royal guard escorted her to a comfortable chair, offering her refreshments.

"No, thank you. I just want to return to the Star Hawk."

———

Tiffany felt a slight bump as the shuttle docked with the Star Hawk. It surprised her to see several executive officers waiting for her as she entered the ship. She blushed, realizing how little coverage she was wearing. "If I had known everyone would be here to greet me, I would have tried to dress up better." She gave a smile.

First Officer Morgan Regan grinned. "We're just happy you're all right. I'll walk with you to your quarters, and we can talk about your disappearance."

Tiffany explained about the deception by Prince Francis. "Other than the lie, he was charming, handsome and someone I could fall in love with easily."

"It's good we could rescue you when we did. That's very elaborate jewellery you're wearing. It looks nice on you and I can understand why you wouldn't want to cover it up by wearing a top."

"I became used to being almost naked. It feels relaxing."

"I see you're wearing a collar."

"Yes. I like it. I think I may have been the only woman on the Star Hawk not wearing a collar. I believe it's time for me to redesign the uniform I wear and wear something closer to Praxton fashions. That includes a collar."

"Good for you. You'll feel more part of the crew that way."

They arrived at Tiffany's quarters.

"Do you need me for anything?"

"No, I'm good. I just need to change." *And remove that butt plug.*

"Okay. Maybe we can have a few drinks later. I want to know more about this Prince Francis."

"Deal. I have a few stories to tell about their entertainment at dinners."

[22]

MORGAN REGAN WALKED with Tiffany Harris down the hallway on their way to dinner. "That must have been worrisome for you, not knowing why the Star Hawk had left."

"Honestly, I just figured it wouldn't be long. I know the Star Hawk was to avoid battles and assumed it was a mission to give protection to a passenger ship. I didn't consider I was being lied to. I really liked Prince Francis, and it hurt when I found out he had been dishonest to me."

"It sounds like he wanted you to stay on Divinus."

"He proposed to me. I would be his fifth wife."

"Five wives? That's a lot, even by Praxton standards."

"I suppose so, but that wasn't a factor in my decision. I told him I wanted to think it over because I like the thought of being married to him. You know, a princess where I would live an elegant life. But I knew I would return to the Star Hawk. This is where I want to be."

"Prince Francis sounds like a very interesting man."

"You have no idea. His mannerism, looks and his voice." She sighed. "He has no trouble attracting ladies."

They reached the dining lounge and sat a table. "You got to keep some nice gifts. The paper contract agreement and leather folder were really special. Master Paul didn't know what section of the Charter of Conduct to use to consider if it was acceptable to keep them." She laughed.

"I wasn't giving them up without a fight. That and the jewellery. The pieces he gave me are worth a lot."

Morgan looked up and saw Janice Maison and Julius Elmwood approach. "Sir, will you be joining us?"

"If you don't mind." He sat. "We received a final communication from Divinus from Elizabeth Harold. She apologized for any misunderstanding that occurred." Elmwood raised his eyebrows.

"Misunderstanding?" Morgan responded. "They lied to her and tried to keep her as a wife to Prince Francis."

"All true, but she also added a personal message to Tiffany. She said she would be staying on the royal floors with Prince Francis. She hoped that she could meet you again under less trying circumstances."

"That's nice. Elizabeth and I had a connection, like friends that had known each other for a long time. It's hard to explain. We just met but got along really well."

"That's good to hear. Let's hope our next mission won't involve you being kidnapped." He gave his order to the server. "Our next Rebel world to visit is the planet Mostert. This is a relatively prosperous world that depends on the export of consumer goods for revenue. They make clothing, cosmetics, jewellery, and leather goods. We have sent a communication to the Mostert government informing them of our visit to discuss a trade agreement."

"Leather is a restricted item on Alliance worlds. I assume that wouldn't be part of a trade agreement." Tiffany said.

Morgan joined in on the conversation. "Mostert has a matriarch government with the monarch elected from among the members of the house of representatives. One thing to note is Mostert does business with pirates and supports the slave trade as well. It may be another challenge for Tiffany regarding curtailing pirating activities." *At least with a matriarchal government, there isn't any danger they will hold Tiffany captive by a prince.*

After dinner, Morgan returned to the command centre. A hyper-space jump was scheduled later, and they required either the captain or the first officer to be present in case of difficulties. She knew the B jump team would do the jump, their first since training. Morgan would also work with the second steermaster. Steermaster Nicole Redding normally worked the day shift unless there was a critical situation. This jump would be the first of three jumps, each one separated by an hour until they reached the outer edges of the Lar solar system that contained the planet Mostert.

"Steermaster McHoul, please prepare our first jump. Execute in twenty minutes." She looked at the young man, who worked through the three-dimensional display with his hands. She walked over to where he sat. "Mr. McHoul, is this your first jump outside of training for the Star Hawk?"

"It is. I've been waiting for this." He touched a few more graphs and sat back. "They're all set."

"How far did you set the jump for?" asked Morgan.

"Eight-point three light years. Our destination is about twenty-one light years. In theory, we could get there in two jumps, but there's no need to push the engines that hard. Besides, it takes longer to recharge when pushing the limits."

"Part of my training for first officer is knowing how to set up a jump destination. It was really difficult, especially anything more than a light year."

"There are a few tricks to it." He gave a small shrug. "After a while it becomes second nature."

Morgan returned to her station, hearing the announcement of the jump in fifteen minutes. She thought about how Julius Elmwood asked her to handle the evening hyper-jump. It was his method to increase her command responsibilities. She wondered about the possibility of being captain of her own ship. When the next Explorer ships were ready for deployment, she expected to be in the interview process as a captain. *What would that mean with my relationship with Julius? It would be a very long distant relationship at best.*

A warning light interrupted her thoughts on her console. She studied her monitor. "Steermaster, we're getting a signal of high gravity perpetrations. What is our situation in relation to the source?"

"It's a black hole, over one-million solar masses. Rapid rotation is causing a distortion in the space-time." He paused. "I've adjusted our orientation and speed and are not in any danger of being pulled in by the black hole."

Morgan looked at the visual of the black hole, appearing as a black torus tilted at a forty-five-degree angle. Red, orange, and yellow light glowed around the circumference. At the centre, blue jets of light escaped from the top and bottom of the torus.

"From a distance, it sure looks interesting," the Communication Officer, Tyler Holson, commented. "Can you imagine the power in that thing?"

"A lot." Morgan heard of the theory that an alternate universe could be reached by going down the centre of the torus, if the ship could survive the tidal forces. She wondered if that was how Nallix Ellis arrived in their universe. *That would be one scary ride.*

"Steermaster, to be on the safe side, let's move up our next hyper-jump as soon as possible."

"I could initiate the second jump engines. We could leave immediately."

"No, we may need that option on our next jump location."

"Understood, first officer."

Morgan sent a message to Captain Elmwood, advising him they were orbiting around a black hole but were not in danger. *He may find it interesting to look at it.*

Thirty minutes later, the Star Hawk had jumped to a new location. Morgan looked at the blackness around the ship, with thousands of stars surrounding them. "This looks better. No black holes anyway." She looked at McHoul. "Schedule the next jump when ready. I'm going for a coffee. You have command."

Morgan wandered down a hallway to a lounge. It was quiet, almost deserted. She picked a table and ordered a coffee and a slice of apple pie. *Pie and coffee sure have improved with Diana. She does wonders with those food formulas.*

She took a drink of coffee when she saw Nallix Ellis enter the lounge, look around, and spotted her. She walked over to Morgan.

"May I sit with you?"

Morgan looked at what she was wearing, a colourful wrap of orange, reds and yellow, and a green top. The top was made of a soft fabric that draped over her shoulders. Like all of Nallix's outfits, Morgan observed, it showed off her midriff and her tattoo. Morgan thought the metallic tattoo was interesting, showing off a creature with a cross between a tiger and a wolf and wrapped around her body. "Sure, is there something the matter?"

Nallix sat in a fluid motion. Her eyes, heavy with green and glittering makeup, stared at Morgan. "The black hole you came across." She stopped, took a breath, and continued. "This is the part of the universe I arrived in, and it must be the same black hole, but there's something wrong with it."

"What do you mean?"

"In my universe, there were two black holes circling each other. Both singularities were spinning rapidly and absorbing mass from gas clouds around them."

"We have only one black hole."

"Yes, but after I went between the two black holes, it's a wormhole created by the distortion of the universe, my instruments were damaged. I was able to determine the mass of the black hole, but I didn't have a visual to show there was just one black hole. The mass of this black hole is the same as the combined mass of the two back holes in my universe. I wonder what that means. In my universe there's two black holes. In this one, there is one. That's a big discrepancy."

"Maybe one black hole was absorbed by the other."

"I suppose so, but in my universe those two black holes should orbit for a million years."

"What are you suggesting? Besides, this universe doesn't match your own."

"I don't know. It's just that it's easier to go between two orbiting black holes than through the torus of a spinning singular black hole. Less radiation and the wormhole is less turbulent. This changes a lot." Nallix stood. "Excuse me. I think I need to go somewhere and have a few drinks and think."

Morgan finished her pie and returned to the command centre. She sat at her console for several minutes and asked, "Steermaster McHoul, what do you know about alternate universes?"

"Not much. It's a field of study for being certified for hyper-space jumps. The current theory holds alternate universes are very similar to our own, although each will have minor differences."

"How about a major difference? Such as a star or black hole disappearing?"

"That would require a mass transiting from one universe to another. If a mass, it could be only a few hundred kilograms, goes from one universe to another, it can have a multiplying effect in the next universe. It's hard to explain, but a sudden appearance of a new mass can cause a strong ripple in the quantum energy of the local volume where the mass appears. Why do you ask?"

"Curiosity. I've heard black holes, especially the spinning singularity ones, are a gateway to another universe. I was wondering what the consequences would be if we were to travel to another universe. Would that change that universe?"

"It would be a one-way trip. If you use a black hole to travel to another universe, your appearance to the alternative universe changes the new universe. Because of the change, you cannot just turn around and go back through the black hole and return to the original universe. The wormhole is a one-way trip. You would go to another universe. But that's almost suicide to travel through the centre of a black hole. Very high radiation and energy at the poles."

"If there were two black holes circling each other?"

"Oh, then one could go between the black holes. That's much safer and theoretically possible. But it is rare to find two large mass black holes orbiting close enough to cause a distortion in spacetime to allow a ship to go to another universe. Again, it would be a one-way trip."

"Thanks. The universe is a strange place."

"Yeah, all of them."

"Ms. Regan, we are ready for our final jump."

"Excellent. Proceed."

Megan heard the warning given over the ship's speakers about the jump. A few minutes later she received confirmation of the successful jump and ordered the normal transit to the planet Mostert. "Steermaster, you have command. Inform me if a situation arises."

Morgan spoke to the ship's A.I. "Where is Nallix Ellis?" A moment later, Morgan went to the lounge, where Nallix was having a drink. She approached her table.

"First Officer Regan. Is there a problem?"

"Maybe. You told us you arrived in our universe by accident. Later you allowed your crew to travel without you to find a way back to your own universe."

"Yes. I don't know if they found a way home or not."

Morgan took a deep breath. "I'm sorry to have to say this, but I think you're not telling me the truth on how you ended here in our universe. If in fact you are from another universe." Morgan watched Nallix's face turn pale.

[23]

"WELL?" Morgan insisted on an answer.

Nallix bit her lower lip, looking ready to cry.

Morgan spoke to her mobile. "Captain Elmwood, I require your presence in Executive Lounge Five. Security, I need two guards at Executive Lounge Five immediately." She looked at Nallix. "Do not attempt to leave that chair."

Nallix nodded, taking rapid breaths.

Elmwood entered the lounge, making quick strides to Morgan's table. Two armed guards followed soon after.

"What's going on?"

"Nallix is either an imposter, a liar, or both."

Nallix looked up at Elmwood. "Please, I assure you I'm not a threat in any way."

"That may be a lie as well." Morgan retorted.

"Maybe you better start, Morgan." Elmwood sat. "What made you conclude Nallix is lying?"

"When we came by that black hole, I had an interesting conversation with Second Steermaster McHoul. He told me one can travel from one universe to another using a black hole under the right conditions. It has to be spinning rapidly so that the singularity forms a torus. In theory, you could travel through the centre to another universe. But it's a one-way trip. If you tried to use that same black hole to travel back to the original universe, you would go to a third universe instead.

"Nallix told us she accidentally travelled to our universe and later she told her crew to try to return home without her. That doesn't make sense. No one accidentally goes through a black hole. Second, there isn't a possibility her crew could return home. They could go to another universe, but not their own. Her story is just not credible."

"Speak." Elmwood stared at Nallix. "The unabridged truth."

A tear rolled down her cheek. "I was with other members of our family, visiting one of the minor planets to celebrate the anniversary of joining our affiliation. The son of their king invited me to have lunch with him and to discuss some art I had been working on. I was a painter of some renown, perhaps because of my social standing. He flattered me with his attention to my paintings, and I agreed to meet him for lunch. It aroused my suspicions when he told the servants to leave us alone after they brought the food in. Then he became aggressive toward me, grabbing at me. I called out for help, but no one came.

"I didn't have a choice but to defend myself. I carry an ornamental knife strapped to my thigh and used it to stab him. He died instantly. My knife went up under his ribcage and into his heart. I pushed him off and decided I needed to escape."

"Couldn't you explain why you stabbed him to the authorities?"

"I could, but if one kills the king's son, the only outcome is an execution. My husband would not protect me in this case. He has to consider what he needs to do to keep war from breaking out. Besides, he has several other wives to keep him company.

"I left the room, telling the servants the prince wanted to rest. I went to the spaceport, where our ships waited. I entered one of the small ships. It was empty, and I ordered the ship to depart. Our ships are programmed to follow the voice instructions of authorized persons. I quickly had the ship hyperjump. As soon as possible, I ordered the ship to hyperjump again."

"You lost their pursuit?" Elmwood asked.

"No, we have technology to follow the wake of a hyperspace jump. I could run, but eventually they would find me. I decided to try to escape to another universe, choosing two black holes in close orbit with each other.

To save my life, I went between the two black holes and ended in this universe. My ship's electronics were damaged from the encounter. To my relief, the hyperjump capabilities were still intact. I made several jumps, although I was blind to where I was going. Eventually I came across a planet with civilization. I listened to the radio conversations and used the computer to decipher the language. I learned to speak well enough to be able to dock at a spaceport. Fortunately, it was an Alliance world. I abandoned my ship, sold a few gems and decided to travel on passenger ships."

"Why did you abandon your ship?" Elmwood asked.

"I fear they could still follow me, even in another universe. When I chanced on being on the Star Hawk, I felt this was the safest place I could be."

"To summarize, you're a criminal fugitive and lied to be a member of the Star Hawk." Morgan pointed a finger at her.

"Yes, but it was in self defence."

"So you claim, and you still lied to us." Morgan frowned. "You must have known it was only a one-way trip through the wormhole. Why were you worried they would try to follow you? Whoever followed you would be stuck in our universe as well."

"It would be a ship operated by artificial intelligence. It would seek out my ship and destroy it. That's the main reason I got rid of my ship."

"Guards, take Ms. Ellis to her quarters and confine her there." Elmwood commanded.

Nallix stood and walked between the two guards, leaving the lounge.

Elmwood looked at Morgan. "Excellent work in discovering she lied to us. What would you like to do with her? And more important, what should we do with her?"

Morgan understood the difference between the two questions. One was what she wanted. But she also knew being in a position of authority meant they had to decide what was best for the Star Hawk. Personal feelings had to be set aside. "I'd like to throw her off the ship and give her to Alliance security. Maybe whip her." She frowned. "But neither of those is the right thing to do. I have to admit, I don't really have a connection with Nallix. She comes across to me as arrogant and self-entitled. And she flirts with you."

Elmwood pursed his lips. "To be honest, I haven't noticed her flirting. But please continue."

"All right." *She touches your arm, smiles at you and tells you that you're in control. How do you not see that as flirting?* "If she's telling the truth this time, I understand why she made a story of being lost from another universe. She likely feared admitting she murdered someone would result in turning her over as a criminal to the authorities." Morgan closed her eyes for a moment. "It seems we either punish her or allow her to continue her role as an advisor. She has proved useful in helping to determine Tiffany was being held under false pretences. If it was my decision, I would let her off with a warning."

"That is what I decided as well. I will inform the guards to bring her to my office in one hour. You should be present there as well."

"Thank you, captain, I'll be there."

Morgan wandered down the hallways, wondering why she felt jealous about Nallix. *I can't let her change the way I act toward Julius. That would put a barrier between us. Maybe it's just her sophisticated 'better than you attitude' that irks me. Regardless, I'll just watch out for what she does and make sure I don't overreact to her.*

She arrived at Elmwood's office and saw him studying a monitor. "Everything good?"

"I think so. Mostert does a lot of commerce and there is a lot of traffic going to and from the planet."

"Some of them pirate ships, I suppose."

"My thoughts as well. Some of these ships are quite large and others travel in groups. I suspect the groups of ships are a case of safety in numbers. It's also possible the groups may be pirate ships."

"This is Rebel space and pirating is legal, or at least not controlled."

Nallix entered the office with two guards behind her. Elmwood dismissed the guards.

"Ms. Ellis, you have put us in an uncomfortable position on what to do with you. Lying on a military vessel is a serious offence and normally leads to a severe reprimand. That you are not sworn in as a member of the crew does not lessen the impact of telling a lie." He folded his hands together and rested them on his desk. "I have considered you were worried admitting you are in fact a criminal trying to escape justice, that you feared for your life. Before I pass judgement, do you have anything to say?"

"Captain Elmwood, please forgive my lack of honesty. I didn't know what you would say if I told you the full story. I didn't know if you would have believed it. I was planning to tell you more at a later date. Captain Elmwood, I'm alone and scared of what will happen to me in a universe where I don't know the rules. I beg you, please help me. Help me survive and be of help to the Star Hawk. I promise I won't let you down, and that if you allow me to stay on the Star Hawk, I will be an appreciative member of your crew. I will swear an oath of allegiance if you want." She began to cry. "Please, please have mercy."

"Very well, I understand what you are saying. Consider this your first, and only, warning. First Officer Regan and I have decided to let you carry on your duties on the Star Hawk as before. I will not tolerate any more surprises that may jeopardize this ship. Understood?"

"Yes, Captain Elmwood." She looked at Morgan. "Thank you, as well, First Officer Regan. I was so worried about what you were going to do me."

Elmwood stood. "You may go, Ms. Ellis."

Morgan watched her retreating back. "She is really sorry and scared or a very good actress."

"Let's hope for the former." Elmwood frowned.

"There's still the discrepancy of her leaving a universe of two black holes and arriving in ours where there's only one."

"I gave it some thought. I think the two black holes in her universe may have collapsed into one after she went through the wormhole. A wormhole is unstable and perhaps the action of her ship going through would have provided the impetuous for the two black holes to combine." He stood and walked around his desk.

"Does that mean in our universe the two black holes combined? Nallix said the two black holes in her universe should be separated for another million years. So is our universe a million years later than hers?" She went with him as he exited the office.

"Possible. But maybe the two universes have a different clock. For example, one runs faster than the other. Another thing to keep in mind is that time slows down in a high gravity field. For Nallix it might have seemed only a few terrifying seconds to travel between the two black holes, but perhaps time slowed down for her such that a million years passed. If the two black holes in her universe also combined, then it's unlikely even an artificial intelligence run ship could survive a journey through the torus of a spinning black hole."

"If that's the case, she really can't ever return home. I could use a drink. Care to join me?" asked Morgan.

"It would be my pleasure."

Morgan walked with Elmwood to a lounge and spotted Nallix sitting by herself with a glass of wine.

"Nallix is by herself. Should we join her, Master Julius?"

"I think it would be the right thing to do. She hasn't had the chance to make many friends yet."

"Perhaps we should introduce her to Master Paul. He's usually by himself as well."

"I'll leave the matchmaking to someone else."

Nallix looked surprised they asked to sit at her table, but quickly agreed. "Please, sit with me. I feel very much isolated on the Star Hawk." She smiled. "I'm under the impression the crew doesn't know what to make of me. I suppose the way I dress and act makes me the odd one."

"There is always a time frame necessary for people to get to know and understand each other. I suggest you introduce yourself to others." Elmwood paused. "Don't be shy. Allow others to know you."

"Thank you. That is excellent advice." She looked at Morgan. "I'm sorry if I have been reserved toward you. And you being the first officer, I find you slightly intimidating. I hope that someday we can be friends."

"That would be nice." *I'm intimidating?* She ordered a glass of cabernet sauvignon, deciding the red wine Nallix was drinking looked good. She noticed Elmwood had ordered a dark rum, his favourite beverage, but she didn't want a higher alcohol beverage in case she had to return to the command centre.

"Compared to the wine in the universe I came from, this is excellent. It is far superior to the wine I used to drink."

Elmwood commented, "Diana Adoria, our food and beverage manager, does remarkable work. Wine is one of her specialities."

"It is helping me relax. I was expecting discipline from you for my mistake."

"May I inquire what type of discipline you were expecting?"

Nallix laughed and covered her mouth. "I'm sorry, it must sound silly, but I thought you might give me a spanking. I had this vision of being placed over your lap and spanked." She shook her head. "I must sound ridiculous."

"Not at all. This is a different culture than what you were used to."

"Thank you for saying that. I'm always afraid of making a social blunder. Sometimes I must appear aloof, but it's really because I'm scared to open my mouth."

Morgan looked at her. *Maybe, but your mouth also admitted you thought about being spanked by Julius. Stop your damn flirting with him.* "Perhaps we can spend some time together and I can help you with what is appropriate to say or do."

"Thank you. I'll take you up on that offer."

Was she being sarcastic or does she really want help? "Of course, anytime."

Elmwood finished his drink and stood. "Ladies, I need to do a few reports. Please excuse me."

Morgan turned her focus toward Nallix. "Tell me, how can I help you with understanding our culture?" She signalled the server to bring two more glasses of wine.

"I don't understand the nuances of men and women on this ship. I was told this is a Praxton ship and therefore, Praxton social rules should follow. I thought they allowed males to have as many females as they wanted, yet when I tried to engage with Captain Elmwood, I got the distinct feeling you felt I crossed a boundary. I don't understand what I did wrong."

Morgan frowned as she stared at Nalix. "You did nothing wrong, other than flirt with the man I'm having a relationship with. I know Master Julius can have more than one female. That is his right. I don't have to like it."

"Oh." Nallix took a drink of her wine. "In my previous life, in the other universe, it did not occur to me to be jealous. My husband had several wives. We just accepted each other." She took another drink of her wine. "But I now understand. The heart knows no logic. I promise not to advance myself toward him."

"Thank you. I didn't mean to come across as being rude." Morgan ordered another glass of wine.

"Not rude. Protective."

"Let's change the subject. Tell me about your tattoo." She thanked the server for the glass and took a drink.

"It took a long time to have it done. Instead of ink, metal was injected into the skin." Her lips tightened at the memory. "It was painful, but I love how it looks. When my husband insisted that I get a tattoo, I designed one that I wanted, a creature known on my world as a yeskat."

"From the part I see, it looks fierce."

"It is a ferocious creature, but it also has beautiful fur." Nallix undid her top, took it off, and stood. She turned around in a circle.

Morgan looked at the yellow, orange and black design of a tiger like creature. The tattoo shined and glittered. Nallix's skin also shined, and Morgan suspected she used a special cream on her skin to achieve the effect. The yeskat head and body covered most of her chest and part of her back. The creature's tail went down past the top of her skirt. "That is beautiful. I've never seen anything quite like it."

"Thank you." Nallix sat. "I'm very proud of it. The tail goes down my leg, but I best not remove my skirt to show it to you."

"You said you designed the tattoo?"

"Yes. I enjoy art and have a talent for it."

"I remember you saying you were a painter." Morgan saw Nallix's eyes open up.

"Yes, it is something I love to do."

"What type of painting do you do?"

Nallix laughed. "Well, usually of people. Portraits. Nudes. I had a reputation of doing quality work. That was partly because I took a long time to paint each subject. I would rather paint than spend time with the other wives who love to gossip and talk about politics."

"You should get paints from the supply department and start painting again."

"You're right. I should do that." She paused. "Thank you for not avoiding me after finding out I lied earlier. I need a friend and I would like you to be mine."

"I can be your friend. Maybe I can help you find a male acquaintance as well."

"That would be nice. Maybe one that would give me a spanking." She grinned.

[24]

MORGAN LISTENED to Captain Elmwood repeat the question to her.

"You want to invite Nallix with us to watch the performance tonight? I thought earlier you wanted a date with just us. Dinner, the performance and some alone time in my suite." He checked the screen of the monitor once more in his office and turned back to Morgan.

"Yes, I said that. But Nallix needs a friend, and I agreed to be hers. I think she's lonely and her mannerisms make it difficult for others to approach her. I thought we could spend some time with her and introduce her to others."

"So that includes the dinner as well?" he asked. "Very well. I appreciate what you're doing to help her. May I at least assume she won't be with us when we return to my suite?"

"About that. She has expressed a desire to be spanked. As the captain of the Star Hawk, you have the right to spank any female whenever you feel it's necessary."

"You want me to spank her?"

"Just a spanking. She has never been spanked before and I think it best it came from you. You know exactly the right amount of pain to deliver and when to stop."

"This is going to make for a most interesting evening."

———

Morgan relaxed with her wine as Elmwood ordered dinner for Nallix and herself. Morgan wore her ship's uniform and saw Nallix wore her own standard of dress, a long skirt and an abbreviated top. The long skirt, light in fabric, hinted at her long legs underneath. The top was of the same yellow material, but the thin material molded to her breasts, hiding little. Nallix didn't wear cuffs, but her wide collar with spikes made an impression. She noted it appeared to be the same style of collar of the beast, a yeskat, wore in the tattoo.

"Captain, may I ask if a male always orders for a woman when dining?"

"A male orders dinner for any female under his control. In this case, it is a formal setting, and I did use a leash on Morgan and yourself. So, I am in control and will order food and drink for Morgan and yourself. Normally on the Star Hawk most females would not be under control of a male. This is a special occasion."

Morgan remembered when Nallix acted mildly surprised when Elmwood earlier attached a leash to her collar, but she didn't offer any objections. Morgan explained, "It's a Praxton custom, and I like the formality of a male being in charge. I can just sit, eat, drink and relax."

"I understand. I'm not used to being escorted like a wild animal." She smiled. "But I can see its merits."

After dinner, Elmwood escorted Morgan and Nallix to one of the theatres. Outside of the entrance, they stopped to chat with several of the ship personnel. The upcoming performance had generated a lot of interest from all ranks of the ship.

Morgan introduced Nallix to several people, hoping they would make a connection later, especially with the men. She saw Paul Thysen was alone again. *The only time he doesn't act stiffer than a steel beam is when he's had a few drinks. He acts and looks better after a few.*

A gong sounded, indicating the doors were now open. Morgan was glad she had introduced Nallix to a few new people. She followed Elmwood to their seats and waited as the crowd moved around them. The lights dimmed and a minute later the red curtain was raised. She focused on the stage where three oversized bed-like frames waited on the stage. In front of them, four musicians stood. A male in the group, wearing a ship's uniform, took a seat behind a set of drums. Another male held a brass horn. The two women musicians were nude, save for stilettoes, cuffs, collars and chains. One held a flute and the other a violin.

The flute player started playing a familiar tune. Three nude women, each wearing only a collar, appeared from the side of the stage. They went to the bed frames and began to work themselves into the strips of cloth attached to the bed frame.

Morgan heard Elmwood whisper to Nallix that the women would be performing fille d'affichage and how it was a very difficult art to perform. A large image screen appeared behind the beds, giving a top view of the performance on each bed. She recognized Teela Mezcal, the technician who helped with the fake audio transmission from Divinus. *She's very good. Smooth movement of limbs.* She looked at the musicians, watching the violin player close her eyes as she focused on her music.

It seemed to Morgan the women were each doing a performance according to their interpretations of the music. Teela, in her opinion, was the best of the three performers, although all of them were fascinating to watch.

The music ended but quickly followed by another piece. Her attention was diverted to the flute player. The slim woman was swaying her body to the music, occasionally taking a half-step as she played. *I'm getting used to seeing naked women on the Star Hawk. A year ago, I would've been shocked to see this nude performance of the women playing music and doing the fille d'affichage. Now it seems natural. Women's bodies are truly appreciated and admired by the Praxton culture. I feel sorry for the men. They're not allowed the freedom of discarding their clothes.*

"Are you enjoying the show?"

Morgan looked over at Elmwood. "Yes, it is very good. I'm surprised at how good Teela Mezcal is at this. She is from an Alliance world and wouldn't have had to chance to learn the fille d'affichage until she arrived on the ship."

"She seems to have a natural ability for this. She's not lightly built but is obviously strong and athletic. She's very pleasing to watch doing this performance." Elmwood added.

"I noticed all the women are nude, but none of the men. Do you ever wish you could take off your shirt? All men must be fully dressed in public, but women don't have those rules."

"Women look better than men undressed, and I guess that is why they're given the option of showing off their bodies. Sure, I'd like to sit around in my own suite in my underwear, but that isn't allowed according to Praxton rules. If that's the price I have to pay to have females walk around naked, then I'll gladly pay it."

Morgan nodded. "I understand what you're saying. I still would like to see some men on stage not fully dressed."

"Maybe during another performance, you will see it," said Julius.

She took his hand. "I'll just have to be satisfied seeing you naked."

The music ended and the three women performing the fille d'affichage stood and took a bow. All three were breathing hard, showing the exertions of their performance. They left the stage to the applause from the appreciative crowd. The music began to play again as the lights dimmed in the back of the stage. Morgan could just make out the three beds being removed and replaced by a larger one.

The music ended and the lights at the back of the stage brightened, revealing two nude women. Both wore body paint; one a blend of blue and green and the other blue and white. They bowed toward the audience and climbed on the large bed.

Morgan looked at the large viewscreen behind the bed and read the text: the two women were to perform a fantasy tale of a battle between the sky and the sea. She saw Teela was wearing the green and blue body paint and was acting out as the sea. She watched the two women interact on the bed, twisting around as they secured their limbs on the long cloth straps.

"This is an interesting performance."

"You would enjoy it." Morgan watched as the sky-coloured woman moved on top on Teela and rolled off her again. The story appeared to be the sky trying to seduce the sea, and with the sea resisting her efforts. "It is rather erotic." Her attention went from the fille d'affichage performance to the group playing music and back again. As the music picked up the tempo, the woman playing the part of the sky slowly seduced Teela. When the music stopped, the battle between the sky and the sea had stopped.

Morgan joined the others in the audience and applauded the

performances of the musicians and the artists. After they left the theatre, she asked Nallix what she thought of the show.

"It was fascinating to watch. I don't know how those women perform such artistic moves using just those horizontal strips of cloth. They must be very strong to make such movements look so graceful. I enjoyed it very much, although I don't understand why the two women playing music were also nude."

"It seems to be a Praxton custom to have women naked whenever possible." Morgan laughed.

"I've heard of worse customs." Nallix looked at Elmwood. "Where are we going now?"

"I thought we could have a drink at my quarters."

"That would be great."

Morgan was amused how Nallix, who normally acted cool and aloft, was acting like a lost teenager. They reached Elmwood's suite, and they entered. Morgan took off her shoes after entering and saw Nallix followed her example.

"I'll make the drinks." Elmwood went to the kitchen.

Morgan indicated the cushions on the floor and placed one near an armchair. She took off her top and kneeled on the cushion. Shortly later Nallix copied her, placing a cushion close to her and took off her top. Morgan whispered, "Females must show submission to a male. Keep your hands on your lap until he offers you a drink."

"Does he know what I want to drink?"

"He decides what you're to drink."

"Oh."

Elmwood passed each woman a tall, clear liquid drink with a slice of green fruit attached to the rim. He held a glass with a gold liquid for himself.

"Thank you, Master Julius." Morgan spoke as she took her glass.

Nallix repeated her response.

Morgan watched as Elmwood sat in the armchair and faced the women. He took a drink and asked Nallix about her tattoo.

"It was done by a special process to marry my skin with metal. I designed the art myself."

"The tattoo is quite large."

"It actually goes to, well, between my legs."

"It looks very nice."

"Thanks. I need to apply cream to the skin to help maintain the colours."

Morgan looked at Nallix's skin. *Yeah, I'm sure that's the only reason you apply cream. That skin is gleaming.*

Elmwood continued to converse with the two women, making sure he included both of them.

Morgan pointed out that Nallix is a painter. "I think she specializes on people."

"I do. I'm getting supplies and will start painting as soon as I find a subject."

"What subject are you looking for?" Elmwood asked.

"I do portraits and nudes. Are you interested in posing for me?"

He laughed. "I can't. Praxton forbids males from appearing undressed in front of females unless they are their guardians."

"Well, how about Morgan? Can she pose for me?"

"For that, you have my permission."

Morgan looked at Nallix. *What just happened here? Master Julius wants me to pose for Nallix?* She decided to change the subject away from herself. "Nallix is interested in receiving a spanking. Perhaps you can help her." *There, I said it.* She heard Nallix take in a quick breath of air and look at her with surprise.

"If she desires a spanking, I would be pleased to administer it." Elmwood put his drink down on a table next to the armchair.

Morgan stood and took Nallix's hand. After Nallix rose, Morgan undid her skirt, revealing a pair of black thong panties. She led her to Elmwood, whispering. "Resist crying out."

Morgan watched Nillax nod, and breathing deeply, gracefully placed herself over Elmwood's lap, her fingertips resting on the floor. Morgan returned to her cushion and kneeled on it, placing her hands behind her back. She saw Elmwood raise his hand and bring it down sharply. Several times he repeated the strikes, alternating between the cheeks and occasionally slapping her thighs as well. He paused to stroke the red skin and struck again. Nallix kicked her legs and gasped as the spanking increased in intensity. Elmwood stopped to pull off her panties, tossing them across the room. He continued her spanking, pausing between each strike.

"How does that feel, Nallix?" His hand massaged her cheeks.

"Very nice. It hurts but feels good too."

"Do you wish me to continue or to stop now?"

"Please, Master Julius, stop now. I'm not used to such a situation."

Elmwood helped Nallix rise. "Do not get dressed." He looked at Morgan. "Undress. It's your turn now."

"Yes, Master Julius." Morgan hurried to remove her skirt and panties. She placed herself over his lap and spread her legs slightly. She turned her head to see Nallix watching her as she stood with her hands behind her back.

She felt his big palm smack her cheeks, causing her body to jolt with each hit. The spanking felt harder than the one he had given Nallix. Elmwood paused twice to massage her ass before resuming her spanking. Morgan groaned and felt a tear fall. She decided the spanking was not only harder but was longer than the one given to Nallix. When he finally stopped, her knees felt weak from her punishment. She stood next to Nallix with her hands behind her back. "Thank you for the spanking, Master Julius."

"You're welcome. Kneel while I refresh our drinks."

"Yes, Master Julius." Morgan winced as her cheeks rested on the back of her heels. She quietly asked Nallix if she enjoyed the spanking.

"Yes, I did. It has left me feeling aroused. I also enjoyed watching you being spanked. Tonight has been a very erotic experience for me."

Elmwood returned with the fresh drinks. "I made these drinks stronger, as you may need to subdue the effects of the spanking."

Morgan took her drink gratefully. *I need to dull the pain a little. That was a serious spanking.*

Nallix explained it was her first spanking, and she was curious why it was so common on in the Praxton culture but added, "I do see its merits and certainly helps ensure males are seen as dominate over females."

"Would you like to be spanked again?" Morgan asked.

"Not tonight, but yes, definitely." She laughed. "I never have thought pain could be pleasurable. I may have to try the other Praxton customs sometime."

Elmwood finished his drink. "I believe it is time for bed. Perhaps you ladies would like to sleep here tonight in the guest bedroom."

Morgan looked at Nallix and saw the small nod. "Yes, Master Julius. That is kind of you to offer." *If she wasn't here, I would get to sleep with him, but Praxton customs means she's going to be my bed partner.* She went upstairs to the guest bedroom and laid down. Nallix joined her and Elmwood attached the ankle cuffs to each of them. He bid them goodnight and left them in the dark room.

Moments later Morgan felt her arm being stroked, then a warm breath on her neck. She twisted her body toward Nallix, pressed forward and kissed her on the lips. Hands drifted over her body and a kiss was exchanged.

Morgan stroked Nallix's hair.

"I think that spanking have me feeling a little frustrated."

Morgan curled up next to Nallix and gave her a kiss. "I feel that way too. I think it'll make our dreams more interesting."

"Sexy dreams are best kind." She returned the kiss to Morgan. "Pleasant dreams."

"Hmm." Morgan drifted off to sleep.

―

Morning came and Morgan felt Nallix stir against her. "Good morning."

"Good morning. What do we now? Get up?"

"You stay in bed. I'm going downstairs and make Master Julius a cup of coffee. After he gets dressed and is downstairs, we'll shower together. He'll be able to watch us."

Morgan went to the kitchen and prepared a cup of coffee. She carried it upstairs, entering Elmwood's bedroom. He was still dressing, putting on a shirt.

"I have your coffee, Master Julius."

"Thank you." He took it from her and tasted it.

"Would you like me to please you?" She dropped to her knees.

"Not right now." He let out a sigh.

"I understand." She stood. "When you are ready, Master Julius, Nallix and I will shower."

"I'll be downstairs soon."

Morgan returned to the guest bedroom and climbed into bed with Nallix and put on her ankle cuff. "We can take a shower in a few minutes."

"Master Julius will be observing us?"

"Yes."

"Are we supposed to do anything special while showering?"

"Whatever we feel like. He will enjoy just seeing us naked showering."

"I'm sure he will. I would like to see him in the shower."

"Unfortunately, Praxton customs doesn't allow that. I've agreed that he is to be my guardian, so I can see him naked." She undid her ankle cuff. "Come, let's shower. He should be downstairs now."

Morgan turned on the warm spray and stepped inside the shower, observing Elmwood below. He drank his coffee as he looked up at her.

Morgan and Nallix took turns washing each other, occasionally fondling each other. Morgan was feeling aroused by the time the shower was finished as the warm air dried their skin.

"I guess we get dressed downstairs." Nallix took Morgan's hand.

"Yes, but only after Master Julius permits us to do so. Let's have a coffee first and then ask if we may get dressed."

Morgan was pleased Elmwood had prepared coffee for Nallix and her. They sat in the dining room and she saw he was occasionally observing a monitor as they talked. "Are you anxious to start work, Master Julius?"

"Yes, the night crew needs to be relieved and have any reports checked off." He looked at Nallix. "You may wear a skirt, but nothing else. I'll escort you to your quarters."

"Yes, Master Julius."

"Morgan, you will remain here. I will cage you until my return."

Nallix put on her skirt and placed her folded top and panties on the dining room table. She stood as Elmwood added a leash to her collar.

"Nallix, wait by the door. Morgan, come with me."

Morgan followed Elmwood upstairs to his bedroom where a corner cage stood.

"Inside you go."

Morgan stood inside the cage and the door was closed and locked.

"I'll return later. I shall inform the crew you'll be indisposed until lunchtime."

"Yes, Master Julius." She watched him leave and placed her hands on the bars. *I wonder what plans he has for me? And does he have additional plans for Nallix? He put a leash on her and ordered her to leave her underwear and top off. That sounds like he may be considering being her guardian as well.*

Morgan waited, determining Elmwood had likely gone to the command centre after escorting Nallix to her suite. She shifted her legs, feeling bored and anxious as she waited. Morgan leaned against the bars, wondering what Elmwood was planning with her.

Elmwood finally returned, and Morgan quickly stood straight on hearing his footsteps.

"Master Julius, it is good to see you again."

He opened the cage door and led her near his bed. "Kneel."

Morgan went to her knees and crossed her wrists behind her back. She watched as he opened his fly and pulled out his stiffening cock. She licked her lips as she leaned forward, her mouth opening wide.

"I speculated on Nallix and you enjoying each other last night. It made my sleep difficult."

"I apologize, Master Julius, if those thoughts caused you distress." She slid her lips around his large member and pushed forward, trying to take the entire length. She felt his hands on the back of her head as he thrusted. Morgan tried to gasp for air when he withdrew before pushing inside again. The fluid exploded in her mouth, and she swallowed rapidly. He continued to hold his cock in her mouth as her face was pressed against the hard muscles of his stomach. She pressed her tongue on his softening member as he pulled away.

She gasped for air as she looked at his gleaming member. "Thank you for allowing me to please you, Master Julius."

"The pleasure was all mine." He grinned. "Let's get you dressed and have a talk downstairs."

Morgan put on her clothes and kneeled on a cushion in the living room, accepting a coffee from him.

Elmwood sat in the armchair. "Morgan, I escorted Nallix to her suite. She told me she enjoyed her spanking very much and I suspect I will be delivering another one to her in the future. You are my primary concern and I trust you're happy with how last night went."

"Yes, very much, Master Julius."

He stood and attached a leash to her collar. "I will now escort you to your suite so you can prepare for the day."

Morgan arrived at her suite and went to her bedroom for a change of clothes. She was pleased how her relationship with Elmwood was going but wondered about Nallix. *I hope it wasn't a mistake to have Julius spank her, but I wanted to help her understand what it was like. And why did she leave her top and panties in his suite? An excuse to return there?*

[25]

MORGAN ENTERED the captain's office. Elmwood studied two different monitors that measured various parameters around the ship, and she waited with her hands behind her back at the entrance.

"Morgan, please come in."

She stepped up to his desk. "You mentioned you wanted me to investigate a situation, Master Julius."

"Yes. I've received reports of unusual activities around the lounges reserved for non-executive personnel. I want you to look into this. I don't believe it's anything serious, but more likely proper decorum isn't being followed. Lounge number eight-B seems to one of the areas of concern."

"I'll look into it."

"Thank you. I want to discuss with you a matter concerning Nallix. I'm pleased you decided to step forward and be her friend and help her learn about the Praxton culture we have on the Star Hawk. I want to emphasise that my intention is still to be your guardian. I will not be pursuing Nallix, or another female, until we have established our relationship and we are living together. As a male, I may be a guardian to more than one female, but I will not exercise that option unless you are in agreement.

"I would like you to continue to help Nallix and be her mentor. I would like to see her adopt more of the Praxton customs, such as adding cuffs and chains. I'm not concerned about her wearing a ship's uniform as what she wears is similar to Praxton style of dress. Not wearing a uniform also relieves us of having to designate a rank for her."

"I understand, Master Julius," said Morgan. "I will continue to help her acclimatize to the way we are expected to act on the ship."

"Excellent. If you feel she is in need of discipline, bring it to my attention."

"Yes, sir. I will inform you of when corrective measures are required."

———

Morgan went down several levels to a lounge used by cadets and other junior crewmembers. As she approached the entrance to a lounge, she saw a group of men and women standing around. They were focused on something in the centre, the sounds they made showed it was exciting event.

"What's going on here?" She snapped out the question.

The group quickly parted and stood at attention.

"At ease." She saw the object of interest, a nude female with her wrists cuffed, holding them at the top of her head. She was also blindfolded, and body paint had been applied to her body. She saw messages had been written on her wishing her a happy birthday. Flowers and other objects were also painted on her. A woman standing next to her explained, "It's Maxine's birthday, so we stripped and blindfolded her during lunchtime."

Morgan walked around the nude woman, observing the different words and painted objects. She noticed her ass was slightly red and concluded it had received a few smacks. She saw her clothes lying on the floor nearby. "Is this a common practice here to celebrate birthdays?"

The woman standing nearby answered, "Yes, First Officer Regan. A few weeks ago we started to strip females with birthdays and paint their bodies."

"Do you spank them as well?"

"Not a full spanking, but just a few smacks from her friends."

Morgan asked Maxine, "Did you feel pressured to do this?"

"No, ma'am. I looked forward to my birthday because of this. It makes my day special."

Morgan asked the woman standing next to her, "I assume you're here to make sure she stays safe. Who has spanked her? Males and females?"

"Mostly females and just one hit from each crew member."

"Are just females the ones that have their birthdays celebrated like this?"

"Yes. Males are not allowed to be undressed, unfortunately," the young woman responded.

I agree with you there. "For now, carry on with your birthday celebration. I will converse with the captain on this particular activity."

"Yes, ma'am. Thank you, ma'am."

Morgan left, deciding to return to the lounge later that evening to see if other celebrations were occurring that might not fit in within the ship's guidelines. She returned to the command centre, checked the Star Hawk's operations, and went to lunch.

She sat with Weapons Officer Kelly Walling, determining other executive officers had returned to duty.

"How are you doing, Master Kelly?"

"Good. Nothing much to do with the weaponry except to run simulations with the crew."

"I understand you're spending time with Khloe Levit."

"Yes. It certainly is an eyeopener how Praxton women view things. They don't like to wear clothes, like being in restraints and treat men like lords. I'm certainly not complaining, but it's quite a change from my background."

Morgan laughed. "Well, it has been an adjustment for myself as well. I wonder if it's more difficult for females or males to adhere to Praxton rules."

Walling chuckled. "I don't know which is tougher, but I do know I appreciate the way the women dress around here."

"Yes, I can see why you'd like that. It's unfortunate males aren't allowed to show off their bodies occasionally as well."

Walling nodded. "I suppose you have a point there, but the female body is meant to be admired. The male body, not so much."

"Says you. Still, I understand what you mean." Morgan finished her lunch and returned to work. She spent the rest of the afternoon doing reports and went to join the rest of the executive team for dinner. She was glad Elmwood didn't ask what she had discovered earlier in the day at the non-executive lounge. She wasn't ready to disclose her finding until she returned to the lounge later.

She declined to stay for drinks after the meal. "Sorry, I'll catch up later. I need to check out the non-executive lounge once more."

"Do you want me to come with you?" Elmwood inquired.

"No, one executive officer probably will make them nervous enough."

Morgan returned to same lounge, entering the through the double doors. Several crew members reacted to her presence, standing at their tables. "At ease." She continued to walk through the lounge. Most of the crew had finished eating and were drinking. She saw several women with their tops removed, noting they wore nipple and breast jewellery, along with body paint on their breasts. She came across a table where two women were using their hands to lean against a table. Two men were standing next to them, one of them spanking a woman as she laughed.

"What are you doing?" Morgan snapped at him.

He froze and stood at attention.

"I asked you a question." Morgan raised her voice.

"Sorry, ma'am. I was spanking Cadet Addison."

"Why were you spanking her? What did she do wrong?"

"Ma'am, she ordered her own drink while I available to do so."

"That is not a reason for female discipline." She turned around and saw most of the lounge patrons were standing and listening to her. "Listen up everyone. The expectation is for everyone to know and understand the rules and policies we operate under. We follow the Praxton rules of social conduct. While that does include female discipline, that does not mean a spanking for your amusement in a public place.

"There will be a notice sent to everyone on the Star Hawk to refresh your understanding of our social policies. That notice will require your acknowledgement so there will no future excuses of a misunderstanding. Until then, female discipline will not be permitted." Morgan left, hearing the whispers among the crew. She returned to the executive levels of the Star Hawk, going to a lounge normally used by the captain. She found him at a table with Communication Office Janice Madison, Steermaster Nicole Redding and Kelly Walling.

"Hi, sorry I'm late for drinks but I needed to check on a situation."

"Nothing serious, I hope." Janice replied.

"No, just a case of a minor indiscretion with the ship's Praxton rules." She spoke to Elmwood. "I'll fill you in tomorrow." Morgan enjoyed a couple of drinks. She observed the Executive lounge was much more subdued than the non-executive lounge. There was another difference that she realized in the uniforms. She wasn't surprised to see a few topless women, an acceptable practice for Praxton social customs. It wasn't nearly as common in the executive lounges, but did occur. The uniform difference she saw was the hemline of the skirts. The women in the other lounge wore shorter skirts. It was one more thing she would review with Elmwood.

━━━

In the morning, Morgan went to the ship's supply store. She sought out the manager, a middle-aged man in his office. The heavy-set man stood behind his desk at her approach.

"First Officer Regan, how may I be of help?"

"I just need some information. Are some female crew members requesting shorter skirts?"

"Yes, we get many requests to shorten the hemline. I have instructed my staff to accommodate these requests up to eight centimetres. Anything beyond that requires a supervisor's permission."

"That sounds reasonable. Are there any other requests regarding clothing I should know about?"

"There are many requests for higher heels on the shoes, but I refuse those due to the safety aspect. Other than that, perhaps a lot of orders for breast and nipple jewellery. I haven't seen anything unusual from the males."

Morgan thanked him and contacted Khloe Levit, who was in charge of the women's quarters.

"Khloe, I'm going to talk to the captain about an incident that occurred near one of the non-executive lounges. Are you available to go with me to his office?"

"Of course. May I ask what the problem is?"

"Naked birthday celebrations."

"Oh. I have heard about those."

Morgan walked with Khloe to Elmwood's office. "So, you knew about this before?"

"I have heard crew members speak about it and have seen it myself."

"You didn't inform anyone about this?"

"No, as far as I could determine, it fell within the Praxton social customs."

"That may be true, but the Star Hawk has a specialized view of Praxton customs. In the future, when you hear of unusual activities, it would be prudent to inform the captain or myself."

"Yes, First Officer Regan. I will do so in the future."

Morgan entered the meeting room and saw Elmwood was seated at one end of the table. "Captain Elmwood, I have the report you requested. Women's Coordinator Levit has knowledge of this situation and I've requested that she join us."

"Very well. Go ahead."

"It appears that there is a tradition for birthday celebrations for the cadets and junior executives to have the female having a birthday to be stripped during lunchtime. She's blindfolded, her wrists cuffed together, and others are invited to apply body paint on her. She also receives a few smacks on her bottom."

"How long is this birthday celebration?"

"Probably less than half an hour."

"I see. Technically, it isn't against regulations for females to be nude when off duty. Doing so at lunchtime is a grey area."

"Yes, sir. I'm not sure this type of birthday celebration should be done during lunchtime and perhaps restricted to after the full shift is completed. There is the matter of this being a military ship, all crew should be ready for action during their work shift. Nude and blindfolded does not meet that requirement."

Elmwood looked at Khloe. "You understand the nuances of the females in the junior ranks. What are your thoughts?"

"Praxton females are expected to be submissive and show off their bodies. This birthday celebration conforms to that. I have seen two birthday celebrations, and both went for less than twenty minutes. I don't believe that is a cause for concern as far as readiness for any emergency. If this birthday celebration is changed to evenings, then drinks would be consumed. A nude female, blindfolded and handcuffed where alcohol is available would make such an event longer with potential for trouble."

"Would you expect most of the junior females will experience this type of birthday celebration?" Morgan asked.

"Yes, after a few did this celebration, it has become the norm."

Morgan looked at Khloe. "Are you aware that many females are having their skirts shortened?"

"Yes, most of the females like the shorter length and it conforms closer to the Praxton standard. They would like them even shorter, but that is stopped by the supply department. I would like to mention most of the younger females enjoy adding decorations to their breasts and feel comfortable with their tops off. Many of them wear only the thong underwear or none at all. I'm telling you this because I believe the junior ranks are more comfortable with the Praxton style of dress. Nudity for them is not an issue. The birthday celebration is just a fun time for them."

"I'm aware nudity isn't an issue on Praxton, but this isn't Praxton. We're on a military ship and need to preserve a certain sense of decorum. Do you have a suggestion on how to handle this?" Elmwood asked Khloe.

"My suggestion is you put a time limit for the birthday celebration. Perhaps fifteen minutes but with tolerance for a few extra minutes."

"I observed a female being spanked for a trivial reason. We need to add that all discipline is reported and must be justified as to appropriateness." Morgan added her opinion.

Elmwood nodded. "I hadn't expected the Praxton culture would be adopted so quickly on this ship." He looked at Morgan. "Write up new regulations and implement them into the ship's guidelines for conduct."

"Yes, sir. I will do so immediately. May I also suggest we do have a need for dress uniforms for special occasions? Currently we just have one uniform for all situations."

"Good point. Please contact Warrant Officer Sheri Richards concerning this. Report back to me when there is a new dress uniform to review."

"Yes, Master Julius."

━━

Morgan asked Sheri Richards to meet with her in a lounge, deciding an informal setting would suffice.

"What did you want to meet about?"

"Our uniforms. Captain Elmwood would like to have uniforms suitable for formal occasions designed. Could you form your committee again and come up with new dress uniforms?"

"Of course. I already have some preliminary designs from when we were designing our present uniforms. Is there anything in particular that the captain wants for the uniform?"

"He didn't say but keep the Praxton influence in the design."

"I will. May I ask how things are going between the captain and yourself? I understand he wants to be your guardian."

"It's going well. He's giving me small commands to follow. I knew him before he was captain of the Star Hawk and we're comfortable with each other."

"That's good, although Praxton relationships are different from Alliance ones."

"Yeah, like being submissive, getting spanked and not being allowed to wear underwear." She grinned. "It makes for an interesting courtship."

"I can appreciate what you're going through. Thanks for the uniform assignment. I was looking for something to test my design skills on."

[26]

NALLIX PEERED at Morgan carrying a bag as she stood at the entrance to her suite. "Are you going to come in?"

"Thanks. I'm nervous about this."

"It's just a painting."

"Of me naked. But when Master Julius said it was all right for me to pose for your painting, I knew it was more than a suggestion."

"I understand. He's in control of you."

Morgan walked inside, standing as she surveyed the suite. A large rectangular canvas, the long side horizontal, stood on a tripod. On a table next to it sat an array of brushes, paints and an easel. Opposite to the canvas, a white couch sat and next to it an armchair. She saw Nallix was wearing just a loose skirt, her tattoo and her gleaming skin.

"But people have seen you naked before." Nallix pointed out.

"Yes, but normally I get to choose the setting. Everyone will see me naked if he puts the painting on display in his living room."

"They will see a painting of a beautiful woman. Clothes, after all, are an option on the Star Hawk for women."

"I know." Morgan sighed. "It's one thing to be nude and another if it's captured for prosperity."

"I hear what you're saying. I tell you what. Let me paint you. If you're not happy with it, I'll destroy it."

"All right." She looked at the open door to the bedroom. "Can I change in there?"

"Of course. What would you like to drink?"

"Gin and tonic. A double, please."

Morgan entered the bedroom. The bedroom, like the living room, was designed in the Alliance worlds' style. She didn't see an ankle cuff attached to the foot of the bed. *I should mention to her that is a requirement for women on the Star Hawk.* Morgan took off her clothes and put on her collar, cuffs and short silver chains, restricting her movement. The collar and cuffs were black and wide, prominent against her pale skin. Her tear shaped nipple clips, connected by a silver chain, featured a diamond centred in the larger bottom part. She carried the end of her leash in her hand as she entered the living room.

Nallix handed her a drink. "A double as requested. I'll make you another as soon as you finish this one."

"Thanks. What should I do? How should I pose?" She used both hands to lift her drink.

"Just relax on the couch and get comfortable. When you feel ready, I'll ask you to pose. Don't think about the painting until then."

"Thanks. Did Master Julius say anything about this painting to you when he escorted you to your room?"

"Not too much. He wants it on a large canvas with you in a horizontal pose."

"Okay." Morgan looked around. "I noticed your suite hasn't been converted to the Praxton style."

"I didn't think too much about that until we went to Captain Elmwood's suite. It had some interesting features."

"You should modify your suite to the Praxton style. For example, you could have the shower visible to the living room."

"That's a possibility. I'm a bit of exhibitionist and showering where others can see me would be fun."

"Maybe have the clear wall face the hallway outside." Morgan grinned.

"I think that would be a bit too much exposure." Nallix laughed.

"I guess I'm ready." Morgan put down her drink. "How should I pose?"

"Stretch out on the couch on your side."

"I noticed your bed doesn't have an ankle cuff." Morgan adjusted her position on the couch according to Nallix's instructions. She ended up holding the end of her leash in a hand, extending it toward an unseen person.

"It does, but I tucked it under the mattress. I do sleep in the nude, as that is a Praxton requirement. But since I don't have a guardian, I didn't feel the ankle cuff was a necessity."

"No, you still have to wear the ankle cuff."

"Okay. I have to admit when Master Julius put the ankle cuff on me, it made me feel aroused, like a captured slave girl." Nallix adjusted one of Morgan's legs, moving the knee higher up. She brushed back a few strands of her hair. "If I fail to wear an ankle cuff, does that mean I would get another spanking?" She smiled.

"You wish. Maybe you would be confined to your room instead." Morgan smiled. "Praxton has multiple ways to discipline a female. Some you may not enjoy. I'll mention to you Master Julius told me to report to him if you were not adhering to the Praxton standards. It would mean you would be disciplined."

"What kind of punishment?"

"Praxton rules allow for a variety of discipline measures. Don't assume you would like them all."

"The Praxton culture takes a bit to get used to. I do like how women can sit in a lounge topless without being harassed by men. Men are very respectful to women on the Star Hawk. I wish I could meet more men but don't know how to approach them."

"Praxton customs prevent a male from being aggressive toward females. There are few ways to let a male you're attracted to them. You can simply ask one to order your drink. That tells him you see him as being in control of you. Or, if you want to be aggressive, hand him the end of your leash and request he escorts you to your suite."

"Maybe I'll have to start carrying a leash with me." Nallix walked to her side to gain a different perspective of Morgan. "I'm not looking for a guardian. I just want companionship."

"If you want to fit in with the ship's culture, you should carry a leash and wear cuffs and chains. That shows you're willing to be part of the Praxton culture."

"Okay, I understand what you're saying. I need to show I'm part of the Star Hawk besides just being a crew member." She put down her brush. "I have enough detail to finish the painting later."

"Good. May I see what you have done so far?"

"Sorry, you can't see it until it's finished." Nallix draped a cloth over the painting.

"All right. I might as well get dressed."

"You're welcome to relax the way you are." Nallix took a drink. "I enjoyed our shower together a few days ago. I wouldn't mind exploring our friendship that way again."

Morgan changed her position to sitting on the couch. "I'm comfortable staying this way, but I would like to know you better before we have sex. I thought you were more into males than females. You said you weren't looking for a guardian?"

"In my universe, I was a controlled wife, having to obey my husband. My life was easy and comfortable for the most part. After I escaped to this universe, I was forced to rely on myself and learned to be independent. Because I wanted to keep my previous life a secret, I sought out men to have short-term relationships with. Men weren't too concerned about details of my life. They just wanted to bed me. Women want a more personal connection before sex. They would ask details about me. Details I didn't want to divulge. That meant most of my partners were men. On the Star Hawk, men want to control me if we have a relationship. After being independent, I'm not sure about having a guardian. Maybe eventually. Right now, women work better for what I need."

"Well, I like Master Julius being in charge of me and giving me orders. I do understand what you're saying. Freedom for one's own choices is good."

Nallix passed Morgan another drink and sat next to her. "I have to admit, my mind was racing when Master Julius led me by a leash down the hallway of Star Hawk. I was receiving a few looks from others. It was rather... stimulating. I guess there are merits to being dependent and being under a man's control." She placed a hand on Morgan's thigh, lightly stroking the skin.

Morgan turned her head and gave Nallix a kiss on the lips. "I like you, but before we get too far, I would like to establish our friendship better first."

"All right, I understand." She returned the kiss.

"I think I should get dressed and maybe we could go to a lounge and have a bite to eat."

"I agree. I'm getting hungry myself."

Morgan went to the bedroom to get dressed. "Thanks for doing the painting. I'm looking forward to seeing it finished." She saw Nallix standing at the doorway, watching her get dressed.

"I suppose I should put a top on as well."

Morgan watched Nallix go to the closet and picked out a bikini style top with long sleeves. She saw her approach her, give her a hard smack on her ass, and take the end of her leash.

"Hey!"

"I couldn't resist. Some time I'd like to give you a spanking." Nallix tugged on the leash. "I'll escort you to the lounge."

"Really? You decided you're in charge of me?"

"I just thought it would be fun to lead you on a leash."

"All right. Just for fun." Morgan went with Nallix to a nearby lounge. After they found a table, Nallix returned the leash to Morgan.

"I thought I better give you your freedom back. If I was in charge of you, it would mean I would have to order food for you. I have no idea how men can feel comfortable ordering a meal for someone else."

"Males are required to have that confidence. Sometimes that confidence can be intimidating or even annoying."

"That's better than having men with a lack of confidence and afraid to express themselves. I've been around men like that, and it isn't very enticing to have as a partner."

"I hear you. I prefer males that want control. Praxton certainly enforces that concept."

After they ordered their food and Morgan continued to ask Nallix about her previous life. "You said you had a privileged life. Was there a big separation between the rich and the poor?"

"No, there was a large middle-class. Big government with lots of social programs. Many people worked for the government or with corporations that provided services for the government. As you know, I was part of the elite class, more symbolic than with actual power, but we were there to ensure the government ruled with integrity. That's a bit ironic considering the elite's lifestyle."

"What do you mean?"

"The elites have too much wealth and time on their hands. Scandals, debauchery and excessive luxuries, and I was part of it. I'm not proud of it, but it was expected I join in a certain amount of the festivities as an elite."

"So, you were forced to do these festivities?" The short chain between her wrists forced her to use both hands together to eat her food.

"Hardly forced. Some were quite enjoyable. But other events were not something a lady would admit too. Truthfully, I'm ashamed of some of the activities I participated in. And no, I will not divulge them." She smiled.

"Okay, so what do you want?"

"I want to have a man who doesn't want to control me. With the Praxton culture as it is, that may be difficult to find. I may have to settle for female friends that are as frustrated as I am."

"So that explains your pass at me. I am committed to Master Julius."

"That doesn't prevent you from sharing moments with another women."

"It doesn't, but I would need his permission first. Maybe not according to Praxton rules, but by my rules. I don't want to do things without him knowing. I don't believe you'll have trouble finding other partners, male or female."

"Maybe not. But I like you. You're strong, intelligent and have that sassy kind of sexuality."

"Thanks. Can I give you some advice?"

"Sure."

"Keep wearing what you're wearing. It looks exotic and sexy. But add cuffs and chains. It helps make you appear vulnerable and approachable."

"Okay. I'll do that."

"And convert your suite to a Praxton style. I can say from experience it is fun to shower visible to others."

Nallix laughed. "Yes, I can see myself doing that again. Okay, I'll have my suite reconfigured."

"You should include wall hooks in the bedroom and living room."

"Maybe."

"You better or I'll use a grade four whip on you."

"A grade four whip? What does that mean?"

"It means it'll be less painful for you to add wall hooks."

"Okay, I get the hint." She stood and took Morgan's leash. "I'll escort back to Master Julius."

"You're going to lead me by the leash again?"

"Yes, I think you enjoy being submissive at times. I'm sure Master Julius will appreciate it when I present you to him."

I'm sure he will. Morgan saw the glances at her being led on a leash as they walked along the corridor to Elmwood's suite. *There is that exotic feeling of being led on a leash to your master. Humiliating, but what a feeling of submission.*

Morgan saw the look of surprise on Elmwood's face when he opened the door to his suite.

"Morgan, this is an unexpected surprise."

Nallix handed the leash to Elmwood. "Master Julius, she's all yours."

Morgan entered his suite. "I can explain…"

"No, don't. I like you this way. Too often you're having to be assertive as your role of first commander. I like you when you're like this occasionally."

"May I retrieve my top and panties from you? I left them here a few days ago." Nallix peered past him toward the dining room.

"Certainly." He stepped back to allow her to enter.

Nallix picked up her clothes. "I best be going. Thank you, Morgan, for your company and advice." She paused to give her a kiss on the lips. Her hand made a quick slap at her ass.

Morgan watched Nallix wave goodbye, a smile on her face. *I'm totally under his authority now. I wonder what he thought of her kiss.*

"Morgan, what should I do with you?"

She dropped to her knees. "Whatever you want, Master Julius."

[27]

Morgan sat across from Elmwood at the corner of the table. She had presented two of the agenda items herself and now waited for Elmwood to introduce the next item.

Elmwood peered around the executive room at the officers sitting around the table. "We have an agenda item here that I'm sure will be of interest to everyone here. Sheri Richards will give us a report on our new formal uniforms."

"Thank you, Captain Elmwood. As with the Star Hawk's everyday uniforms, we used the Praxton style of clothing. We kept the same colour scheme of blue with red trim. The uniforms for non-military personnel it will be blue-grey with the red trim. I will show the male military uniform first." She paused to activate a rotating hologram floating above the conference table. It was approximately two-thirds the height of a normal male. "As you can see, the jacket is loose fitting at the shoulders but tapers at the waist. The jacket is held together by two buttons and has epaulets to indicate rank."

Morgan looked at the floating image. She liked the dark blue jacket with red trim at the top and bottom of the sleeves, with the white shirt underneath. Morgan thought the shirt deviated from the Praxton style by having a small collar and being open at the front to the stomach. *That shirt is more like an Alliance style. It's rare to see male skin in clothing. That's a nice change.*

"The blue pants are loose along the leg with a red stripe along the exterior of the leg. The top is fitted with a wide black belt, which has a strap to hold a riding crop. We utilized the high waist of Praxton style and incorporated a wide decorative fly. The fly, as you can see, is a weave of blue and red cords and is see-through. Our model is wearing red underwear, but blue would also be acceptable. The black boots have a thick sole with a high lace."

"I really like the uniform. It seems to have the best features of Praxton and Alliance styles. I have to ask, is the only option for underwear red or blue?" Communication Officer Janice Madison gave a smile. "Perhaps none at all?"

Sherri grinned as the sound of chuckles filled the room. "I suppose there is an option to go without, although it has been my experience the men on the Star Hawk are conservative in that regard."

"May I ask about the riding crop?" Khloe Levit asked. "I understand it was a common item early in Praxton's history to help maintain order among the slaves."

"Yes, that's true. Our research showed it was carried by all adult males during the early years of Praxton colonization. Incidentally, it wasn't unusual for males to be shirtless, or have their shirts open. The full coverage of males is a more recent trend. We decided the open shirt does fit in with the Praxton and Alliance style."

Morgan studied the riding crop. *If Julius was wearing that uniform with the riding crop in his hand, I think I would be on my knees fairly quickly.* "May I ask if the riding crop is intended to be functional?"

Laughter erupted before Sheri responded. "Our intention was for show only, but perhaps female crew members may want to be on their best behaviour." She waited a few seconds and continued. "If that is all the questions concerning the male uniform, I will now show the female uniform."

Morgan watched as the male model was replaced by a female one. The new model wore a sleeveless blue dress with a red trim at the hemline that reached mid thigh. The front of the form fitting dress had a scooped neckline, but the back was bare down to the top of her cheeks. The cleavage at the front was mirrored at the low back. The model stood on red high heels, matching the colour of the cuffs and collar. The wide, soft cuffs were joined by its counterpart by a silver chain. Besides the ankle and wrist cuffs, a set of cuffs were attached above the elbow with the chain draping behind her back. *That is one sexy outfit.*

"We decided to use wide, leather-like cuffs to make a statement that the females on the Star Hawk are submissive. The collar is made of metal and is meant to restrict head movement and the leash helps enforce the submission of the subject. As with our present collars, the rank of the crew member is shown as rings embedded in the collar."

"Is the leash optional?" Janice Madison asked.

"No. As per Praxton customs, all females at formal events are escorted by a leash."

"I guess I better get used to being escorted by a leash."

Morgan listened to the mostly positive comments on the new formal uniforms. *The female uniform is certainly interesting. Nothing at the back. I like the elbow restraints. That's a nice touch.*

"I'm curious about the neckline, the lower back and the hemline," Steermaster Nicole Redding stated. "Are they fixed or can they be adjusted for individual styles?"

"There will be minor accommodation for different body types. We will permit increasing the scoop of the neckline or lowering the back. Was that your concern?"

"Actually, I was wondering about raising the hemline. I like the back. It could go even lower."

"That's because you have a nice ass." Janice Madison retorted as laugher erupted.

Sheri waited until the laughter died down. "Yes, you can raise the hemline. Or lower the back. Just don't do too much alterations."

"I must raise an objection to the riding crop on the male uniform and the number of cuffs and chains on the female uniform. I believe the issue can be best described as perpetuating the notion women are to be submissive to men. This is against the Charter of Conduct principles." Paul Thyssen laid his arms flat on the table.

"Paul, I believe what we have here is an issue of a misunderstanding," Elmwood responded, as he clasped his hands in front of him. "The formal uniform is for special occasions and the riding crop is simply part of that uniform."

"I still believe these uniforms puts women in a vulnerable position. The dress is revealing and the collar add to the image of being submissive."

"Master Paul, this dress is meant to follow Praxton's customs," Sherri answered. "I want to stress that by Praxton's standards, this is a conservative dress for evening wear. Many of the dress styles are much longer on exposure, including being topless. I believe it would be beneficial to review how Praxton views women. They believe the female form is to be admired and put-on display. Thus, our dress meets that requirement by showing off the back. The second factor is for females to be protected and controlled by males. The collar shows the female is protected by a guardian, while the cuffs represent being under control. Our dress, while conservative, meets the requirements of the Praxton culture."

Paul Thyssen stared at her and finally nodded. "While the Charter of Conduct Office cannot condone the wearing of a collar and cuffs, I accept your explanation and withdraw my objections."

"That concludes our discussion on the new dress uniforms," Elmwood announced. "The final design will be implemented as soon as they can be manufactured."

Morgan approached Thyssen as they exited the room. "Master Paul, may I ask why you withdrew your objection to the formal wear?"

He frowned. "I had put myself in an untenable position by my objection. After I said it, I realized it would not prevent the dress design to be accepted by the captain. I remember the captain advising me that objecting to every possible infraction of the Charter of Conduct Laws was making me an unpopular figure.

"The second part is that the formal dress, along with the collar and cuffs, do not break the Charter of Conduct Laws. There is a provision within the document that permits almost any activity, including what a woman is wearing, for special events. For example, the re-enactment of a military battle allows for the use of guns, which is normally forbidden. The formal dress is for special occasions and thus is exempt from normal regulations.

"So, to answer your question, I admit I was wrong in my objection."

"Master Paul, when you withdrew your objection, that surprised a few people. It also gained you a measure of respect."

"Thank you, first officer, I don't hear that very often."

"Master Paul, I assure you that you are a respected member of the Star Hawk. You just need to continue to let others see who you are. I'm going for lunch. Would you like to join me? I'll likely sit with the captain and other officers."

Thyssen hesitated. "Yes, I believe I will. I must make more of an effort to talk to others."

"Have you had a chance to talk to Nallix?"

"No. I haven't seen her much and I suspect she hasn't noticed me. I do use much of my time working in my office and doing reports. I don't spend much time socializing."

What is there to do reports on? Some infraction's that's occurring on the ship? "You won't meet many people in your office, Master Paul."

"True. You can call me Paul without a title. I don't follow the Praxton social customs."

"I understand, but I do. I could be disciplined for not using a proper salutation to your name."

"Do you really enjoy following all the Praxton customs?"

"At first, I found some of them odd, but I like the structure it brings."

"Does that include the collar and the cuffs?"

Morgan believed she heard a condescending tone in his voice. "Yes, Master Paul. The collar and cuffs make me feel secure and I like the look of them. Do you really dislike how they look?"

"It's what they symbolize. They make you appeared captured."

"I suppose they do." She looked at him. "Is that necessarily bad? Don't you find this look appealing as a man?"

"Yes, you do-do look, attractive," he stuttered. "Bu-but my point is that —is that it is wrong to force women to wear them as they represent slavery."

"You must wear your uniform, and some people feel the Charter of Conduct uniform represents the intolerance of choices." She entered the lounge with him.

"I suppose you have a point, although I believe stating the Charter of Conduct represents an intolerance of choice is simplistic and doesn't properly convey what the Charter is about."

"I agree with you. And in the same vein, saying these cuffs represent slavery is simplistic."

They reached a table where Elmwood, Sheri Richards, and Senior Diplomat Tiffany Harris were sitting.

Morgan sat across from Elmwood. "Master Julius, may I have tea instead of coffee for lunch? I've had three cups of coffee this morning and would like a change."

"Of course."

Morgan saw a server approaching their table and turned her attention to Sheri. "I really like the formal uniform you presented, both male and female. I'm glad the male uniform shows a more of the body."

"Thank you. It's harder to design the male uniform as the requirement for Praxton males is to look as large and powerful as possible. That means loose-fitting clothes normally. We had to investigate earlier Praxton fashions to find something that wasn't full coverage. The riding crop helps present the male as someone who is powerful and in control."

Morgan heard Elmwood order her meal for her. She would have preferred the vegetable instead of the chicken soup, but the rest of the food met her expectations. She said hello to Tiffany. "This is nice that you've joined us for lunch."

"Thanks. It isn't a coincidence. I wanted to meet with Sheri. I want to use her expertise to help with the design of a new diplomat uniform."

"That's exciting news," Morgan said.

"I'm looking forward to wearing something not so officious and drab. I'm even going to have a collar as part of the uniform."

"Wonderful." Morgan smiled. *I can almost hear Paul having a heart attack.*

[28]

"MASTER JULIUS, you wanted to see me?" Morgan stood at the entrance to Elmwood's office. A second doorway led to his suite.

"Yes, come in. This is both a business meeting and personal one."

"Oh." She stopped at the entrance and removed her shoes. She saw a cushion near his desk and kneeled on it, placing her hands on her lap. Today she added a chain between her ankle cuffs and a chain went from her collar to her wrist cuffs.

"Business first." He gave a tight smile. "The planet Mostert, as you're aware, is a matriarch society. From the reports we have received, it appears they prefer not to deal with men. Therefore, you will be heading our delegation to the planet. I'm hoping we can conclude a trade agreement with them, although when they see the women from the Star Hawk wearing collar and cuffs, it may give them pause."

"I can instruct our delegation to leave the cuffs off. It isn't a requirement like the collar is."

"Good suggestion. Let's consider that option when we have a meeting with Senior Diplomat Harris prior to landing on Mostert." He stood and walked in front of his desk. "I've been neglectful of my responsibilities of ensuring you are behaving and being under my control. I noticed your interaction with Nallix a few days ago. A kiss and a pat on your ass. Are you wanting to have a closer relationship with her?"

"Yes, I do, Master Julius. I won't without your approval. My preference is one more friendship with her than as a sexual partner. She is lonely and seeks female and male companionship."

"Our supply department has a device called a devotion belt. Are you aware of it?"

"Yes, Master Julius. It is a wide, tight fitting fabric belt. A lockable chain goes from the front to the back between the legs. The chain prevents penetration of the female and the chain is a constant reminder she is under a master's control."

"Good. I have one for you and you'll wear it after leaving my office."

"Yes, sir."

"Now, undress and lean over my desk. You're in need of discipline."

"Yes sir, thank you, sir." She removed her uniform and saw him holding a flogger. She placed herself on his desk, her arms reaching in front of her. Her breasts felt the cool surface of the desk, her nipple clips squeezing her engorged nipples. The sound of the whip whistled in the air, and then he struck. Her skin felt the lashes striking her back and move down to her ass and to her legs.

"This is a grade three whip. It will sting more."

"Yes, sir. Thank you, sir." Morgan took deep breaths. She felt his hand slide over her tingling skin. Then he hit again with the whip, this time with more authority. She groaned. The lashing continued, the strikes overlapping previous marks.

"Very nice." His fingers stroked her skin. "I like the marks the grade three whip leaves. From now on I believe this will be what I'll use on you."

"It does hurt more, Master Julius."

"It's supposed to."

"I understand, Master Julius. Thank you for disciplining me."

"Stand. I will add the devotion belt."

Morgan stood and twisted around to see the red stripes at the back of her legs. *I can imagine what my back must look like.* She stood with her hands behind her neck as Elmwood approached with the belt. He secured it around her waist and gently pulled the chain from the back up and between her legs. His fingers slipped the silver chain against her vagina. He paused to massage her clitoris. Morgan moaned.

"The whipping made you wet."

"Yes, Master Julius. I feel very sensitive to your touch." She felt the chain being tightened and then heard the lock holding the chain into place.

"I will give you a key so you may undo the chain if the need arises. Otherwise, I expect you to wear the devotion belt for the rest of the day and wear it again tomorrow."

"Yes, Master Julius. Thank you for this."

"Now, I have a meeting in a few minutes. You will remain here during the meeting, as I may require your input. Keep your hands behind your neck and stand against the wall with your back against it as well.

"Yes, Master Julius. Thank you for whipping me. I deserved it." Morgan placed herself against the wall and waited as Elmwood returned behind his desk. Shortly later, she heard the door chime.

"Enter." Elmwood stood.

Morgan saw Lieutenant Khloe Levit, who was in charge of the women's quarters, enter the office. Khloe took a quick look at Morgan and stood in front of the desk, her hands behind her back.

"Thank you, captain, for seeing me."

"I understand you want to implement changes in the women's quarters." He sat and gestured for her to sit in one of the chairs.

"Yes, sir." She sat and looked at Morgan. "I'm pleased to see she is wearing a devotion belt. That is one of the items I wanted to discuss."

"Go ahead."

"I want to see more effort and consistency of the females adhering to Praxton standards. I believe there should be a greater emphasis on exercise, makeup, wearing chains and showing poise. The devotion belt, I feel, should be worn by females in a relationship at least part of the time. I've noticed the females are wearing shorter skirts and going topless after work. This falls under expected Praxton culture, but the females are using this freedom to tease and flirt with males. That is wrong, as they know the males cannot be aggressive toward them. I have seen females, not wearing panties, lift their skirts in a lounge to attract attention. This is not proper behaviour according to Praxton rules."

"What are your suggestions on how to remedy this?"

"I want to visit each section and clarify the expectations of how females are to dress and act. I want to lay down rules for them to follow. I want them not only to wear cuffs and chains properly, but also act properly. Discipline needs to be increased. One verbal warning is sufficient before harsher measures are to be used. I will also discipline the supervisors if their group are not acting correctly."

"Morgan, what are your feelings on this?"

"I agree, sir. My visit to a lounge of the non-executive officers showed a lack of decorum. The women were often openly flirting with men. With alcohol involved, I'm surprised we haven't had serious incidents. The women have a right to sit topless in the lounge, but they shouldn't be daring men to act on it."

Elmwood sighed. He tapped his fingers on his desk. "Khloe, I support your initiative in visiting the women's quarters and improving their attitude. The time I have spent on Praxton, the women were usually reserved, self-assured and maintained a femineity that invited respect. We don't want to lose that quality. I am also of the opinion that the men must also step forward on this issue. If a female is acting poorly, they should speak up and ensure she does not cause problems for others or herself."

"I agree with Master Julius. He makes sure I act properly," Morgan replied. "I know if I was to sit in a lounge topless and giggle like a cadet, I would find myself over his lap in a hurry."

Elmwood nodded. "Khloe, I believe you should also speak to the males, perhaps in large group at a formal meeting. You can inform them of their responsibilities. Failure on their part can also have consequences. While males are never spanked or whipped, we can suspend their drinking privileges or ban them from the drinking lounges."

After Khloe left, Morgan put on her skirt and top. "I think Khloe is right about the female behaviour. I need to improve on my own appearance. I should use the body paints and makeup more. I'd like to sit topless in the lounge occasionally but need to apply breast paints first. It takes practice to use the paints."

"Good, you can help set an example for the others."

"Thank you for the devotion belt. It makes me feel owned and protected by you. I also find it arousing." She looked at the whip lying on his desk. "I liked that you went to a grade three whip. I now know what will happen if I misbehave. I support what Khloe is doing. She's helping prevent future problems."

"I agree. Let's hope our future missions will run smoothly with a well-trained crew, a crew that understands the aspects of the Praxton culture."

"Yes, sir. Mostert will be an interesting place to expand our trade plans to. I wonder how a world governed by women will react to a culture where women defer to men."

"As long as both parties want to trade goods, then obstacles can be overcome."

"So you don't foresee any problems with Mostert, captain?"

"I didn't say that. We just need to be prepared for anything different, because we all know how minor issues can suddenly become large problems."

[29]

Planet Mostert, Lar Star System

"CAPTAIN, we have reached the edge of the Lar solar system. Shall I prepare a course for Mostert?" Steermaster Redding asked.

"Yes. Fifty percent of light speed."

Morgan approached him. "Captain, the Lar system actually has two habitable planets."

"Why is it that we only know of one?"

"Mostert is the second planet from their sun and it's in a warmer, temperate zone. The third planet is larger, approximately one point one Earth in size, and is located in a cooler temperate zone. Much of the planet is covered in ice but at the equator plus twenty-five degrees of latitude there is a habitable zone of moderate temperatures. I suspect Mostert has colonized the planet and we're not dealing with two different civilizations."

"Recommendations?"

"We adjust our route to Mostert and swing by the third planet. We can collect data and analyse it before we begin negotiations with Mostert."

"I concur. We want to avoid surprises during our first meeting with them." He spoke to the steermaster. "Nicole, adjust our course to pass by the third planet."

"Yes, captain. I can adjust the course to pass by eight-hundred thousand kilometres."

"Proceed."

———

Teela Mezcal studied a monitor and changed the settings to look at another set of graphs. The holographic images revealed information to her. She made a summary of the data. "Corporal Karlson, I have information on the third planet. Should I send it to the command centre?"

Karlson looked at the screen. "Yes, that's very comprehensive. Excellent work, again."

"Thank you. That's not a place I'd like to live. Cold and with polluted air and water. The mining is open face. It makes for an ugly world."

"I tend to agree." She frowned. "I hope Mostert is a better taken care of."

———

Morgan followed Elmwood in the executive meeting room and sat at the corner of the table next to him at the head of the table. Already sitting was Charter of Conduct Officer Paul Thyssen, Special Envoy Nallix, Senior Diplomat Tiffany Harris and Weapons Commander Officer Kelly Walling. She noticed the senior diplomat was wearing a blue metal collar that matched a three-quarter sleeve form fitting shirt. The shirt was closely buttoned at the front with a lace collar.

Elmwood spoke. "It appears that there may be a surprise or two waiting for us at Mostert. One, as Weapons Commander Walling has noted, is that the planet is heavily armed. There's significant traffic of large cargo ships and may explain a need for some of the military vessels. However, there seems to be more than the usual firepower for protecting travel ships. It is if Mostert is planning for a possible war."

Walling added. "That doesn't mean the Sky Hawk is in immediate danger. Not only can we defend ourselves against a host of attackers. We can also hyperjump to safety. As Captain Elmwood points out, their military seems excessive if they are not planning to engage in hostilities, but we learn of their reasons later."

Elmwood continued. "As you see on your tablets, there is unusual activity on the third planet. Our analysis show that the planet is being used for its resources. Unfortunately, the mining methods used are polluting the air, water and likely harming life forms. There seems to be a total disregard for the environment."

"Is it our assumption that Mostert is operating the mining operation?" Nallix asked.

"Yes. Cargo ships are travelling between the two worlds. It is safe to assume Mostert is exploiting the resources of the third planet."

"What Mostert is doing is not only a serious violation of Charter of Conduct laws but also an affront to how humans should respect the environment. I'm appalled at this disregard for indigenous lifeforms and the environment." Thyssen raised his voice, causing the others to look at him in surprise.

"Unfortunately, Paul, the Charter of Conduct laws do not apply here. We have to remember the Rebel worlds may have their reasons for acting the way they do."

Morgan looked at the upset face of Thyssen. "Perhaps when we meet with the Mostert delegation we can express the need to respect the environment. We could offer Alliance world technology that would reduce the impact of their mining activities."

"I do understand our first priority is to reduce or eliminate the use of Alliance citizens as slaves. But we would be remiss if we didn't address our other concern." Thyssen took a drink of water, looking like he was trying to control his appearance. The stress in his voice remained. "My apologises for raising my voice earlier."

"Quite all right. We appreciate your passion." Elmwood looked at Harris. "Tiffany, it seems like you'll have a full agenda of topics to discuss when you meet with Mostert representatives."

"Yes, I will. I'm scheduled to have a video conference with the head of the Mostert trade delegation later today to discuss when and where to meet and any special meeting requirements."

"Excellent. Please keep me informed of your progress."

The meeting ended and Morgan watched Thyssen hurry after Tiffany Harris as they left the room. *I'm sure he's asking to be included to the delegation. I wonder if his passion for the Charter of Conduct laws will be helpful in these meetings.* For the first time she saw the rest of Tiffany's new uniform. The skirt was forest green, long and attached to a brown belt by loops. Tiffany had shifted the skirt to reveal one side of her left leg, exposing part of her cheek. *That's an interesting feature. She can adjust the skirt to show less, or more, according to her mood.*

———

Morgan met with Harris and Elmwood in his office later that evening.

"I assume you have an update from your video conference, Tiffany," Elmwood inquired.

"Yes. I will meet with them in two day's time on the planet surface. It will be at their capital, Brunet. I learned the third planet is called Rudis and it used for mining. No one lives there and the only people there are contractors to facilitate the mining operations. I suspect slave labour is involved in the extraction of the ore but my questions about Rudis were ignored. I felt it wasn't because they were being secretive but rather it wasn't important to warrant any conversation."

"That may be problematic about addressing our concerns about how they mine."

"I agree. Their meeting requirements are a bit unusual. They want a female as the lead negotiator and that the majority of delegation be female as well."

"I see." Elmwood gave a small shrug. "Fortunately, you are the head of delegation so that won't be an issue. Have you considered who else will travel with you to Mostert?"

"I have decided to include Paul. I do have reservations about him, but eventually his input will have to be considered when we draw up any trade agreements. I'm hoping he'll come to realize that the Charter of Conduct laws have little weight on the Rebel worlds and a compromise is the only way we can extend influence.

"I wanted to include Jeremy Lawson, the second ranking diplomat, but the female majority requirement makes that difficult. Althea Rossa, the third ranking diplomat, will be included instead. I would also like to include Morgan. Since Mostert obviously prefers to deal with females, they may be influenced that a female is also a high-ranking officer on the Star Hawk."

"Good point. A delegation of four seems reasonable. Will you be taking military personnel with you?"

"No. That may send the wrong message why we're here. If they were to attack our shuttle, I doubt the presence of soldiers would be an effective deterrent."

"Fair enough. I would suggest you consider taking Teela Mezcal with you and have her stay on the shuttle. She may be able to obtain more information for you by monitoring the signals on Mostert."

"I will do so. Mostert is a matriarchal society and government. I expected they would be more receptive during my video call with them. However, the representative I talked to was not friendly. Stern would be an appropriate description. I'm under the impression they don't trust us and consider the Star Hawk a nuisance."

Morgan walked with Tiffany after the meeting. "I like your new uniform."

"Thank you. It took me a while to decide on what I wanted. The collar was a big decision, but I thought the diplomats should try to blend in with the philosophy of the Star Hawk. I like the collar. It feels strange to wear it at first but now I'm use to it."

"That skirt can be adjusted, I assume."

"Yes. I'll close it up when I go to Mostert."

"I think Paul was shocked when he heard you were going to wear a collar."

"I'm sure he was. I thought he was going to say something to me, but he never did."

"I do hope he doesn't say anything that will cause problems on Mostert."

"Me as well. I will talk to him before we arrive and tell him our objective is to stop the piracy and the kidnapping of Alliance citizens.

End of Book six of the Praxton Series

⊏───⊐

Don't miss out on your next favorite book!

Join the Melange Books mailing list at
www.melange-books.com/mail.html

THANK YOU FOR READING

Did you enjoy this book?

We invite you to leave a review at the website of your choice, such as Goodreads, Amazon, Barnes & Noble, etc.

DID YOU KNOW THAT LEAVING A REVIEW...

- Helps other readers find books they may enjoy.
- Gives you a chance to let your voice be heard.
- Gives authors recognition for their hard work.
- Doesn't have to be long. A sentence or two about why you liked the book will do.

ABOUT THE AUTHOR

Nick Howard lives near Grande Prairie, Alberta where winter is never far away. There he pursues a dream of writing and taming weeds on an acreage. So far, the weeds are winning but perhaps the writing will allow him to feel a small measure of victory. He shares the green jungle with his wife, and a dog that thinks itself as human. Rumors that the dog assists him in writing are greatly exaggerated as the dog is horrible at grammar. One last thing, thank you for reading this story, and I do hope you enjoyed it.

nshwrd@yahoo.ca

ALSO BY N. S. HOWARD

Praxton Series

Slaves of the Rogue World

The Battle for Freedom

The Proposal

A Vote For Change

Voyages of the Star Hawk

The Missing Diplomat

Novels

Haven

The Witch and the Hairbrush